KING OF
SPADES

KING OF SPADES

A novel by

Kiniesha Gayle

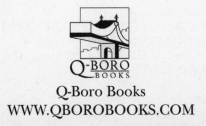

Q-Boro Books
WWW.QBOROBOOKS.COM

An Urban Entertainment Company

Published by Q-Boro Books
Reprint Edition Copyright © 2006 by Kiniesha Gayle

ISBN 1-933967-06-4
First Printing March 2005

10 9 8 7 6 5 4

Cover Layout & Design - www.mariondesigns.com
Editors - Melissa Forbes, Candace K. Cottrell, Shonell Bacon, Lissa Woodson, and Stacey Seay

Q-BORO BOOKS
Jamaica, Queens NY 11431
WWW.QBOROBOOKS.COM

DEDICATION

I would like to dedicate this book to my step-grandfather, Hubert Williams. You always believed in me, I remember when I was only seven years old, and you asked me what I wanted to become and I came up with a whole bunch of occupations. While everyone else told me I could only choose one, you told me, "It's okay to have more than one. Be the best you can be." You were a grandfather to me, more than my real grandfather. And even though you are gone, you live on in my heart. I miss you so much, Granddad.

ACKNOWLEDGMENTS

First and foremost all praises to the Creator, without him this wouldn't be possible. There were days I never understood your doings, and I would always wonder why I struggled so much, and never had the support I needed from others. Through my struggles, you showed me that as long as I leaned and depended on you, then no one else mattered. The road was hard, but I am glad you're guiding me through.

To my son, mommy loves you so much. You're my inspiration. I hope I made you proud, and I want you to know I am proud of you. Whatever dreams or aspirations you have, it can be done, because can't is never in a black person's vocabulary. You have seen what I've been through; don't let such a cycle repeat itself.

My best friend and road dawg. Sherry-Ann Burgess. Remember those days' girl? We were two bad mothaf**kers, look at us now. Although we both got ourselves in some deep shit streams, I am happy that we became two mature young ladies. I love you, sis. You supported my project from the moment the idea popped in my head, you had my back like a real friend no matter what. Thanks.

To my mother, you are a piece of work. God listens to you every night while you pray. You're a fighter and you'll survive anything. I love you. My grandmother, I love you dearly, my grandfather, I love u too.

My father, though we don't communicate much, I still have love for you. My brothers and sisters, Peter, Omari, Marvin, Kimberley, and Julian. My uncles Wally, Kirk,

Egbert, Errol, Hilary, Carol, and Norma. My cousins Freddy, Anna, Stacy, Damion, and Lexie, there are more but the list is too long.

Prof. Conrad Wynters, thanks for standing by me on this project. You listened to my ideas on becoming a writer, and never once have you discouraged me. I will ever be grateful for that. Rosa Perez, you're the best. Lord knows, I hated you in the beginning. Yes I did! You were constantly on my ass in high school about my grades. Thanks Ms. Perez, the lecturing did pay off.

My editor Lissa Woodson, you are the best editor anyone could have. You go beyond the call of duty: the late night phone calls, staying up until five in the morning working on my book. Trust me, the industry doesn't have any idea of how powerful you are. I can't say thanks enough.

Author Kwan of *Gangsta, Road Dawgz,* and *Street Dreams,* thanks for having my back. You would constantly check in to see how a sista was doing, and extended your hand and offered very powerful advice. Trust me, I retained all that info. Dwayne Joseph author of *Womanizer,* and *The Choices Men Make,* you were the first to open my eyes to the hidden danger of the publishing world. I must say, that advice paid off. Winston Chapman author of *Caught Up* and *Wild Thangz,* you kept it real, and I am very appreciative of everything you did for me. S.W. Smith author of *The Connection,* thanks for answering all of my emails, and helping out whenever you could.

Mark Anthony, my publisher and author of *Paper Chasers* and *Dogism,* thank you so much for believing in my work, and giving me an opportunity to become a published author. Trust me when I say, "you won't regret it".

My attorney Kirk Palma Esq., and also Courtney Smith Esq. for diligently going over my contract, and making sure I got the best deal possible.

My friends, Able Staff—especially Ray, Lisa, and Roberta,

Tamesha, Gladies, Sherrie, Anthony, Mark, Tia, Tameka, Timair, Diana, Alisa, Rudy, Jhonelle, Nashae, Malik, Michelle, Nicole, Marlon, Bull, Dee, Grampie, Kimberely, Nashaun, Karen, Sonaye, Tannisha, J. L. Woodson, Jennifer, Hasan— for always offering good advice, Vernon—you recognized my talent before anyone else did.

Now to a special friend whom I hold dear in my heart, Anthony "Tone" Stepney. Thank you so much. You were my biggest fan and supporter from day one. And although we had our differences, at the end of the day we overlooked it. Aside from Sherry, I could always tell you about my struggles and you never judged me. You are always there with a loving arm, and offering friendly advice. There were days when I cried and you consoled me. You look beyond my feistiness and saw the sweetness in me. Thanks Tone my Clyde in everything.

Terrell, my brother in Christ for praying with me, and offering spiritual guidance along the way. You listened to me, and when things seemed out of control we prayed about it. You taught me how to pray, and I am ever grateful.

Carvis, my photographer thank you for working on my photos diligently so they would be nothing but perfect. You have been a friend through this.

Everyone on lock down, stay strong and hold your head up, they might imprison your body, but never let them imprison your mind.

To the readers, bookstores and street vendors, thanks for supporting and pushing this book.

If you don't see your name it's either of two things, I forgot you, so please don't hold it against me I still have love for you, or you fell in the next category: you already know what you mean to me and I don't have to spell it out.

Last but not least how can I forget the haters and fakers, what more can I say, the book speaks for itself.

KING OF
SPADES

CHAPTER 1

CHIN

Tha Hustle Recording Studio: July 19, 2004, 3:23 p.m.

*T*he sins of the past will always come back to haunt the success of the future. I read that somewhere. In my case, those words would not come true. At least, I hoped not. Making every effort to get away from the drug game and spread my wings into a legitimate business—the restaurant business, the music business, any business where death was not an everyday thing—had to count for something. Maybe then I could sleep without nightmares. Maybe then I could stroll down Adam Clayton Powell Boulevard without looking over my shoulder.

As the last words of Dragon's song played over the speakers, I knew we had finally hit the jackpot. Making sure the lyrics were right for this last track took a lot of hard work on everyone's part at Tha Hustle Records. But, finally, my spirits were soaring higher than an eagle on a mountain flight.

Smoke from cigarettes and something a little stronger created a white haze that barely allowed us to see beyond a few feet. The final track for Dragon's first album still spun on a disc deep in the recorder. The beat was tight, the words to the song were catchy, and the sound was a classic blend of hip-hop and R&B. If we played our cards right, the album would reach number one faster than a speeding bullet could hit a frozen target.

"Yo, man, that's hot," I said, pushing a button while trying to yell over the music. I waved for Dragon to come out of the tiny recording booth that barely fit his solid, muscular frame.

As Dragon swaggered out of the booth, past the engineers, producers, and background singers, a smile creased his thick lips and excitement glazed his dark brown eyes. This talented kid's hunger matched my own. Before he had a chance to take the leather chair next to me, the glass doors to the studio burst open. Several heads snapped around to see who would be bold enough to interrupt a closed set.

"What the hell!" I shouted, pushing the swivel chair back from the control panel, glaring at the massive figure bearing down on us.

Tony Moreno, my partner of Tha Hustle Records, marched in the studio with a sour expression on his face and a red flush to his golden skin. His thin lips were twisted into a frown, and the tiny veins on his neck throbbed to the beat of music only he could hear. His black suit only added to his menacing image. The man was pissed with a capital "P."

A silent prayer went up as I hoped it wasn't any more bad news. Bad news had been plentiful this week. The sins in my past were plentiful and my enemies weren't so forgiving. The studio spot had been under constant police surveillance and shipments were being jacked—stolen en route to my warehouse. Somebody who didn't have a clue was truly fucking with my patience.

"Sup, Tony?" I said, giving him my undivided attention. No one moved as they waited for him to say something, anything to lessen the tension in the studio. As he removed his jacket, tossing it on the nearest chair, the tattoos on his arms stood out. Chinese letters were on one forearm and a scroll with a brief synopsis of his life story was engraved on the other. When he spoke in a quiet but cold manner, his deep voice would often draw everyone's attention. But under that deep voice, he would always remain calm, something I hadn't mastered yet. Maybe Tony having to deal with a hot-headed nagging wife and two young children had something to do with it. Mostly, I think it had everything to do with me.

"Problemo, Chin."

The two words spoke volumes. Tony barely used Spanish words in conversation. When he did, either someone was about to get into some serious toe-curling sex, or someone was about to bite a bullet.

The flash of anger in his eyes indicated the need to talk in private.

"Hey, team, I'll be right back. Keep working," I said, following Tony from the studio while ignoring the curious stares from everyone.

As soon as the office door shut behind him, he blurted out, "We just took another hit."

"What!" One vicious sweep of my hand and everything on the desk hit the carpet. Pacing the floor, trying to still the angry beat of my heart, I asked, "How much supply was stolen?" The silence expanded between us as I moved away from my desk and went to the safe.

"I don't know yet."

Only halfway through the combination, I turned to face him. "What the hell do you mean, you don't know?"

My fist came slamming down on the top of the safe, causing him to wince before he said another word. Pain shot through my hand, but I barely noticed. What I did notice was that Tony was taking things a little too calmly for me. This latest development hit his pocket, too.

"Something ain't right, Chin." He tried to keep his voice steady, but his eyes narrowed suspiciously as he peered out the window. The wind whipped viciously against the plate glass window of my office, signaling that the rain, which had threatened to come for the past few days, would finally make good on its promise.

"What the fuck's going on, Tony? I can't afford any more losses. Bills have to get paid. This company doesn't run on charity." Slipping back in my leather chair, I felt a knot tightening in my stomach and my perfectly laid plans slipping through my fingers. "The ink isn't even dry on the deal for the clothing line and now this shit."

Sighing heavily, my eyes dimmed and my fingers tapped solidly on the cherry wood desk. I glared at Tony. Waiting. Watching. He avoided eye contact, something that didn't sit too well with me. Was my partner somehow involved in the robberies?

"You ask me," he began in a solemn tone, "we need to get out of this game a little faster than we planned. Shit's getting foul real quick." Tony sighed wearily as he leaned back on the money green leather sofa. Strangely enough, I had purchased that green furniture when I first opened Tha Hustle Records, when the money was rolling in like ocean waves. Now something—no, someone—had tried to make sure those waves rolled back out to sea, emptying our pockets along the way.

"Change the plans? Hell no!" As if nature agreed, the wind outside whirled in a frenzy turning the sky a darker shade of blue. "I keep telling you that's out of the question, Tony. I'm not giving up anything that I worked so hard to build. Until Porsha's finished with the paperwork making all of our businesses legit, we stay put. We need the cash flow." Jumping out of my chair, I paced the carpet again like a meter maid doing a ticket run on 42nd Street.

Turning my attention to the window, the skyline came into view. The wind had died down for just a moment. Things were deceptively peaceful and calm—the total opposite of what I felt inside at the moment.

"I'm not saying that we should give up anything, Chin. I'm just saying, maybe it's time we pack this shit up. Focus on music, clothing, and your nightclub." Tony tapped a cigarette pack, pulling out a single smoke and putting it between his lips. "We're already making crazy loot. We have three of the hottest rappers in the industry right now, so why are we still holding on to *el juego*? We should've been out of the drug game months ago. I don't see what's taking Porsha so long."

Music from the studio wafted in through the closed door. Unlike a few minutes earlier, Dragon's song no longer gave me the good feeling that more success was within my reach.

Tony definitely had a point about getting out of the drug game. I was already sitting on millions. Money was not an issue, although I wasn't any Bill Gates. So, why was I still in the drug game? It was insurance for me. I needed to know for certain that I would never be poor again.

Tony took a drag from the cigarette, letting the smoke curl around his face like a halo. "Man, we need to cover our asses. It's only a matter of time before the FBI will be on to the fact that we're running a multi-million dollar drug empire through the companies. You know we got the police over here on lock, so there's no worry in that corner. But the FBI?" He shook his head scornfully. "Man, those mothafuckas are hard to buy off."

Glancing down at the business contracts on my desk, then up to the pictures of awards from the organizations that received donations from us on a regular basis, I said, "This is the last thing I need right now, Tony." A canceled check for Encore Records Group lay on the desk as proof of the fact things were finally on the right track. The distribution deal with them had hit the newspapers in record time, and suddenly Tha Hustle Records was on the map. "Somebody wants me out and we still have no idea who it is."

Tony cleared his throat, swiped the bottle of Hennessy off

the desk, took two tumblers out of the credenza, and poured us both a drink. "I say we do a thorough investigation. Trust me. It could be one of our workers."

That thought had already crossed my mind, but hearing him voice it was a different story. Taking a long, slow sip of the warm liquid, I watched him over the rim of my glass. "Who do you *really* think it is?"

"To be honest, I'm not sure. But the way it's been going down means it's someone from the inside. It's a game and everybody wants to win. Today it's all about you, so people are envious. There's always another man waiting to take your *comida*—food. Danny's dead, and somebody's crew keeps tapping our reserves," Tony said, swirling the crisp brown liquid in his glass. "I say we cut and run. Leave what's left to the vultures."

The more I thought about things, the less I liked his suggestion. "I'd rather die than watch someone else control what's mine. Find them. Dead or alive, I want them. I don't care if it takes me a million dollars to get a hold of them, because when I do, this box of bullets right here will be waiting for them." I tapped the carton in the upper right hand drawer next to my weapons to make my point. "Find them before I do. 'cause then the game is really over—for everybody!" I didn't have to tell Tony that his ass was on the line, too.

Tony rose from the chair, placed his empty glass on the desk, and walked toward the door. As the door closed on his disappearing form, I turned to face the window, watching as a little sliver of sun dipped beyond the clouds and out of view once again. I wondered about the state of my empire. Was it setting or just hiding behind the clouds? I knew death was inevitable in this game, but I hoped it wouldn't come by my hand again. Well, at least not quite so soon.

Draining the last of the drink, my gaze traveled over the books in my library. The blue book with a black spine grabbed my attention as I realized where I had read that saying:

The sins of the past will always come back to haunt the success of the future. Then I remembered the rest: *Will you fall into the trap of easy money and painful ways, or will you travel the path to a higher calling and purpose? The choice is always yours.* Naleighna Kai had said it best in her novel, *Trio.* Now I only hoped I could find the path that led out of the drug game and into a more legitimate lifestyle.

My train of thought was interrupted by the ringing phone. Thinking it might be Tony calling back with some other vital information, I snatched it up.

"Hello."

"Chin, Porsha's on the line," Tracey announced in her soft, sexy voice—one of the reasons she landed the job as my assistant. Within seconds, Porsha's soft humming flowed into my ear as she greeted me with an excited, "Hello."

I tried to conceal my anger. "Hey, lady."

"Hey, baby, how are you?" Porsha's smooth, sultry voice lightened my dark mood.

"A'ight."

"Is everything okay, Chin?" she asked, a slight worried tone entering her voice.

"Somebody robbed one of our Harlem bases. They took a good amount of cash and a few bags of white lady."

"Just money and cocaine? Is anyone hurt?"

The studio music had changed from daring new Hip-Hop beats to a slow R&B tune. I wished I was there being part of the more pleasant side of life, instead of having to tell Porsha, "Danny's dead."

Her sharp intake of breath made my heart pause for a moment. "Chin, baby please, I keep telling you, the drug game is not for you." She sighed, sounding wearier than she had moments earlier. "You've got to get out while you can. I'll only need one more month and things will be fine on this end. Just pull out now! I love you, baby, and I don't want to see you strung up in some hospital, behind bars for life, or worse yet, in a coroner's bag."

Tipping the bottle over, I filled the glass to the rim a second time and took a long swallow. "I know, baby. Trust me, I have it under control."

"You sure?"

"Yes, baby," I said with a voice as strong as I could manage while wishing for the hundredth time that she would not talk about my business over the phone. No matter how many times I have mentioned it, she ignored me, believing that if anything came out of it, her legal skills would get me out of trouble. Personally, I didn't want it to go that far. "So how was your day?"

"Not bad. My partner and I are still working on the murder case I told you about. We're trying to put in a motion for a change of venue to have it tried in the suburbs. The case has been too highly publicized for city folks to give my client a fair trial."

I swiveled in my chair, effectively changing the view from the pouring rain to the wall that displayed several accomplishments. "You think the judge will be okay with that?"

"I don't know, baby, but I'll try."

Another swig of Hennessy, and a slight bit of a buzz tickled my temple. "Good luck."

"I'll need it," she replied softly. This was the first time I'd ever heard her less than her normal, confident self.

"Please! You've got this, woman. So go show the courtroom what my girl is made of. They don't call you Ms. Invincible for nothing," I laughed, hoping that changing the topic had made her forget that I still had something heavy weighing over me.

"You're right! I should kick some asses in there to remind them just who they're dealing with," she bragged, laughing along with me. I could envision her sitting up straight in her chair, head held high once again.

"That's the spirit," I said, knowing that as one of the up and coming attorneys at Leland and Mitchell Law Firm, kicking ass and taking names came with the territory. Porsha wasn't new to the legal game; she was smart, sassy, and walked a little bit on the edge. These were all reasons why I loved my wifey so much.

"Will you be home for dinner?"

"I'm not sure," I lied smoothly, knowing that a few more drinks would pass my lips before I had time to cool down and work out my problems. "I'll call you later."

"I love you, baby," she said in a breathy whisper.

"I love you too, sweetheart. And try to at least touch the speed limit on the way home. It's raining like mad out there." She chuckled and broke the connection, knowing she had no intention of slowing down. Placing the receiver back on the cradle, my mind instantly sprang into strategic planning mode.

My anxiousness to find out what really went down increased. A quick call to Lou, the super of the building, would have security tapes in my office first thing in the morning. Lou always took them to a separate location since the police had once gotten wind of the ones he kept in his apartment.

It wasn't like I didn't trust Tony, but in this game, a real businessman had to find out more—and not just from the usual sources. Tony didn't know that I had installed the cameras. He also didn't know that before too long, hidden cameras would be in every part of the building. Sometimes I met the electricians at three in the morning, just to make sure no one else was around. I'd find out what was going on for myself.

Lou's phone rang quite a few times before it went to voicemail. I didn't leave him a message since I didn't want it to fall into the wrong ears, *if* they were listening in—illegally, I might add. But what could I do? What we were doing was illegal—for now. I hung up the phone and made a mental note to get in touch with Lou later.

CHAPTER 2

PORSHA HILTON

Manhattan, NYC: July 19, 2004, 9:53 p.m.

I raced my convertible along the Westside Highway. The rain had stopped and now the cool summer breeze blew through the window. My jet-black hair with ruby-red highlights whipped around my dark brown face, sometimes blurring my vision, but I refused to put the top up. I loved New York at night. There was something so mysterious and on the edge about the place. No wonder I was attracted to Chin. He had an edge, too—one that became deadlier with every setback. I felt every bit of the pressure. I was the one who demanded he change into a more acceptable line of business. And he didn't fight me on it. He challenged me to make it happen. Once the corporation papers were accepted and documented by the State of New York, everyone could breathe easier.

After a frustrating day at work, I just wanted to get home, lay down next to Chin, and forget that the forecast on winning my client's case seemed a bit cloudy. The judge might not allow the change of venue, forcing me to find jurors who hadn't already decided that my client was guilty. Talk about a needle in a haystack. If some break didn't unfold to save his ass, the man would soon be on a bus going up north to serve a lifetime sentence for murder.

Easing in and out of the light traffic, I smiled at the image that stared back from the rearview mirror. My feathered hair brought out my skin tone. Curls from yesterday's hot ironing were still intact, thanks to the spritz whose citrus scent still lingered, crinkling my pert nose. My big brown eyes sparkled, which made most men melt when I flashed them a quick glance. A dark amber complexion and flawless skin were definitely signs of good breeding and visits to Elizabeth Arden Salon twice a month.

Position and money definitely had its privileges. It didn't hurt that I had become one of Leland and Mitchell's criminal defense attorneys. I had set my sights on making associate partner by my twenty-ninth birthday. Given my track record and winning caseload, I would definitely make it. Well, if this case didn't sideline everything I had worked so hard to achieve. I wondered who on top wanted to see me fail. What other reason did they have for giving me a case for a man whose guilt was obvious? A printout of his criminal record could span the entire State of New York.

L&M, a small but prestigious law firm with corporate assets totaling over forty million dollars, had connections with some of the country's best and brightest. Joining the firm was definitely a move my parents approved of, although I was equally sure that meeting Chin would give them a mild stroke, if not a flat out heart attack. So I kept the love of my life a secret, and Chin didn't mind one bit. Parents were not his thing. He barely kept in touch with his folks back in Jamaica.

Although I'd worked at L&M for almost four years, I never felt as though I was part of the firm. All of my co-workers dated judges, prestigious lawyers, doctors, and the list went on. They were on a "power begets power" trip. Everyone that is, except for Chyna, my crazy friend who could never keep a man. The poor woman's heart was set on a lover who had forced her to get an abortion. She swore the man would come back to her—one way or another, and he would pay.

I, on the other hand, seemed to purposely go out of my way to find the nearest cliff, just to see how close I could come to the edge without falling off. My relationship with Chin, though he was unquestionably a gift sent from heaven, worried me because I knew the slightest wrong turn could send him over the edge and take me with him. But life with him wasn't boring, and that had to count for something.

Raised in the *perfect* family, with the *perfect* nanny, and two *perfect* brothers and sisters, I attended the *perfect* school and did all the *perfect* extra-curricular activities and clubs. So plunging into a career in the justice system wasn't just an option, it was damn near a requirement. But I lived my personal life on my own terms.

I longed to trade places with my friends who got bussed into other schools and were exposed to the hip-hop lifestyle. Oh, just to live the fast life for a minute. I didn't date until I turned nineteen. The guy my family wanted me to bring home had to have no less than an A average, a decent family pedigree, and be able to provide me with the finer things in life.

Well, that may have been every lily-white girl's typical dream, but I wanted a bad boy, or even better, a romantic thug—the type of guy my girlfriends dated back in high school and college. No pedigree, no manners, no mistaking who was in charge. And, of course, he had to be a man that could fuck me until my hair fell out from the roots!

Who gives a damn about having a man with money when I have my own money, I would always think as my parents lectured me on "acceptable" men. I wanted the type of man who dressed decent but was a gangsta down in his soul, the horny type who would take it anytime and anywhere. Chin was that man. He dressed in Armani, but thought and acted like Scarface or even Nino Brown.

I met Chin outside of a celebration party for Curtis Lawrence, an entertainment lawyer at Dunn and Givinchy who had just made partner. Chin, one of Curtis' clients, came as a guest. A heated argument jumped off, and Chin punched a Latino man in the face with twenty or more witnesses lurking nearby. Chin jumped into the first cab he found, putting much distance between him and an assault charge.

"Excuse me, what the hell do you think you're doing?" I yelled, startled from the back seat as I clutched my belongings close.

"Listen, I'm sorry, but shit just popped off and I really have to get out of here," he explained, flashing a grand piano smile and turning on the charm as he settled next to me on the seat. After a quick glance, I saw that his smooth forehead didn't have an inch of sweat to prove that he had been in a scuffle.

"What kind of shit are you talking about?" I asked, hoping my indignant tone would put him off, or at least make him get out of *my* cab. "And is it something I might not want to remember in the morning?"

He nearly glared at me. "Well, aren't you a little too fucking nosey?" Chin spat as he slammed the door, tapping the glass divider to signal that the driver could take off. "Besides, a fine lady like yourself shouldn't know about situations like this," he said smoothly, moving closer to my side of the seat. The scent of his cologne swirled around me in an arousing haze; his intense gaze seemed to see right through me.

Maybe his arrogance or the way he phrased the compliment sparked my interest. Either way, my panties moistened as "little Porsha" throbbed in response.

"May I remind you that you're in *my* fucking cab," I

snapped, a little angry that my body melted for a total stranger so fast. "Actually, I saw what went down. I can either help or hurt. I'm an attorney, so I do know about things like this." I reached into my purse just at the point the cab whipped down West 14th Street. "On second thought, maybe I should call the police. You might need some assistance." I flashed him an equally bright smile, wondering about his next move.

"You're from the hood, sweetheart?" he asked, giving me a second glance, then turning his attention to the view of the stores in downtown Manhattan as the cab drove faster than the speed limit. "Shit, you coulda fooled me. What type of attorney?"

Chin stared at me longingly, so I leaned into him, touching his shoulder. While I lowered my gaze, I gave him a flirtatious smile. I knew my touch moved him because he quivered as I used my hands to stroke along the side of his face.

"Now you're interested," I said, laughing lightly, pulling my hand away. "A minute ago I was too fucking nosey."

"Well, Miss . . ." Chin waited for me to supply my last name. Instead, I glanced out the cab window, pretending to ignore his sudden interest.

He shrugged, chuckling to play it off as he continued, "I know you were only bluffing when you mentioned calling the police."

The cab driver now made a sharp turn onto 6th Avenue off West 14th Street, so the approaching red light wouldn't catch him.

"Don't push my buttons, because I will," I retorted, opening my cell phone with a single finger.

Leaning in, he closed the phone and kissed me lightly on the cheek as the musky scent of his cologne enveloped me. "If you were really going to call, it would've happened before I told the driver to take off." Chin glanced out the window and then tapped the glass partition once again. "Cabbie, can you pull over at this corner?"

Suddenly, I didn't want him to leave. "Where are you going?"

Chin looked back at me, his lips parting in a sexy smile, while putting his fingers to my lips. I trembled slightly from the connection.

"Thanks for not calling the police. Miss . . ."

"Hilton."

With that, he gently brushed his lips across mine. Then he winked, stepped out of the cab, strolled across the street, and hailed another cab. Maybe it was the kiss that had me mesmerized. His lips were so soft and electric. But then again, maybe it was his way of doing things. His manner was so . . . thuggish. Damn, the brotha had my panties wet!

Settling back in the torn leather seat, I watched as his six feet tall, 185-pound frame disappeared into cab and took off. His eyes were chinky—slanted in a way that would disappear if he laughed too hard. The Cavalli suit draped his muscular form as though it was made especially for him. But those lips . . . "Damn, they have to be his best attribute."

"Did you say something, Miss?"

"No, um . . . no, driver. Just thinking out loud."

The man had some Asian in his blood, and the emphasis he placed on certain words revealed that he had a little Jamaican floating in him, too. "Hmmm, Jamaican and Chinese. Not a bad combination." The icing on the cake would be his abs. I'd brushed against him and could tell that those didn't happen without constant trips to the gym. The boy had it going on and I couldn't be mad at him. I regretted that I didn't ask for his name and number. Now I would never get to . . .

As I turned my head, a small business card that lay in the spot he once occupied caught my attention. Excited, I quickly picked it up and flipped it over. "Tha Hustle

Records, Andre Chin, CEO." A small grin spread over my lips as the cab whizzed past West 46th Street, pushing toward Central Park West where I lived. At the time, I felt it was my lucky day.

A few days later, I called him.

"Tha Hustle, this is Andre Chin speaking. How may I help you?"

I took a deep breath before diving in. "Mr. Chin, this is Miss Hilton. I was wondering if you were still in need of a lawyer. I wanted to offer my . . . *services.*"

"Now see, I thought we'd worked that out," he said coyly, his smooth masculine voice had the wetness in my panties dripping at forty miles an hour.

"Well, you never know. I need to review some things to see if my memory lapse is still permanent or just temporary."

He roared with a hearty laughter. "I'll tell you what, my secretary isn't here, and I can't find my schedule. But right now it's just me and my partner. So, if you can make it down here today, I'll see what I can . . . work out."

I could envision the smile on his handsome face. I could also imagine exactly what his words implied. I instantly calculated the effort to revamp my schedule. "I'll be there in an hour."

Actually, I made it in thirty minutes, never realizing that the chance meeting in the cab would damn near cost me a glowing future and my life.

CHAPTER 3

NATALIE "BABYGIRL" SMITH

Harlem Hospital: July 21, 2004, 1:17 p.m.

I hate hospitals. Anyone who knew me understood that fact. Someone who was supposed to have my back had forgotten that one detail. It was the main reason I was so angry with Sandy. Her carelessness, and her ability to always think with her pussy instead of her brains, was the reason I ended up with one bullet lodged in a place where only tattoos and armbands should be, and the other lodged in a spot close to my heart. That bitch almost got me killed!

Midday, on a warm July afternoon in New York when I should've been out smoking and drinking, I sat upright in my bed cursing out Sandy-Ann Richards for the nineteenth time that hour. My record had been thirty times in sixty minutes. Sleep last night didn't come easy with the nurses constantly walking in and out, taking my blood pressure and temperature, and checking my bandages. The tray of food from lunch still sat on the table. I never ate nasty shit like that in high school, so I certainly wouldn't make an exception for Harlem Hospital.

On the other hand, my hospital roommate, who looked a

bit on the masculine side, gulped her lunch down like she hadn't eaten in weeks. When she was done she looked my way as though she wanted to ask for my leftovers. "Shit, she can have all that nasty stuff if she wants," I mumbled, but I wouldn't offer. The heifer would have to ask. I don't give anybody a damn thing. We both wore identical blue and white striped hospital gowns, looking like twins. But her arm was strung up to an IV, while mine had been bandaged from a gunshot wound.

After being cooped up in Room 563 for almost a week, my release date had arrived. It didn't come fast enough for me, 'cause I was ready to put my foot up Sandy's ass something terrible. Not only did she mess up the assignment and land me in the hospital, she was filling PitBull's ears with some things that weren't her business.

"You didn't eat anything," the nurse said, breaking my concentration and looking at me over her thick glasses. *Damn*, I thought as her eyes seemed to swim on the other side, *could she actually see anything out of them?*

"Eat this crap? Hell no," I snapped, glaring at her, then down at the food. "Would you eat that shit?" She turned on her heels and strolled out the door, mumbling something I couldn't catch.

I got tired of them asking me the same questions everyday and wondered why they didn't get tired of my answers with the same damn attitude. To top it off, they always made a note of anything I said on my chart. What did my attitude have to do with my gunshots? Actually, on the street it had plenty to do with it, but what did these quacks know? Not a damn thing.

"Damn, would those mothafuckin' police get here so I can *go*?" My angry voice sent another nurse scurrying out of the room before she made it all the way inside.

I had already made it through the first round of questioning, and two more officers were on their way. I had no problem telling them that something had happened. My biggest worry was if they found out what *really* happened. My arm injury wasn't that bad, just a flesh wound, but the one near my heart took surgery and a week's worth of recovery time.

I dressed quickly, putting my things into a plastic bag before slipping back into the bed. As I adjusted my pillow, trying to find a more comfortable position and hoping to take some stress off my mind, there was a soft knock at the door.

I quickly glanced at my roommate, who shrugged and turned her attention back to the television.

"Who is it?"

"Girl, quit acting like you don't know it's your homegirls coming to visit you," Dimples bellowed as she pushed open the door and Sandy followed cautiously on her heels. Her broad smile only deepened the deep crevices in her cheeks—dimples—which is how she gained the nickname. The two women came over and wrapped their arms around me. Dimples was never the type to dress in sexy clothes, so I was shocked to see her in a baby blue and white knee-length halter dress.

On the other hand, it was expected that Sandy, who couldn't think beyond her next fuck, would dress like a ho. She did not disappoint. Who else would stroll into the hospital in a mini skirt and strapless shirt, exposing all the goods? I glanced at them both once more, and I must say, Dimples looked good. Sandy wouldn't look good until I smashed my fist in her face a few times. Black and blue would certainly be a better color for her.

"I thought it was the police," I said, making room for Dimples to sit near me, and not caring if Sandy stood all day long. "They said they were coming back today."

"Police!" Sandy shouted, as she leaned over the bed and glanced at the door before moving to stand next to the bathroom.

"Yes, the police," I answered rolling my eyes at Sandy. "Their asses came up in here wanting to know how I got shot."

"Did you tell them?" Dimples' light brown face furrowed with worry as she glanced at Sandy, then back to me.

"Do I look like a fucking idiot?" I said, a little harsher than I intended. "What I told them will hold them for now."

"You think so?" Dimples asked, her serious tone irritating me just a bit. "Because if it did, they wouldn't be coming back a second time."

"Trust me, they bought the story. They just want to make sure what I said *yesterday* is what I'm going to say today."

"And can I ask *what* you told them?" Sandy asked, folding her arms over her chest.

"You'll know when they get here," I said, glowering at the woman. "Right now you've got other shit to worry about." And she did; twenty separate things—all my fingers and toes.

If Sandy had a brain, she would have been beautiful. With a golden complexion, she stood about 5 feet, 7 inches, and weighed 165 pounds. Her hazel eyes blended perfectly with her short, bleached-blonde hair. The mole on her broad nose was obvious, fitting perfectly with her childish facial features. She didn't have a lot of curves, but that wide ass more than made up for it. She wore nothing but skimpy outfits, and smoked weed all damn day, keeping the neighborhood dealers in business just on her habit alone. Her philosophy about life was simple and fucked up: "Once you have street smarts, you can never go wrong." Either she didn't understand it, or she had made that up, because instead of getting smarter, she got dumber as the days went by.

"So what time are you leaving?" Dimples pulled up the chair next to the bed. Both women ignored my roommate and the fact that she turned the volume up on the television.

"Soon as Five-O does their thing, I can leave."

"Good, because your ass is going to smoke a blunt and sip

some Moet with us." Dimples leaned back in the chair and tapped her purse. The bottle answered with a ping.

"I really don't think it's a good idea for me to be getting drunk and smoking chronic when I'm on medication." The pain pills were practically burning a hole in my pocket, but the shots they gave me burned their way through my veins, pushing away every inch of pain, so I didn't need them.

Sandy finally found the nerve to say something else. "BabyGirl, chill. One drink ain't gonna kill you, much less a little puff, puff, pass."

"Whatever, Sandy, whatever. Besides, if you weren't smoking that shit, maybe your brain could function like it's supposed to. Then maybe we'd already be having that drink instead of sitting in the hospital waiting for the police to show up. What do you think about that?"

Sandy huffed and folded her arms across her chest again as her gaze landed on my roommate's screen. Damn straight. The heifer should keep her trap shut. Sandy was normally vulgar and loud to the point where anyone could stand a mile away and hear her. And just by looking at her, anyone could peep her whole game: "Sex addicted, will spread legs once money is involved."

I never wanted to be a part of the type of lifestyle she lived. Soon, I would find a way to use her stupidity in my favor. I had figured once I got into the game, I'd adapt a strategy where I could always stay on top. This was easier said than done.

"Get up, bitch. Ain't no lying around gonna help your ass recuperate." Dimples snatched the blanket off my fully-dressed form. "What you need is some weed, a glass of Moet, and to shake your ass, then you'll be fine."

"You think you know it all," Sandy shot back, as she swiped the bottle from Dimples, who reached for it but missed. "What you need to do is tell homegirl *why* we're celebrating."

"Please." Dimples stood face-to-face with the petite blonde-haired girl, looking at Sandy as if she was a giant. "I don't think. I *do* know it all."

I glanced at both women, hoping they wouldn't break out in a fight in the hospital. "Hey, fill a sista in. I'm missing the fucking picture here!"

"Child, please, let me sit right here and give you the 411." Dimples plopped on the hospital bed and Sandy joined her, but kept her eyes toward the door. "We did such a good job, PitBull bought us a Lexus."

"Say word!" I tilted my head back and snapped my fingers. "We're finally coming into some real shit."

"That's why you need to hurry and get the fuck outta here so we can celebrate." Sandy pointed the bottle back to Dimples, gesturing to the plastic cups on the tray.

I immediately pulled them out of reach, asking, "So each of us is getting a Lexus?"

"Girl, please, don't be greedy now." Sandy laughed hard. "He ain't rolling all like that just yet."

"Damn, Sandy." Dimples lowered her dark brown eyes at the woman. "Your gold-digging ass should tell him we each need our own ride since digging is what you do best. And fucking PitBull is the only thing you seem to do right."

"Fuck you, bitch," she said, slapping Dimples upside the head with the pillow. "Ain't shit for free, not even pussy. So get that straight. He's tight right now, so don't front. Believe me when I tell you, his ass will come up off another car real goddamn fast. I want my own shit, too. Trust!" Sandy wrapped her hands around the neck of the bottle. She was known for taking people to task over some bullshit. Sandy was scarred in a way that only therapy could help. *PitBull had better watch his back.* And I thought he only had me to worry about.

"You're right, Sandy. We all need our own," Dimples said. We both nodded and glanced at Dimples who did the same.

Dimples, an "on the grind person," stood an inch shorter than Sandy. She had the complexion of a Hershey bar, weighed 160 pounds, and had a tiny face with almond-shaped eyes. Her medium length, baby fine, curly hair was an obvious gift from her Cuban father.

Unlike Sandy, Dimples never lowered herself to a level where a bad reputation preceded an uneasy footstep. I didn't hang with Sandy too tough because they always say birds of a feather flock together, and I certainly didn't fly the same unfriendly skies as that girl. Some birds needed their own nest.

Seeing Dimples brought a smile to my face. I considered myself lucky to be alive. A week ago, when I felt the burning and the weakness in my body, I thought God had sent the Angel of Death, instead of a second chance at life.

Now, with Dimples gazing at my bandaged hand, and Sandy keeping her eyes to the door, I wanted all of us to pray and thank God for allowing me to pull through. Just as I opened my mouth to ask my friends to bow their heads, a hard knock at the door interrupted me. Two men strolled through the doorway with pens and pads in their hands. Dimples barely managed to keep Sandy from passing out. *Stupid bitch. She could blow the whole game.*

"Good afternoon, Ms. James," the African-American cop said as he entered the hospital room. "My name is Detective Jenkins, and this is Officer Perez."

"Good afternoon to you too, officers," I said to the men, while chancing a quick glance in the corner at Dimples and Sandy. They looked as though they had seen a ghost. Dimples tried to get Sandy out the door, but somehow nosiness won over fear and she stayed put.

"How are you doing today?" Officer Perez asked, his wavy black hair, tan skin, and Hispanic good looks making him a better candidate for Hollywood than the police force.

"I'm doing fine, officers," I said in the most proper language I could manage. "Just ready to get home, my friends came to pick me up."

"We can see that," Officer Perez's gaze narrowed at the two women glaring back at him from the corner.

"Ahh, if you don't mind, officers, I would really love to get home. My arm is killing me."

"Fine with me, just a few details and you're out the door," Detective Jenkins replied. His dark skin glowed under the hospital's florescent lights. "Could you tell us what happened the other night and where all of this took place?"

The nurse walked in, looked at the officers, and backed away, disappearing out of the door faster than a deadbeat dad misses a child support payment.

"Like y'all already know, it took place in Harlem on 155th Street. I was on my way to pick up my friend, Danielle." Officer Perez scribbled quickly on the pad as my girls looked at me, puzzled. "We were planning on catching a movie at Loews Theater on 3rd Avenue. When I got out of the cab, there were a lot of people standing around two buildings, some playing dominoes, and some listening to music. As I made my way into the deli to get a bottle of Snapple, I felt something hit me in the arm and then a pain in my chest. I didn't know what it was until I placed my hands where the pain was and saw blood."

"Did you see the shooter or the direction the shot came from?"

"Like I told the other officers before," I said, not bothering to hide my irritation, "everything happened so fast, I couldn't see much. The only thing I could do was lay flat on the floor."

"Do you know that drugs were found in the building?" Perez asked, leveling his eyes at me. "And that one person is dead?"

"Drugs? Shit, I couldn't have known all of that." I glared at Officer Perez and his silent partner. "Especially since I don't *live* there. As for the person who died, I didn't know him. Once I realized I was hit, I fell to the ground. I didn't want to take another hit. I mean, I know you fine officers can understand that, right?"

Officer Perez grimaced, sent a knowing look to Officer Jenkins, groaned, and whipped the notepad into his jacket pocket. "Okay, well that's it. We'll let you know if we come up with anything."

"In the meantime, get better," Jenkins said before closing his pad, handing me a business card, and following the Hispanic cutie out the door.

This time the nurse came in, glaring at me before taking my less-than-talkative roommate for a walk. As surly as my roommate happened to be, the nurse should have used a leash. Maybe that was the reason for the IV.

"Miss . . . James?" Dimples teased, chuckling heartily.

"I don't have any fucking insurance. Besides I don't need any cops up in my business. I'm better off giving some jacked-up name so they can't find me."

"Girl, you're good." Sandy joined Dimples' laughter. "I think you would've made a great lawyer. You can look a person straight in the face and tell a boldface lie."

"I guess it comes naturally with certain lifestyles." Then I looked her square in the eye. "Just like hanging your girl out to dry, forcing her to catch a bullet."

"Let's save the chit-chat for later," Dimples said, helping me out of bed. "Let's blow this joint."

Grabbing my bag off the floor, I looked at my friend. "I couldn't agree with you more."

CHAPTER 4

CHIN

Tha Hustle Records: July 19, 2004, 10:29 p.m.

Porsha called to let me know that she had made it home safely. Thank God. The girl drove like if she didn't get from point A to point B as fast as possible, she'd die from shock.

I depended on her so much, and I'm sure that her firm would have bounced her out of the door if they knew how involved she was in my business. As we created legitimate businesses, only a little of the money from my other businesses trickled in, and Tony's money played a larger part in our finances. His money was legit and traceable. As time went on, Porsha helped me create a financial cushion within each company she incorporated, that meant my legit life would be just as comfortable as the one I had already mastered.

I owed the woman more than could ever be repaid. I thank God that she had the presence of mind to pick up that business card and call me. She made an appointment to see me only a day after we met in the cab.

As I waited for Miss Hilton to appear at my office that sunny day four years ago, the studio music filtered into my office and this time it was loud enough to compete with the Notorious B.I.G.'s record playing in my personal stereo. Picking up the remote, I switched my stereo off and tried to figure out who had just come into the studio to lay down some tracks in the off peak hours. Exactly half an hour later, a knock on my office door distracted me from the paper-work that had kept me bound to the desk all day.

"One second," I yelled, slipping out of the leather chair. The soft scent of a woman's perfume drifted in. I took a look in the mirror one more time before opening the door.

Since I didn't have a business meeting or any other seri-ous commitments that day, I decided to rock denim shorts, a white T-shirt, and white Nikes—or uptowns as most people called them. The du-rag and hat were too much. I took them off, closed the closet door, slipped back into my chair, and said, "Come in, Miss Hilton," then mumbled under my breath, "I wasn't expecting your fine ass for another thirty minutes, but that's all good. It shows you want this."

The doorknob turned and she entered my office in a sexy outfit that gave me the shock of my life. The professional woman I met days before had been replaced with a ghetto chick. She had on a white mesh blouse, exposing her baby blue push up bra, a white Polo mini skirt, and high heeled sandals to match the outfit.

My dick swelled to attention, and it got harder when she bent over to adjust her heel. The Fendi shades covered her eyes, so I couldn't tell if she was trying to read me. The white Prada pocketbook looked cute under her arm. The girl's taste shouted, "high maintenance, but I'll give you a dis-count if you have the right attitude." I definitely had the right attitude.

As she walked up to the desk, her long chocolate legs took one lovely step at a time. By now, homegirl not only had my dick hard, but if she kept it up she would soon make me crawl on top of the desk because of the way her hips swayed and her tongue slipped out to lick her lips.

"Why are you looking as if you've seen a billion dollars?" she asked, a small grin parting her lips.

I lost every bit of my cool. "Well I have . . . Damn, you're fine," were the only words I could get past my lips.

"Well, thank you for the compliment," she said simply, brushing me off as though she didn't see my eyes were locked on her. "I just stopped by to drop off the business card you dropped in the cab."

Bullshit, I thought, but instead I said, "You're definitely not dressed for the courtroom today."

"I do have a wild side, you know." She leaned forward, breasts jutting out proudly.

My mouth drooled like a teething baby. If I hadn't wanted her before, damn skippy, I wanted her now. Her gaze lowered, then met mine head on, lips moist and ready, teasing me. And my ass was falling right into her trap.

"I see that you've calmed down compared to when we last met." She glanced at my left hand. "Should I take it that you're single and ready to mingle?"

Surprised by her boldness, I burst out laughing. "Who the hell told you that I was single and ready to mingle?"

Miss Hilton shrugged, smiled, turned, and walked toward the door. Running around the desk, I caught up with her, grasped her hand and pulled her close. I planted a slow, exploratory kiss on her luscious lips. As the kiss deepened, her slender arms wound around my neck. She melted into me, her body pressing against mine as though nothing else mattered at the moment. Truthfully, nothing did. Moments later, I offered her a seat and apologized for my rudeness. Quickly wrapping up the details of my day, we were soon out the door, headed to B. Smith's Restaurant for dinner.

Four years later, in the very same restaurant, I asked her to marry me. The woman had my heart on lockdown, so I had no other choice. At the time, with Porsha by my side, Tony investing his cash, and my business taking off, I thought nothing could go wrong.

"Chin, I've tallied up how much that last robbery cost us," Tony said as he stuffed the last of dinner into his mouth. Between bites he managed to say, "If shit like this continues, pretty soon we'll be out of business. Supplies will dry up and money to pay the workers will disappear."

Unable to say anything at first, I gave my partner a narrow glance. He should have answers, not more problems. My partner is supposed to watch out for me and catch the things I missed. We were exact opposites in temperament and in the way we looked. The majority of the time Tony was easily mistaken for African-American, even with his golden complexion, but when he opened his mouth to speak, his Puerto Rican and Dominican heritage came through. Tony spoke a little Spanish, infusing simple words and phrases into his speech here and there: Like problemo (problem), beso mi colo (kiss my ass), or matilda madre (motherfucker). I learned at least that much Spanish because he said those three on a regular basis these days.

"I think PitBull knows more than he's letting on," Tony said. "He's too slick in all this. Don't you think he might have a problem with the fact that he's working for you as a middleman instead of being your partner?"

"That's his problem. If he was stupid enough to get his ass locked up, then he couldn't afford to be a part of this empire."

Tony shrugged uncertainly. He stopped eating for a moment as he looked me square in the eyes. "He might have a problem since you fucked his girl while he was away. That shit can run deep."

"Then she should've kept her legs closed," I snapped,

quickly becoming irritated with Tony's logic. "Find out what he knows."

Tony snatched up the phone, dialed, and then punched the speaker button.

"Hello," a masculine voice answered from the other end of the line.

"PitBull, it's Tony. We need to see you at the office right away."

"A'ight. I'll be there along with Chico."

"Chico?" I asked. A small stab of alarm tore into me. "Where's Shotta? Please don't tell me that someone else is dead."

"He's over his girlfriend's house," PitBull responded in a hushed tone as though unwilling to give us that bit of information.

"This is fucking business!" After a slow intake of breath, I said, "Tell him that we don't have time for that bullshit. If that nigga wants to be down, he better get his mind off his dick and bring his ass down here."

I disconnected the call, hoping PitBull had gotten the message.

CHAPTER 5

MARVIN "PITBULL" WHITE

Harlem Base—145th Street: July 21, 2004, 1:40 p.m.

I pulled the receiver from my ear, glaring at it as though it carried some sort of disease. "That nigga has no idea who he's talking to like that," I growled through clenched teeth. "One day he won't be able to disrespect me. By then, he'll be too dead to realize how wrong he was."

I should have been the one giving the orders. I still hadn't received an explanation for how Tony had slipped into my spot. My plans and ideas were what put Chin into the game, and now he let some Rican from outside deal the cards? Not for long! I would have to suck it up and follow the rules, but I had other plans for Tha Hustle Records and every single one of Chin's new businesses. I'd also take Porsha as my woman since Chin so willingly "helped" Chyna out while I did a stint in Marion Federal Institution.

Not wanting to waste any more time, I woke Chico up and explained the situation and the fact that we had to get a move on.

"Yo, who the fuck them cats think they be?" Chico snapped. "Talkin' all sorts of bullshit. All they do is sit around that office and collect big checks. They ain't in the street seeing things like we see them."

I agreed, but I still had my keys in hand, ready to make that move at a moment's notice. I knew when to talk and when to act. And I understood the bigger picture, something that Tony and Chin had forgotten I had in me.

Chico, on the other hand, wouldn't let it ride. "I mean, to be honest, nobody's guaranteed to see tomorrow, but our chance of living to see tomorrow is greater than theirs. I'm telling you, man, it's about time you take over their shit, and show them niggas who we be."

"Word, dawg, but everything takes time," I said cautiously, glancing out the door to the parking lot of my apartment complex where a Cadillac Escalade sat in the first space. "If we're going to do this, we have to make sure it's done the right way. We can't rush things. See what I'm saying?"

"Yeah, I feel you, kid. Get Shotta on the phone, man. Tell him to meet us down there so we can see what these bitch ass niggas gotta say."

After dialing Shotta to tell him to get moving in the studio's direction, I dialed BabyGirl's extension at the hospital. One of the nurses answered and informed me that she had already left. I hung up, rushed out of the apartment, and pulled off at top speed. I had a secret weapon that should bring Chin down in such a way that he wouldn't know what hit him.

CHAPTER 6

PORSHA

New York City FDR Highway: July 21, 2004 Time, 10:30 p.m.

Take-out instantly became a better option for dinner after I navigated the heavy traffic on the FDR trying to get to Chin's and my Central Park apartment. Besides, Chin had just called again and said he would not be coming home until late, so he wouldn't be eating dinner tonight anyway. Although I understood the fact that Chin had business to take care of, I was still disappointed that two days in a row, he hadn't had dinner with me. Lately, he consistently chose business over me, which settled hard in my belly. If it wasn't for me, he wouldn't have a business right now.

"Well, I guess my little plan for tonight is history." My voice echoed in the empty house as I placed my car keys on the side table. Taking off my clothes piece by piece, I walked to the center of the living room and pushed the button on my answering machine. The only call was from Chyna, a co-worker and my best friend, calling to remind me about a presentation scheduled at the office tomorrow.

"Yeah, yeah, you don't have to remind me."

With nothing left to do, I picked up the phone, dialed the number for a Chinese restaurant, and ordered my favorite:

General Tso's chicken with white rice. Forty minutes later, I had polished off my meal in bed while the space next to me lay quiet and achingly empty.

As I snuggled into the pillow, longing for Chin's touch, his smell, and his taste, I distinctly remembered the times when we couldn't get enough of each other. Like the time he first invited me to his house and I learned that Chin was my soul mate. That night, I made perfectly sure that he, too, understood he couldn't do much better than Porsha Hilton.

Doing a 360-degree turn in front of the mirror, I made sure the Dolce and Gabbana lace mini-dress hugged the curves on my body properly. Though this wasn't my first date with Chin, it was special because I had taken off that weekend to stay in the Hamptons so I could visit him at his home out there. We had held off on making love, and I knew that this time, our time together would be about more than just dinner.

Underneath the lace dress was the best lingerie money could buy. Hell, just looking at myself in the mirror made me hot. I could only imagine what Chin's reaction would be.

I threw a few condoms in my purse, ran out of the house, and prayed I wouldn't run into any traffic jams that night.

CHAPTER 7

CHIN

Tha Hustle Records

I looked at the phone for the eighth time, knowing I should call Porsha and wish her a good night. As I waited for the business meeting to start, my dick throbbed, aching to be with her. After all the shit I went through to make her mine, it seemed the more problems with business increased, the less I saw of the one woman who made all of this possible. When I got the chance, I'd have to surprise her with another candlelight dinner like I did when I first met her. Remembering that night put a smile on my face, as though it had just happened a few hours ago.

As I lit the second candle, I looked around my home, which had a Southern style and a little bit of Mediterranean influence in the architectural work, to make sure everything was perfect. The lights were dimmed perfectly, and the baked and jerked chicken would be ready about five minutes before Porsha arrived. Those dishes would join all the other dishes I had prepared and already sat on the table. My stereo filled the whole house with the melodic sounds of Luther Vandross. The plan was simple: as soon as she hit the driveway, the water would fill the Jacuzzi, then there would be dinner and a little dancing, and then finally, the games would begin.

Just thinking about the woman brought a rise to my dick. Those sexy ass legs, wide hips, and gorgeous breasts that were more than a mouthful, could make a man jump in the ocean without knowing how to swim. I didn't give a damn what she'd be wearing; slipping her out of everything so I can get a full view of her naked body was a top priority. Even if the night didn't lead to the sex, I wanted the chance to cuddle, tease, play with her, and possibly taste her.

Damn you're getting soft, boy, an inner voice teased while I checked the status of the house once again.

Usually, if I'm not in the drawers the same day, I guarantee they're coming off the next. With Porsha, I couldn't call it. It was beyond belief that I'd actually waited three months for her to put some lovin' on me. And with the way I felt about her, waiting another three months would be worth it, but judging by the way my dick expanded when I was near her, holding out for much longer might be a bit of a stretch. A good one.

To speed things up, I filled the Jacuzzi with all hot water and when it reached the right level, I switched off the spout and poured in some bubble bath. She would arrive in forty-five minutes, the water would cool off some, and then I could add a little cold water to mellow things out if necessary.

"Well, that's it for now," I said, backing away from the edge of the Jacuzzi before walking to the kitchen. Dinner could make or break a date. I definitely didn't want a single thing to burn. Everything had to be perfect. Just perfect.

CHAPTER 8

PORSHA

Of course, I ran into a bit of a snag trying to get to Chin's place in the Hamptons that night.

"Fuck," I yelled, hitting the steering wheel of my convertible. "I can't believe the traffic's bumper to bumper on Sunrise Highway. I won't make it on time." I blew a strand of hair out of my face, wishing I had taken Chin up on his offer to have his driver bring me up to the house.

With each passing moment, I was more powerless to change the situation. Switching on the CD player to soothe my nerves, Mary J. Blige's *My Life* CD flowed into the car. Soon my fingers tapped on the near-frozen steering wheel, and then my head bopped to the infectious beat. The music eased me through the traffic, and by the time I looked up, I had made it to the second stop before my exit. The digital numbers on the dashboard flashed 7:15.

"Good, at least I won't be that late."

Pulling onto Church Lane, I took one more look at my notepad to make sure I had the right address—698 Butter

Lane, Bridgehampton. I paused as I checked the address again.

First of all, homeboy had a house in Virginia, a home in Staten Island, an apartment not too far from her Central Park place, and one in the Hamptons. Of the four places, the Hamptons home was something to talk about. Before I drove up on his property, I announced my arrival into an intercom. I didn't miss the two concrete lions that stood on each side of the gate, whose eyes angled toward the intercom. The black eyes of the lions suddenly turned toward me, indicating that they were more than just decoration.

Chin's sexy, tenor voice crooned through the intercom. "Who is it?"

"Who else are you expecting?"

He chuckled lightly. "Halle Berry promised to stop by."

"Boy, quit fucking around and open the gate," I snapped as the car's engine purred beneath me.

"Oooh, did you know your feistiness is a turn on?"

"Chin!"

The lion's eyes went back to their original position. The black iron gates opened, slowly revealing the well-trimmed garden and a huge concrete fountain in the center of the driveway. The outside alone painted an impressive picture. I couldn't wait to check out the inside.

The garage opened and I drove into the one empty space, parking right beside his H2 Hummer. A quick glance to my right showed that the man truly believed in transportation. Along with the Hummer, the garage held a Bentley, a Lamborghini, and a Ferrari. Getting out of my car I noticed a Denali, a Benz, a Range Rover, a Jaguar, and the latest Honda Accord were parked outside. I paused at the last car.

"An Accord? Must be the car he uses to drive around in the hood."

The entry door was made of thick glass with colorful elaborate designs. But it was the gorgeous man inside the door who held my attention.

"You look beautiful," he complimented as his eyes glanced at my legs, and then traveled up the rest of my body.

"Thank you." I followed him inside. The wonderful aromas wafting in from the kitchen brought an unladylike grumble from my stomach. Thank God Luther's voice covered it up.

The house could have been pulled from a page of *Architectural Digest*. In the center of the foyer, a baby angel sculpture holding a vase poured clear water into a fountain. Abstract artwork covered the walls of the doorway entrance. One picture stood out, a painting of Chin, which had been situated in such a way that his eyes "followed" anyone walking through the door.

I followed Chin into the elegantly modern dining room, so caught up in admiring everything, that I barely heard Luther's mellow voice singing one of my favorites.

Chin's large hands closed over mine. "Are you a'ight?"

"Yeah, it's . . ."

"It's what?"

"The house, the atmosphere is . . . beautiful."

"Thank you," he answered, grinning like a kid at Christmas. He placed a slow kiss on my lips, tasting me, teasing me, and making my panties moist before I could even sample the wonderful dinner he had prepared.

Versace dominated the table, from the tablecloth, down to the silverware, and even the candleholder. A crystal chandelier hung over the table, reflecting brightly off the marble floor. As much as I loved the set-up, I knew that such a massive display of wealth made him vulnerable to the watchful eyes of the IRS. A man couldn't live in this much luxury and not have a decent explanation for the money. If he would trust me, I could change all that. One thing at a time.

Chin didn't release my hand as I followed him into the

kitchen. My mouth fell open at the sheer size of the most used place in the house. From an eight-burner stove and a walk-in freezer, to the large island, there was enough space to prepare food for an Army. The cupboards were all cherry wood, glistening with a polished shine. This kitchen was too pretty to cook in, but if you knew how to burn a few pots, it was definitely the spot to put a smile on any chef's face.

The salad, along with dessert, had already been neatly placed on the counter. My stomach grumbled again, and this time Luther didn't help cover the sound.

"Hungry?" he asked, removing the chicken from the double oven.

"Starving. Can I help?"

"You're a guest."

He walked me into the dining room, pulled out the chair next to his at the head of the table, and settled me in. "Give me a minute and I'll have everything on the table. Then you'll see that my talents don't all . . . *lie* in one place." His steely gaze bore down on me as he said, "You're not the only one who's hungry."

Hmm. Not only did Chin want to eat dinner, seemed like he also had plans to eat me for dessert. I trembled with anticipation.

Chin left the table and walked to the buffet where he removed a china plate. As he did so, he glanced back at my eyes, which were taking in the roses and card that sat on the table before me. I leaned in and took a deep breath before removing the card that contained his poetry, which said:

"My love for you is like a cabbage, the leaves I give to others, but the heart I give to you."

"Cabbage?" I burst out laughing.

"What's so funny?" Chin asked me with a sound of disappointment in his voice.

"Of all the other words in the dictionary, you used *cabbage* to describe your love?"

"Listen, a nigga ain't poetic. I was trying to impress you with a little sumthin' sumthin'."

"Baby, you already impress me," I said with a little laughter still left in my voice. "I'm even more impressed with all of this. So don't worry about anything. You've already proven your point."

"Oh yeah?" Chin stood and walked toward me.

Placing his lips on my neck, he gave me a gentle tongue massage and I felt my body shiver in such a way that it was easy to tell I had been without a man for a while.

"Baby," I whispered, holding on to his neck.

"Shhhh. Enjoy," Chin whispered back while placing his index finger on my lips, then replacing it with his own lips.

Removing the bunch of roses from my hands, Chin then poured a glass of Dom Perignon 1982 and served dinner. I kept staring in his direction, and with each passing moment, my stares became more lust-filled.

While he leaned over to serve me a helping of potato salad, my hands traveled downward to his dick.

Chin almost dropped the plate. "No, not yet."

With a determined look on his face, Chin removed my hands from his dick. "Tonight we're going to do it my way, so you need to exercise a little *self-control*," he said.

Self-control, I thought and almost fell out of my chair laughing. But his firm tone and serious demeanor meant that laughing wasn't a good idea. The whole way he went about doing things turned me on to a point where I was grateful I had on panties, and not a thong. My dress would have been soaked by now.

Chin lifted his crystal goblet. "To a night filled with surprises."

"To a night of pure pleasure," I added, giving him a wink.

By this time, his body was calling me. Self-control went out the window.

"You look so good, baby," I said, after nearly polishing off the scrumptious meal. "I feel like throwing you on the table and spreading dinner on top of you to get a real taste of . . . things."

He responded by getting up from his seat and walking back toward my chair.

Leaning over my shoulder, Chin's hand glided gently down the center of my chest. A small moan escaped my lips, indicating that I was all his. Feeding off of it, he pushed back my chair, knelt in front of me, opened the front of my jacket, and slipped one of my breasts from the lace bra, suckling softly on the nipple.

Removing his lips from my now-moist breast, he blew a soft, cool breeze on it, sending a chill through my body.

"You like that?" he asked, his voice ragged with lust.

"Unh huh," I groaned, arching my body, giving him full access.

Without saying anything else, he slid his hands down my legs, pulled my dress up, and moved my panties aside so his fingers could gently tease my pearl.

"Mmmm . . . Ahhh baby," I moaned, feeling a wave of heat flow through me.

The louder my moans grew, the more intensely his fingers teased, then slid into my wet pussy.

"Don't stop," I screamed. "I'm about to cum."

Suddenly, he pulled his fingers out, replaced my panties, lowered my dress back over my thighs, put my breasts back into the bra, grabbed one of the wet, rolled towels from the center of the table, wiped his hands thoroughly, and picked up his fork to continue eating.

My anger surged to an all time high. *That motherfucker!!* I took a quick sip of champagne before turning to him. "Ain't this a bitch? How the hell are you going to leave me hanging?"

Instead of replying, he smirked, held up his glass up, and said, "Let's enjoy dinner."

After dinner, much to my disappointment, Chin resumed the position of host, rather than seducer. This time when he came around to my chair and pulled it back, he firmly held onto my hands while leading me to the living room, leaving no room for sexual play.

Slipping off our shoes, we crossed the wall-to-wall white carpet to sit on the white leather sofa. Mirrors reflected our images from several points in the room. Crystal center and side tables and glass statues of lions reflected the light from the flower-shaped light fixture. The man had a thing for lions. The big screen plasma television sat directly across from an enormous fish tank where tropical fish swam rhythmically, as if they enjoyed the sounds of soothing R&B classics.

After leaving the white room, we walked slowly to another room. I stopped only to notice the new room was a "mini-club" with strobe lights and fog machines. Pink and white rose petals led up to the center of the floor.

"Wow, baby, all of this is for me?"

"Anything for you, sweetheart," he said, lifting my chin and kissing me softly.

A quick flip of his remote and the stereo switched from Luther to old time hits like Roger and Zapp's "I Wanna Be Your Man," to Al B. Sure's "Nite and Day," to modern hits like Joe's, "I Wanna Know," and Dru Hill's "Beauty."

We danced under the wonderful, constantly changing club lights. Our time together was beautiful and magical. Like nothing I had ever experienced before. Just when I thought things couldn't get any better, he ordered me to follow another set of rose petals—this time peach and white—which took me up the stairs and ended at his bathroom door. At first I hesitated.

Chin's lips brushed mine gently. "We don't have to if you don't—"

"It's all right." I kissed him, taking the lead by opening the door. The Jacuzzi had been filled with bubbles, and scented candles stood around the edges, illuminating the bathroom. Keith Sweat crooned the words, "Nobody can love you like me."

Chin undressed, exposing his well-toned mocha body. Using my hands, I traced every single inch of his six-pack abs. I closed my eyes, pretending that chocolate syrup flowed over his body as my tongue caught every single drop before it hit the floor. Slowly opening my eyes, I saw prince charming lying in the Jacuzzi and awaiting his princess.

"That was quick," I said, placing my left foot into the water to test the temperature.

"Shhhh, less talking and more undressing."

Since he had been teasing me all night, payback was definitely in order.

I began by undressing slowly, but seeing Chin lying there butt naked in the water made me more eager to join him. Seconds later, the only item left was my panties. I quickly took them off, stepped into the warm water, and let the bubbles glide over my body.

Chin reached for me, kissing me passionately. It didn't take long for moisture from the hottest of places to build, nearly making me explode. His tongue darted in and out of my mouth as he caressed my breasts. My nipples were so hard the tight little knots hurt, and Chin didn't waste any time sucking on them like a newborn draining the last drop of milk.

I wanted him inside me so bad; I thought my body would drown with pleasure. Sliding down in the Jacuzzi, I placed one of my legs on the edge of the tub. Chin continued sucking on my breasts as I angled my body so the warm water spurting from the jets splashed on my pearl. The intense waves of pleasure almost made me pass out. *Self control? Fuck that!*

"Sit here," Chin's strong voice broke through my thoughts as he patted the edge of the tub.

I didn't bother to question him. Suddenly, warm water from an attached hose sprayed off all the bubbles, tingling my skin.

A plate sat on the floor beside the Jacuzzi, one side filled with whipped cream, the other with strawberries. I turned to him, one eyebrow raised. He moved to within inches of my center, resting his arms on the outside of my wet thighs. He took one of the strawberries, dipped it in the whipped cream, placed the other end of the strawberry in his mouth, and ran the end from the center of my chest to beginning of the small nestle of curls just below my navel.

"Mmmm . . . baby, baby," I groaned as he caressed one of my breasts.

Chin continued, running the strawberry against my clit, and then slowly placing it in his mouth where it disappeared on contact. Instead of using another strawberry, this time he placed a single finger inside my opening, stroking with a slow rhythm while using his tongue to tease my clit. The more I moaned, the faster he stroked until he replaced his finger with his face.

"Ahhhh . . . Ahhhh. . . ." I screamed while holding on to his head, using my other hand to grip the edge of the tub so I wouldn't fall.

"Baby, don't stop, Mmmm . . . I'm about to cum, Daddy . . . Ahhhh," I moaned while licking my lips, then biting on the bottom one, but it still couldn't contain my screams.

After a massive orgasm, I collected my wits and kneeled in

the tub as Chin stood in front of me. I wrapped my lips around his dick, nearly gagging at first, but eventually, I adjusted to his size and caught on to the rhythm, angling him so I could deep throat as much of him as possible. Minutes later he growled as he shot off, his thick cum joining the water swirling out of the emptying tub.

From the Jacuzzi to the den to the bedroom, that night we made love in every single position we could dream of, but the grand finale was when I got on top of him, riding him like the New York City Subway. I leaned back, angling my body for a smoother ride, fucking every single ounce of energy out of him. His eyes would open from time to time. That is, when they weren't rolling upward as though he'd had a stroke. Chin was definitely on the edge. I could feel his dick bursting with cum.

My gaze bore down on him as my tempo increased. "What's my name?"

"Por—Por—Porsha," he stuttered.

"That's right." I suddenly stopped all rhythm and gripped the base of his dick to stop him from cumming. "And if you ever *think* of straying, remember this." With that, I let go and increased the rhythm to a frantic pace. Chin reached for me as he trembled in his effort to release. I gripped him again, tighter this time. Then I began moving even faster. He stuttered uncontrollably as he tried to wrap his mind and lips around my name. As I finally allowed his orgasm to break through, his moan was almost deadly as his seed filled me, then spilled out of my moist center.

"Porsha . . ." His voice, weak and spent, barely reached my ears.

I looked down at his still form, smiled softly and said, "Don't you ever forget it. Don't you ever step out on me. I don't forgive that easily."

*   *   *

Now, it seemed he had forgotten that one important thing. As I lay in our home, alone and aching with my need for him, I wondered who Chin was sleeping with. I hadn't seen his dick in ages. Maybe Chin didn't realize that I had sacrificed a lot to make sure his dreams came true. Maybe he needed a little reminder.

CHAPTER 9

BABYGIRL

Harlem Hospital: July 21, 2004, 2:11 p.m.

Sandy sat with me in the lobby of Harlem Hospital as we waited for Dimples to get the car and meet us at the main entrance.

Sandy broke the five-minute silence between us when she said, "Yeah, party over here." As she got up from the lobby's chair, she laughed so hard that I couldn't help but join in. Then she almost made me bust my stitches when she got up and started shaking her ass in the middle of the hospital's waiting room as if the Soul Train line had pulled into the room.

The stares from people in the room didn't trouble her one bit. Thankfully, her little performance was interrupted by the sound of Dimples' car horn.

She rolled down the window of her Toyota Camry and yelled, "Come on."

As Sandy and I strolled slowly across the linoleum floor, we heard Dimples honk the horn again and yell, "Hurry your ass up."

"Bitch, I'm sick, so calm your nerves down," I said. Couldn't she see me walking like an old maid?

With Sandy's help, I took my place in the back seat, but leaned over and popped my finger on Dimples' temple just for good measure. As the car sped down Lennox Avenue, I slouched down a little, leaned my head against the window, and went to sleep.

My eyes fluttered open as Dimples drove along the Harlem River Drive South. With my head plastered to the cool glass, I had left a bit of oil from my long jet-black hair on the window. Soon, my mind reflected on recent events and I wondered if my life would get any better. And if so, how?

I was different from Dimples and Sandy, so I should be able to make it without needing to pull these assignments for a living. I had enough money now to go to college, but my mind wasn't settled enough. Until my parents' killer was found, I couldn't rest. My life would begin once that issue was resolved. I had to recover fast and get away from PitBull and his crew.

What stood out about me, unlike the other two ladies, was that I was a sweetheart. But like Dimples and Sandy, I also loved money and played a good game. Dimples and Sandy called me "the chameleon." With the first three sentences from a man's lips, I could tell if he was smart, just played the game, was the educated type, or the hang-out-with-his-boys type—the kind who only smoked weed and got drunk. After a man's first words, I adjusted to whoever he was, so the conversation flowed and I could get into his head. I thought this skill alone would help me adjust to my new lifestyle. And having a tight ass body could only make things better.

I stood at almost five feet, three inches tall, tipped the scale at 140 pounds, had a caramel complexion, blended green/gray eyes, curves in the right places (at least I thought so), a not-too-broad nose, and a great sense of humor. I never classified myself as a bitch, but if it came down to it . . . Mainly, I was easy to get along with. Well, *kind of* easy to get along with, as long as someone didn't rub me the wrong way. Then, I could be straight-up gangsta.

When I first got in the game, I had no idea what I was getting myself into. All I saw growing up was the business side of things—money changing hands for drugs, and drugs getting into the hands of the sellers. Mostly, I remember my father playing spades and joking with his buddies in between shipments and sells. Nothing hard about that, right? Supply and demand. And in my mind, the game was an easy way to go.

After Dragon, one of my dad's workers who I had a major crush on because of the way he handled things as far as protecting me, took me back to his place when I was released from the psychiatrist's care. College was on my plate, and being married to Dragon was definitely part of my plans. I had no intention of getting in the game. Actually, Dimples forced me into it, and for that I'll never forgive her.

Security wasn't part of the job. A lot of risks were involved. My bullet wound could attest to that. There were days when I wanted to get out and leave with my ass intact. However, a quick peek at the job market showed that even people with college degrees couldn't get a job. The ones who were lucky enough to land a 9-to-5 still didn't bring in the amount of cheddar I did. That alone made me question if working a legit job made sense. But the one thing a legit job wouldn't do was force a person to make life and death choices on a daily basis. With each assignment PitBull gave us, I felt less like the BabyGirl that I've always known, and more like a hardened criminal. I didn't like that feeling one single bit.

Dimples' cell phone snapped me out of my thoughts and shifted my attention.

"Hello," Dimples answered softly, then listened for a moment before saying, "Yeah, she left already." Dimples nodded to me, listening once again. "Good looking out," and with that, she put the phone away and this time, she glanced at me through the rearview mirror.

I sat up and leaned my good hand on the headrest. "What?"

"Things ain't looking too right."

"When were they ever looking right?" I asked, not bothering to mask my sarcastic tone.

"BabyGirl, don't even start right now." She took a quick look at Sandy, who applied another coat of lip-gloss to her already overdone face. "We just gotta lay low a while. There's a lot of speculation about Danny's death. Mad police and FBI are investigating."

"Duh! Don't you think that when a crime is committed there has to be some type of law enforcement involved?" I asked, slipping back into my comfortable position. "What crime scene you ever seen without them? Now you're acting like Sandy."

"Shut the fuck up, bitch!" she shot back.

The vein on my neck throbbed. "Don't be mad at me just 'cause your ass forgot your thinking cap today."

She glared angrily at me in the mirror, rolled her eyes, and concentrated on driving. She punched the gas and the car tore down Van Wyck Expressway. The police, FBI, and all the other bullshit didn't worry me unless they put two and two together with me being shot the same night as Danny. A sampling of the blood work would show that someone else besides the one they knew about had caught a bullet. No way would I get out of that one. If they didn't find us the normal way, somebody who had probably witnessed the whole thing might be ready to snitch, especially if a reward was part of the deal. I only hoped that by that time I would have found my parents' killer, and I would be out of the game for good.

CHAPTER 10

PITBULL

Chin's Office—42nd Street: July 21, 2004, 4:17 p.m.

After leaving the office for a brief minute to check on the girls, I walked back in the meeting just in time to hear Chin and Tony wrapping up their plans.

"Like I said, dead or alive, I want these niggas. One million dollars for the person who captures them," Chin shouted while everyone in the room watched him clean his Glock.

"Damn, Chin, you really want these niggas so bad to the point you're willing to dish out that much cash?" Chico inquired, shifting in his seat.

Chin's steely gaze bore down on the wiry man seated to the left of Shotta. "Let me tell you something Chico, and if you never knew this, then know it now. When it comes to my money, no one messes with me. I will lie, cheat, and kill for what I want. But when it comes to someone crossing me, I will create a massacre. I don't care who it is."

Everyone remained silent after that comment. Perspiration began gathering under the arms of my throwback jersey. The glasses of Hennessy all remained full because no one had the nerve to grab their drink first.

"Now, here's the deal," Chin said, eyeing each of us seated at the long glass table in the conference room of the recording studio. "Tony and I discussed things. We want you guys to go down in Harlem and start posing some questions to the street hustlers down there. See if anyone's running their mouths about the robbery. You know all a nigga gotta do is say there's a million dollar hit on a person's head."

Chin's gaze connected with Tony's before he stared directly at me. "If you find somebody that's willing to talk, bring him down here so I can talk to him *personally*." Chin's eyes narrowed on Chico as he watched Chico squirm again.

"Because the majority of the time, cats be *lying* since there's money involved," Chin continued. Also, I want us to hit my club Big Tymers later tonight or sometime this week." A quick check of his watch and he said, "Better yet, later this week, because I want to see if there's any ordinary cat who's flossing now that wasn't flossing before."

"Anything else you want us to do?" I asked.

"Go strapped and wrapped. Be prepared at all times for a shoot out."

With that said, the almighty Chin concluded the meeting and joined the hunt.

CHAPTER 11

BABYGIRL

My first real taste of the game was when my father took me to his base on 145th Street off of St. Nicholas Avenue. I was ten years old at the time and everyone knew me as Natalie Smith. My father was a drug dealer; not a kingpin, but a warehouse distributor. He was a step above the street corners, but nowhere near the real power. The drugs, guns, and all that stuff they had in the apartment caught my attention. But all that fast money accumulating in the corner of the room was what had really fascinated me.

My mother knew about his "job," but she would probably have fainted if she ever knew that he let me hold a .45 loaded with copper shot.

This is the shit right here, I thought, imitating my Dad's words and mannerisms, admiring the metal piece as his friends played spades on a rickety old card table. *Man, if I ever get in the game, this is what I want under my pillow at night.* The heaviness of the gun and the fact that it was loaded made me want to give it a little test.

"Daddy, I'll be back," I told him after slipping the gun into my waist, hoping he wouldn't notice.

Without looking up from his cards he asked, "Where are you off to?" Dad had a Boston hand and would probably have the balls to play it too.

"I'm just going to sit outside on the bench and watch the kids swim in the pool." Maybe it was his instincts as a drug dealer or maybe my inexperience with concealing a weapon, but his next words stopped me cold.

"Would you please put the .45 down on your way out?"

Damn, I screamed in my head. I wanted so badly to bust this damn gun to see how it felt. But he ruined everything.

Since my father was a drug dealer, one would expect my mother to be some timid sort of female just laying around waiting for the money to come in and doing everything my father told her.

Nicole Smith was the exact opposite. Anthony Smith's wife just happened to be a parole officer. People are so right when they say opposites attract. Maybe the money had something to do with it, or my father's gangsta ways, but whatever the reason, her ass sure was weak when it came to him.

One thing I'm grateful for, is that Dad's money made sure I wore only the finest clothes and attended the finest schools. I got bored with private school and demanded to go to a public one like my friends. Clinton High School in the Bronx would have been the ideal place since it had a high rating, but it had a ghetto-ass student body—kingpins and queenpins in training.

On one hot steamy day in August, the stupid guards had all of us outside in the boiling sun waiting to get in. Cursing was normal, but one girl was out of control. While all of us stood in line sweating like pigs in hearty shit, she got into a heated argument with another girl over some bullshit.

"Fuck! You just stepped on my white sneaker," the Puerto Rican girl snapped at the black girl standing next to her. I craned my neck to look at the shoe, and sure enough a black footprint stood out.

"I'm sorry," the other girl replied softly, then turned her back.

"Bitch, sorry ain't gonna cut it," the girl with the creamy yellow skin said, waving her hands to make her point. "You better buy me a pair of brand new white sneakers."

Miss African-American jumped in her face as people swarmed around them. "Like I said, I'm sorry. But I ain't buying you shit."

To be honest, I don't know the next words that were spoken, but the black girl scooped an empty bottle off the ground, broke it, and sliced the girl right under the chin.

A sudden wave of gasps came from the line of people as they stepped back.

"Keep fucking with me like this, and the next time it'll be your windpipe, bitch," the black girl said, yelling so the girl and everyone else could hear.

As security walked over, the Puerto Rican girl ran off, hopped her ass to the nurse's office, and we later found out she was sent home for the rest of the day. I bet she wouldn't come back to school stepping to the black girl either.

When I walked into math class, the subject I disliked most, the black girl sat near the back of the room. I slipped into the seat right beside her. That day we exchanged words for the first time, and from then until now, Dimples and I have been inseparable.

Dimples was not as fascinated with guns as I was. She was all about the Benjamins. Every single word that came out of Dimples' mouth had something to do with money. She slept on money, woke up with money, and every thought was on ways of getting money. A native of Brooklyn, she moved from there to the Bronx with her mother and brother. At first it was difficult for her to adjust, but eventually she met me and mellowed out a little.

Her favorite thing to say when we were high school was, "Pussy is a mothafucking bank, believe it. We have all control. If a nigga wants to get up in there, he better be investing some serious dough, because this bank does not take small change. Once you give a nigga the idea that pussy's free or your pussy's cheap, then he expects to run in and out of the bank without investing a dime."

Each time we would meet a guy, Dimples would repeat these words. I have no idea where she got this philosophy, but in most ways, I must agree. Besides, it was a far cry better than Sandy's philosophy.

Dimples, known in the real world as Natasha Crawford, was a criminal mastermind who started out simple enough. She had a bike selling business at age nine, where she would find an old bike, have it repaired, then jack up the price and make a nice little profit. It was only a matter of time before she moved up from selling bikes to robberies, and by then, she was taking me with her. That was the beginning of my criminal career.

I was sure money would be Dimples' downfall one day, along with the flashy things that life has to offer. Hustling was one of the main reasons she dropped out of high school and began hanging with Sandy. Now Sandy was another story all together.

The three of us ain't nothing nice, and somehow we'd just scored big enough to let the whole world know. PitBull was cashing in and sharing a little of the wealth, but I knew he was holding out.

Little did I know, that the moment I refused to sleep with PitBull, my fate was sealed. PitBull had plans for me that didn't include just money. PitBull wanted me dead.

* * *

The day that changed my life was when Dimples came back on campus to bring me into the street life. Some days I consider it a blessing, other days, I wish she had never shown up at Clinton High School.

After Dimples dropped out of school, it was kinda boring. I could never find anybody who could keep it real like she did.

The snow fell heavy that Friday afternoon and Dragon was late picking me up. He was probably doing a run, so I had no choice but to use public transportation.

Although I ran up the block trying to catch up with the Bx28 bus, it pulled off without me. And I know that bus driver saw me running.

As I made my way across the street, a car horn blared, and I thought I heard my name. My gaze spread across the area, hoping Dragon had come, but nothing looked familiar. Continuing toward the bus stop, the horn blew again. This time I saw the sound had come from a white Honda Accord parked across the street. I didn't recognize it, so I kept walking, but I made sure to glance in the direction of the vehicle just in case something was about to jump off.

"Bitch, would you walk your ass over here and stop acting like you don't know me." I would recognize that voice in a crowded lunchroom.

I turned in Dimples' direction. She leaned lazily out of the passenger window, and then got out of the car. Another girl sat in the driver's seat.

"Oh my God!" My spirits lifted as I ran across the street with open arms, grateful to see my friend after such a long time. It had been three months, but it seemed like three years.

"I was not about to let you walk home in this cold." She gestured to the car. "So I asked my homegirl to stop here to pick you up."

Opening the door so I could get in, she introduced me to

Sandy, who, by the amount of jewels that laced her neck, the blunt in her ashtray, and the two-ounce bag of weed she had in the car, gave me the impression she must have been in the same business as Dimples.

Sandy nodded once and simply said, "Whassup!"

"Nothing much," I replied, peering at her suspiciously. Sometimes, when you first meet a person you can tell that something's not right about them. Dimples immediately laid out Sandy's history, only adding to my suspicions about the girl.

Sandy wasn't the typical female hustler. To some, she may have been a baller, but to me, she was just another ho on the block getting laid and getting paid.

Dimples' constant praise for her line of work was a complete mystery to me. Fucking and collecting dough from poor niggas who had no sense wasn't top-of-the-line work. I always figured that once everyone knows you have some good pussy, there shouldn't be a problem getting money. But I guess Sandy's game skills weren't all that tight, so sometimes she'd settle for any bum who rolled by.

Sandy was five years older than us, and for someone to be in the game so long, the bitch should've been pushing a Bentley, instead of a Honda Accord that looked like a good wind could put an end to it. Unlike Dimples and Sandy, I decided to stick out high school until graduation. College was a sure thing in my future, and a Ph.D. in psychology would come next.

But life has a fucked up way of laying out the cards. Just when I thought life had dealt me an excellent hand, someone shuffled the deck and slipped me a fast one off the bottom.

Two years earlier, on a cold winter day a week before Christmas, people were so hungry for drugs they resorted to drastic measures to get them.

My father's business had been going good, not as strong as it had been in the summer due to his recent arrest, but something that could make ends meet without meeting the end. He had just finished selling off his last batch of cocaine, and sat at his desk counting out the money. The next morning, he would give a report to the boss explaining how much profit they raked in.

Since Dad had made plans to take us out for dinner, my mom and I waited at the base until he was ready to leave. My mother sat in the upstairs apartment—the "office"— watching the evening news, and I sat in the spot right next to her with my head on her shoulder. I suddenly remembered that I had left my sneakers in the downstairs apartment, so I ran down to get them.

A knock at the door was followed by a female voice asking to use the bathroom. The guns and money were laid out on the table, so he said, "Hold on, I'll let you in the downstairs apartment." The lady was pregnant and Dad thought she was harmless. Pregnant females always had to use the bathroom. That day my father underestimated the whole situation.

After all business paraphernalia had been tucked into a chest in the corner of the room, he opened the door, locked it, and led her downstairs.

I remember him saying, "I know how it is when you females are pregnant. My wife went through the same thing. Seems like every five minutes she was in the can."

"Really, you have kids?" the Mexican lady inquired.

"One daughter."

As my dad tried to close the door behind him, a gun clicked behind his head. I ducked into the closet and watched through the half-opened door.

"Pussy! Where's the drugs and the cheddar?" Two guys burst into the room, bringing a blast of cold New York air with them.

"I don't have shit."

"Yeah, you don't have shit. Search him," said the taller of the two men.

They searched his pants, found the keys to the upstairs apartment, and six hundred dollars in his back pocket.

"This is for being so kind to a stranger," one of the men said before discharging his gun. My heart felt as though it had stopped beating. My father's lifeless body fell to the floor, making me wince as it landed.

The silencer on the gun muffled the sound. No one would know what happened. No one would come and help. I shrank into the closet, hoping they wouldn't find me or my mother. But killing my father was not enough. Hearing one of the stranger's voices upstairs had my heart nearly pounding out of my chest. Then I heard my mother's scream tear through the air and my heart. Tears poured from my eyes, blurring my vision. I didn't have to be upstairs to know what they were doing. The man with the tattoo was still nearby searching for the drugs. The one upstairs had decided to take more than just money.

My mother screamed over and over again. My heart hurt and my head began to pound. Then suddenly, everything became still. I prayed for my mother's life. I heard nothing else except for a few mumblings. I thought God had answered my prayer until a loud thump on the floor signaled that my mother's body had hit the floor. Was she still alive?

When the doors closed, I crawled out of the closet as quietly as possible and peeked out the window. The killers and the pregnant lady ran out of the warehouse and moments later, they drove off in a dark gray van.

The license plate number became etched into my brain, even to this day. I called the police and had no trouble telling them that one of the guys had a funny walk, and another one had a tattoo on his neck.

A frantic search of the apartment showed my father and

mother shot in the head, and the place scattered with left-over money and drugs. I ran out of the apartment, frantically screaming at the top of my lungs, banging on the neighbor's door for help.

The memory of my parents' silent bodies laid out in pools of blood, their eyes wide open and staring at me could still make me tremble in pain. I broke down, crying so hard my head nearly burst, and seconds later my world went black. The last thing I remember before losing consciousness was the lingering scent of Issey Miyake cologne.

The next day, I woke up in a hospital. The smell of antiseptic and death swirled around me like flies on a piece of dead meat. I left, vowing to find my parents' killers, but I met dead end after dead end. I did find out about the pregnant girl they used as bait. The killers didn't need her after she got them into the warehouse, so they killed her along with her unborn baby and dumped her body in the East River.

The week that followed my parents' murders, I had a nervous breakdown. I tried to join them by slitting my wrists. After the funeral, my doctor admitted me to a psychiatric institution for a period of time. After being released into Dragon's custody, I was okay, but I still wouldn't give up on finding the killers. Dragon, with his sexy self, was doing a good job of taking care of me, so I didn't want for much. Dragon would support anything I decided to do. But once he landed in jail, which I later found out was the reason he didn't pick me up that snowy day, my only escape was life on the street. And I had two of the best teachers in the world—Dimples and Sandy. They introduced me to the game, and I put the search for my parents' killers on hold until Dragon was released and my life could go on.

CHAPTER 12

PITBULL

125th Street—Harlem: Several months earlier

I walked down 125th, heading in the direction of Magic Johnson Theatre. The temperature had reached seventy-two degrees, with a nice breeze blowing through every now and then.

I inhaled deeply, taking in the sultry smells of Harlem—shish kabobs and fried corn from the street vendors, CD bootleggers yelling out prices—two CDs for five bucks—, and book vendors directing readers on which books were hot off the presses. The little tired eyes of the Hispanic guy who sold the mango, cherry, and coco ices on the corners could be seen as the sun bore down on him. Everyone had something to sell. Harlem represented the true hustle. Who could be mad at that?

Inhaling once more, I thought to myself: *it sure feels good being out of prison. This time, it's going to stay that way.*

Sentenced to fifty-four months in Marion Federal Prison Institution for possessing one kilo of cocaine, I got out in only forty-eight months due to the rehab program. Making it only to a place where I simply *worked* for Chin was despicable by anyone's street standards. I was named PitBull because of my aggressive nature, so there was no way I could let this shit slide.

Chin wouldn't even be in the game if I hadn't pulled him in, or let him escape with the three kilos of cocaine we stole from the base. And Chin showed me exactly how grateful he really was, the moment I left the concrete and fenced-in areas of the prison. He gave me the last of the cash that was made before I went into the joint, and a measly little job. Not half of what was owed to me, but just a "job."

Seeing the signs of Chin's success everywhere and knowing that I wasn't a part of it made my blood boil. We were boys. I had Chin's back, and Chin had mine, like Bonnie and Clyde. But all that came to an end as soon as I got busted. Then Chin kept going with our original plans to open the record label, and somehow he put Tony Moreno in the game. He didn't know that nigga from a can of paint, and now he ran things? And I answered to Tony?

To top it off, word on the street was that for a time, Chin was fucking Chyna—my main lady. Some had said Chin had even gotten her pregnant. But I let that shit slide too—because we were boys. Bitches didn't matter in the game. Well they *shouldn't,* but Chyna did matter to me. Even though Chin held me down while I did my time, I wished that courtesy had extended to me when I stepped back into the mainstream.

I had high expectations when I was released, but people and things change once a man is locked away for a while. Revenge was necessary, but the one thing I wanted most was Chin's empire. Not just his piece—the whole fucking empire. Revenge wouldn't be an issue if Chin had given me a bigger part when he hit the streets again. No, Chin would rather give a stranger top billing than do what's right. Tony wasn't there the night that we hit that joint. He wasn't there when the police came looking for us because someone had given our license plate number. Tony hadn't lifted a finger then, but his fingers were all in the pie now. And I was going to slice off every single finger and take the pie for myself.

Chin would be sorry he ever crossed me. Very sorry. Chyna had come up with a brilliant plan, even though I knew that her motives were strictly about revenge. Now that I had the perfect team to pull it off, that empire was just as good as in my hands. Although pulling one of the women into the team was creating a major problem, I decided I would keep trying.

CHAPTER 13

BABYGIRL

Home—Watson Ave—Da Bronx: March 25, 2004, 6:27 a.m

The spring sun had just started to creep up into the sky. Its bright light poured in from my bedroom window. I lost the apartment after Dragon's incarceration. When his lease ran out, I was too young to sign, but his landlord said he'd overlook my age if I gave him some pussy. I wasn't that desperate. So, I had no other choice but move to move into Sandy's three-bedroom apartment.

As with so many other things in Sandy's house, blinds were missing from the window, so I threw the sheets back over my head in order to block out the sun.

Sandy's raspy voice plowed through the pillow as a heated argument ensued between her and PitBull. Maybe PitBull had caught her in bed with someone else—again. I tried like hell to shut out their voices, hoping to get back to dreamland.

As the minutes rolled by, the argument got louder, making sleep impossible. Seconds later, a crash against the wall made my head snap up. Scrambling out of bed, I didn't bother to slip on my flats as I sprinted to Dimples' room. I listened at her door and heard nothing but silence on the other side.

I wrapped my knuckles against the dark wood.

"Who's that?" was the whispery response.

"It's me," I said. "Let me in."

She unlocked the door, then trudged back to her queen-sized bed and threw the pink floral comforter over her head.

"You hear the commotion going on in Sandy's room?"

"Yeah," she said, punching the pillow into submission.

My head whipped to the door as something new crashed against the wall. "You think we should go and check?"

"Hell naw. That's Sandy's problem. Let her work that shit out," Dimples warned. "Besides, that bitch and her man are always fighting. I'm used to it. When she starts screaming, *then* we make a move."

"But what if she can't scream?"

Dimples turned over and glared at me like I was the enemy. I should have just taken her advice. The girl knew Sandy better than anyone. She had been living with her since freshman year.

After several arguments with her mother about late night parties, smoking, and drinking, Dimples was given a choice: school or the door. Dimples packed her bags, hit the door, and hadn't been back since. She dropped out of high school and moved in with Sandy.

Since I hadn't started in the game at the time I moved in with Sandy, my funds were a little low. I had taken only a little of Dragon's money, and for a while that kept me afloat. So I helped out by cooking, cleaning, and doing other little household chores, knowing it was only a matter of time before I had to do something more, I had a plan for that, too.

Ten minutes after I walked into Dimples' room, the argument ended only to be replaced with loud sexual moans and the bed creaking like it was getting a serious workout. I stormed back to my room and dropped onto my bed. That would be the last time worrying about Sandy's trifling ass would keep me awake. They could tear the house down for all I cared.

When I eventually woke up, the clock had just hit one in the afternoon. I went into the kitchen to make breakfast. The three of us ate in silence until Dimples got up the nerve to ask if Sandy was all right.

"Yeah, I'm okay." She spoke softly and kept the left side of her face from our view. She didn't have to hide the large bruise. It shouted "see me" from the moment she stepped into the kitchen.

"We heard arguing this morning," Dimples said, sliding back from the glass kitchen table and her near empty plate. "We just wanted to make sure you were okay."

Suddenly, Sandy's lips pursed into a tight, grim line, but she didn't speak. I sensed trouble. Big trouble.

"A'ight Sandy, what the fuck's going on?" I inquired in a hard voice. The cool breeze from the open kitchen window made me wish I'd worn a robe instead of my favorite thin gown.

"It's PitBull," she said, breaking several minutes of silence. "He's having a problem with y'all living here and not working for him."

"So he wants us out of the apartment?" Dimples asked, a slight bit of anger creeping into her voice.

"Not really."

"What the fuck is *not really*," Dimples snapped. "Listen Sandy, this ain't the time for no fucking games. Now tell us what he wants or keep that shit to yourself."

She took a deep breath and gazed uneasily in the direction of her bedroom.

"He wants y'all to work for him."

Dimples slumped down in the chair and didn't say a word.

I leaned forward so that Sandy's shady eyes were directly in my line of vision. "You mean join the drug game?"

"Yep!"

Dimples glanced at me, then to Sandy. Sandy looked away, waiting.

"Well, that's no problem." Dimples' wide smile lifted the mood. "When does he want us to start?"

"Whenever he gets here, I'll talk to him and set up a meeting for y'all." Then she swallowed hard before looking my way. I felt an instant of panic before she said, "Also, he wants to sleep with you, BabyGirl."

I nearly jumped from the table. "He wants to do *what*?"

"He wants to sleep with you," Sandy whispered, her eyes sad but determined.

"What the fuck's wrong with your pussy? That's your man, let him fuck *you*."

"Listen bitch, you're gonna do whatever he wants," she said slapping her hand on the glass table. "He pays the bills around here. If you don't get with it, you'll go from having a roof over your head to being homeless. It's your choice."

Dimples watched both of us and backed up to give us space.

"I'm not doing shit," I said, glowering at the woman. "I don't mix business with pleasure."

Sandy jerked out of the chair and stormed over to me. I swiped a knife off the counter, holding it firmly in my hand, aiming for the center of her chest. She backed away slowly, her eyes widening with shock.

"You think about what you have," she said, her voice wavering just a bit. "And how far ahead you can go. Keep up this bullshit and your ass will be out of here so fast you'll never know what hit you!"

After lecturing me, she turned to Dimples, "Talk to your friend. If you don't want to see her homeless—"

Dimples whirled to face Sandy. "Bitch, you're acting as if your house is a damn palace or some shit. You think we can't survive without you and PitBull? Get a grip!"

Sandy looked us up and down and laughed hard. "Baby-Girl ain't got no parents and your ass can't go home. From where I'm standing, it looks as if you're drowning, waiting to take your last breath."

Even though words from Sandy shouldn't have hurt, pointing out that I didn't have any family was painful. It felt like someone had run a knife through my heart, took it out, and ran it back through again. Though she was right about the fact that I couldn't put a single piece of clothing on my back, or food on the table, she didn't have to do things this way.

Sandy should have known I would feel this way about being forced to sleep with someone. She'd escaped the same sort of thing when she left home at an early age. That should have made her more compassionate. Instead, it made her cold and hard.

Sandy-Ann Richards was one of Harlem's own. At the tender age of nine her stepfather began crawling into her bed during the late hours of the night when everyone else was asleep. He forced her to have sex, taking her virginity and innocence in a way no little girl should experience.

After months of this, she would burst into tears at school, on the playground, at church—wherever. She couldn't keep the secret anymore. She turned to the one person who should have been able to make things right. Her mother called her a liar, and then followed the insult with a severe beating. Deep down in her heart Sandy knew her mother knew the truth, and only later in life, after Sandy began to have one abusive relationship after another, did she understand her mother's need to hold on to a man at all costs.

Finally, at age twelve, Sandy took matters into her own

hands. Late one Saturday night, her stepfather had just polished off a bottle of Vodka, took off his shoes at the doorway, and crept quietly into her room. After the first time, Sandy always slept with one eye open and fixed on the bedroom door, so she was ready for him.

"Don't you take another step mothafucka, 'cause I will shoot," twelve-year-old Sandy whispered in a stern voice, holding a .22 purchased by her best friend—a friend who told her that shooting the man in his dick would put an end to her trouble.

"What are you doing, sweetie? Daddy loves you." He stood frozen at the door.

"That's what y'all say. This is America, nigga. The law's on my side. I could lock your Nigerian ass up or kill you. Your choice."

"Put the gun down, and let's talk about this."

"I'll put the gun down when you leave my room."

Without saying anything else, he left the room and never laid a hand on her again. He wouldn't even make eye contact with her. Sandy kept the piece on her at all times. But her stepfather spun a tale for her mother so far from the truth that soon the climate in the house went from tepid to hot—as arguments and beatings became a daily way of life. Soon, Sandy packed her bags and bounced around from one friend's house to another until she could fend for herself. Then she hooked up with PitBull after he got out of the joint. Now she was trying to serve up game by hooking me up with him too, just to keep him happy.

With my parents gone and only a high school diploma, life would be rocky for me. Maybe the only way to keep some clothes on my back and a roof over my head was to join Dimples and Sandy in the game for now. But I'd be damned if I would sleep with PitBull for the privilege.

My heart belonged to Dragon. I didn't want anyone but him. He was due to be out soon, and I could spend my days in a shelter until then. The first time I mentioned where I was staying, he told me to keep a watch out for PitBull. Even in the joint, Dragon had found out some information. Pit-Bull's name had come up a few times in connection with the killing that frigid night. Some other guy named Andre was part of it too. As soon as Dragon got out, we would take care of things. But for now, he wanted me to stay put and keep my eyes and ears open.

I turned to Dimples, my one true friend, in the middle of Sandy's kitchen that hurtful day and said, "You heard what Sandy said. I have to sleep with him."

She shrugged. "I know, BabyGirl, that's why you just go along. Do what they want." She reached for my hand.

I slapped it away. "You've got to be kidding! You're straight with this bullshit, too?"

"Look at it this way—"

Running a single finger across my throat before she could even finish her sentence, I left the air silent. I didn't want to hear what she had to say.

"I can't believe you, Dimples. I thought you were my friend."

Dimples could afford to be reasonable about the situation. No one was asking her to sleep with anyone.

Watching my parents get killed by the man with the tattoo on his neck had taken the first part of my innocence. Then when they released me from the hospital right after my parent's death, Dragon picked me up and took care of me. I actually had a crush on the man, but he said he wouldn't touch me until I turned eighteen. Damn, the months went by so slow. The day he got picked up and put in jail meant I was on my own again. I took the cash he left in the bottom left-hand drawer of his dresser and put it into an account for him to use in jail. I figured I could always make more money on the outside than he could in jail. I continued going to school, and nobody knew that I was taking care of myself. That also took some of my innocence. Then Dimples and Sandy showed up. Now with Dimples teaming up with Sandy and PitBull, the rest of my innocence was gone.

I ran out of Sandy's house to the bus stop, caught the Bee-line Bus to Rye Playland Beach, and stayed there watching the waves for the rest of the day.

When I strolled back into Sandy's house hours later, I had come to a decision. I went to my room and started packing my bags. My choice was easy because sleeping with PitBull was nothing I planned to do. Not because I was being an ass, but everybody knew the rule—that business should never be mixed with pleasure.

When I first heard the name PitBull I was looking for someone ugly who actually did look like a pitbull. Sandy's boyfriend wasn't that bad looking after all: dark complexion, dark brown eyes, clean shaven and Caesar haircut, well built, (the prison build—as if all the oil he had stored up in his five feet, nine inch frame had turned into muscle). He weighed probably about 200 pounds, and had a long telephone cut— a sharp scar extending from his right ear to the corner of his lips. No matter how built and sexy he was, he still wasn't my type. Like any other hustler, he dressed in designer clothes and gator shoes. One would have sworn he was a kingpin. All anyone had to do was listen to the way he talked, and they would find out that PitBull was not the type to fuck with.

"Where are you going?" Dimples asked, watching me sling the few things that I'd brought with me into my bag. I only managed to pull out the most important things from Dragon's house before the new people came in and took over. At that moment, even though she agreed with me now, I didn't trust Dimples anymore. Seeing how she switched sides so easily made me glad that I hadn't told her about Dragon. I would never know what she would keep to herself or what she'd let spill to Sandy or PitBull. That thought left a hollow feeling in my heart.

"I'm leaving," I said without looking up. "I'll see if I can get started somewhere else."

I plucked the bottles of perfume off the rickety dresser, one that I kept cleaned and polished as though it had come straight from Ethan Allen's showroom floor. The smell of Perry Ellis 360 filled the air—my mother's favorite fragrance. Actually, the bottle I held in my hand was one my dad got her for Mother's Day, the one we celebrated just before she passed.

"BabyGirl, where the hell you gonna go?" Dimples reached out, taking the bottle from my shaking hand. "Come on, just close your eyes and do what the man wants. It ain't no big deal."

I shook off her hand. "You know, out of everybody I thought you were the one who would understand me the most." I paused to shove the last piece of clothing in. "You know that's not my style, and it'll never be my style. So instead of degrading myself, I'd rather live on the streets."

"I'm sorry. You're right, if you don't feel like sleeping with him, then don't. But don't be a chicken and run off." She stood toe-to-toe with me, her hot gaze bearing down on me like a ton of bricks. "Stand up and tell that nigga you ain't gonna do it."

I brushed past her, and continued packing. "Like he wants to hear that."

"Who gives a fuck what he wants to hear? You're here to work for him, not fuck him. Sandy's his bitch. Let her take care of him, like she's done all those other niggas she fucked."

CHAPTER 14

PITBULL

125th Street—Harlem: March 25, 2004, 2:10 p.m.

After my big argument with Sandy earlier, I fucked her, gave her instructions, and left the house. She would put the new girl in check. Later that afternoon, I walked back into the house and pulled Sandy into the room. I lowered my voice because the walls that separated the girls' bedrooms were thin.

I smacked Sandy on her wide ass. "So what did she say?"

"She's packing her bags. She'll be gone in a few minutes," Sandy informed me with a smug smile.

"What the fuck?" I jumped off the bed, strolled down the hall, and knocked once. BabyGirl didn't bother to answer. I went in anyway.

"Going somewhere?" I asked, crossing my arms over my chest while leaning on the doorjamb.

"I should be outta here by tonight when my ride comes to get me." She didn't make eye contact and didn't stop packing, either. I saw my plans for Chin going down the drain, all because I'd rightfully demanded a piece of ass.

"Where you gonna stay?" I inquired while pretending to clean my already immaculate nails.

"It doesn't matter if I have to sleep on the street corner, PitBull," she snapped. "It's better than lowering my standards to sleep with you."

Damn, the woman was cold and had heart, too. "Sleep with me?" I laughed, trying hard to hide my disappointment. "So what's wrong with me?"

"Nothing's wrong with you, it's just that I don't mix business with pleasure." She stood, snapping the suitcase shut before glaring at me. "That's a rule I've always had, and I'm not changing it for nobody."

I walked over to stand in front of her. "Why should I bend the rules for you? Dimples had to spread 'em, too. It shows loyalty. It's always been done *my* way."

"Loyalty?" She smirked. "Do you ask the guys to bend over and take it up the ass?"

I froze. I couldn't come up with a quick answer. *Damn, the bitch had a point.*

BabyGirl's eyes connected with mine. "Thought so. All I see is that you're getting a free ride. And you're doing this because we're female. Well, I'm not doing it." She didn't back away from me or show an ounce of fear. Her lips spread into a wide grin. "What's up? You never had somebody refuse you before?"

"Nope," I said, shrugging. "Especially when their next meal depends on me."

Sandy ducked in, but inched away when she saw us still talking. Dimples hid right behind her as they peeked into the room, believing that I couldn't see them. They needed better skills at creeping if they were going to be part of my team.

BabyGirl snatched the suitcase and her book bag off the bed. "There's a first time for everything. Deal with it." Then she turned to face me. "And now, my next meal won't have anything to do with you. So what do you think about that?"

A moment of silence passed before I said, "You know

what? I like your style." Gently taking the suitcases from her hands, I tossed them back on the bed. "You've got a lot of fire and I like that. You ain't afraid to speak your mind and fight for what you believe in."

"That's right," she said, slinging the bag over her shoulder and reaching for the suitcase again.

"Don't even sweat it, sweetie. You can stay here, so start unpacking."

She didn't move. Her eyes just stared at me, trying to take in my words. Dimples did a little happy dance as Sandy tried to get her to move back with a swipe of her hands.

"You ain't gotta sleep with me. And you won't have to worry about me creeping into your room at night. I'm not a rapist."

BabyGirl stood frozen, peering at me suspiciously. The bag slid off her shoulder as she slumped onto the bed.

"But you are gonna work for me. Don't think your ass is gonna get out of that one."

"Work? Now *that* I expected."

"Oh, expect a lot more, BabyGirl, because I have big plans for you, big plans."

Little did I know, BabyGirl had even bigger plans for me. But then again, didn't everyone have their own agenda when they played the game?

Since BabyGirl decided to stay, I now had three girls to pair up with Chico and Shotta—two other members of my team.

Chico and Shotta were niggas I recruited off the street once Chin wanted me to run the new base in Harlem. Recruiting niggas wasn't easy. Trying to find people who'd be loyal and stay true to the game when shit was going down was a rare thing.

I chose the two men because their reputations reached all the way to my cell block in prison. On days in the yard, stories ran rampant about Chico and Shotta, two Harlem cats who were running Harlem red. They had their whole street on lock, and if you crossed them, there was no living to talk about it the next day.

They were ruthless, but it took very little to get them to join up with me. Every nigga in the drug game wants to reach kingpin status—the top of the line. Few get there, and most reach an early grave trying.

All I had to do was tell them about Chin's empire, and how other plans would soon come into play. Taking over Chin's business was top priority, and who would help me run an empire better than two who were on their way to kingpin status? Then I knew I'd have to split off part of the businesses with them. They could have the drug business. I wanted the legit shit.

Did they buy the story? They jumped in with both feet once they found out I had been Chin's partner and that I would run Chin's Harlem base. Ain't no way a man would leave anyone to run his drug base if trust wasn't a factor.

Base was set up the first week. Then a few people crawled in to cop as many grams of crack as they wanted.

Within a month, the base was doing well enough to knock a few competitors out of business. Now, if I could only knock Chin and Tony out of the way, the game would be all good.

CHAPTER 15

BABYGIRL

Watson Avenue: March 25, 2004, 7:41 p.m.

PitBull watched me unpack and then called Dimples and Sandy into the room. They didn't have too far to go since they'd been lurking outside my door. Sandy looked happy while Dimples glared at me before she smiled. What was up with that?

"Ya'll get your shit together and squash any beef ya'll have about what happened," PitBull said. He looked at me, then at Sandy. Somehow Dimples didn't factor into it, although she had actually hurt me the most. "I'm not gonna have ya'll out there as street hustlers. I'm changing the game." His gaze went from Sandy, to Dimples, then to me. "You three will be female drug robbers."

Robbing drug supplies wasn't a problem for me. Taking from criminals wasn't the same as stealing from a square. Dimples felt the same way because her money-loving ass didn't mind being grimy for a little dough.

Later that night, PitBull returned with two other guys. One man was so fine, I couldn't help but stare. His light skin looked almost white, his dark hair was braided, and the sideburns were lined up, connecting with his beard. Dark brown eyes, sexy lips, slim—but well-built— body, and a strong romantic voice were a lethal combination.

He introduced himself with a simple word as I stood there staring. "Chico," he said, extending his hand, while running his fingers across the center of my hand.

"BabyGirl," I responded while biting my bottom lip, then doing a quick lick around my lips with my tongue. Chico grinned, giving my body a thorough inspection. PitBull cleared his throat three times. We ignored him.

The other guy was darker than a New York midnight. Everything about Shotta was rough, from his voice to his outward appearance. He stood six feet, one inch, with wavy hair, dark brown eyes, and lips darkened by constant weed smoking. He never smiled, and he greeted us with a simple, "Hi," then stood ramrod straight as though he'd been in the military.

I leaned over to Dimples. "Damn, he need some good pussy to soften his ass up," I mumbled under my breath. Chico heard me and laughed. I turned away, blushing for the first time I could remember.

I waited for Chico to say something smart, or "put me in my place" like so many men had tried to do and failed. Instead, he just smiled and shook his head. Being curious about Shotta, I decided to be a little smart ass, and asked, "How'd you get that name?"

"They call me Shotta because I never shoot and miss." The room fell silent as he looked at each one of us. "Let's put it this way, I never shot a nigga and they lived to tell the tale."

We understood him the first time. The second time let me know he was short on brains.

After the introductions were done, PitBull stepped up to give us the details.

"The Tahoe will come pick you up tonight at eleven, so be

ready." His gaze fell to all five of us at the kitchen table. "Now, the house is set up in a way that we don't know where the drugs or money are."

I leaned back in the hard wood chair. "So, if y'all don't know where they are, how are we supposed to know?"

"You'll find out when you get there."

"Isn't that a little too late?" Dimples dipped in, taking a swig of Alizé Red Passion from a glass she hadn't touched since PitBull had walked through the door.

"Naw, you run up in there anytime I tell you." PitBull pointed at her, signaling for her to put the glass down. She complied. "Okay, there'll be a female in there. Her man leaves to drop off some supplies around eleven thirty every Thursday. Once he pulls off in his green Lexus, y'all run up in there, tie the bitch up, and get the information you need."

"What if she don't wanna talk?" I asked.

PitBull's thick head swung in my direction. "Beat the shit outta the bitch 'til she does."

Dimples nodded. "I have no problem with that."

"What if she *still* don't wanna talk?" I insisted. I didn't agree all the way around with Dimples' sentiments.

"I don't care," he snapped. "Get her to talk. I'm giving ya'll ten minutes to complete this assignment, not a minute longer. If you come out in ten minutes and one second, you failed the mission and you can kiss any other assignments goodbye."

"Okay, so when do we go on this mission?" Sandy inquired, glaring at me to keep my mouth shut so PitBull could calm down.

"Tonight." His gaze lingered on mine. "Are ya'll ready for this?"

"No problem," I responded.

When PitBull left I sat in my bedroom thinking, *How are*

we going to carry out this assignment and we have no real gun training or experience in this shit? Only once had my father let me shoot a gun. I truly regretted that Daddy didn't get a chance to teach me much else.

Maybe the game left no time for lessons. Everything was done *now*, and whatever hit at the present time was both a lesson and a test. Passing depended on how fast the brain and the body reacted. My father, definitely one of the smartest men I knew, made a gross underestimate of a simple situation. The mistake cost him his and my mother's life. Would I join them in death, or would I live to reap the benefits of the game? And would I ever find the person who had changed my life forever?

Later that night the clock read ten p.m., and everyone was ready—except Sandy. The slow jam music from the tiny radio in the kitchen faded as I walked down the hallway to her room.

Peeking in, anger welled inside me when I saw her lazy ass stretched out on the bed. "You're not going?"

She turned over to face me. The soft red blanket was pulled up high over her breasts. "I'm not feeling so well."

"What's wrong?"

"My period. These cramps are a killer."

"A'ight. So if you're not feeling well, don't come. Dimples and I will hold it down for you, okay?"

She was balled up into a fetal position, but managed a weak, "You sure?"

"Yup, just rest. We got you tonight."

"Thanks." Her lips spread into a small, sad smile. I understood her pain. Cramps could lay even the strongest woman on her back.

Dimples stopped me at the living room entrance. "What's wrong?"

"Sandy's not coming."

"What the fuck you mean she ain't coming?" Her nasty attitude made Chico and Shotta turn in our direction.

"She's having bad cramps."

Dimples folded her arms over her flat chest, glaring angrily at me. "So because she's having her period, she can't come?" She stormed down the hallway toward Sandy's room, but I managed to stop her. "That's bullshit!" she snapped. "What the fuck they make Tylenol or Advil for? To stop cramps. Women have to deal with periods every fucking month. And plenty of 'em don't let that stop 'em from handling their business. So why should she be any different?"

Damn, the woman had a point. "I don't know, Dimples. I told her we'd hold her down."

"You did what!" she shouted, almost busting my eardrums. Shotta and Chico rose from the table. Dimples waved them back down.

"I told her we'd hold her down this time."

"You fucking buggin', BabyGirl," she snapped, her brown curly hair waving about. "You can't do that shit. This isn't a fucking kid's game. Ain't no holding down nobody in this shit. Especially when they're not your partner. If it was me, I'd understand. You don't even like the girl—"

"Listen, the girl is sick, and I just—"

"Fuck that! *You* hold her down. Me? I'm on my own." Dimples stepped forward so that we stood toe-to-toe. "Any money I make tonight belongs to me and me only. So you share *your* money with that stupid bitch." She turned to walk away, but then whipped around to face me again. "And I think there's more going on to this shit than just her fucking period. So think about that shit, too."

CHAPTER 16

CHIN

42nd Street—Manhattan: March 26, 2004, 8:37 a.m.

Walking down 42nd Street, I stood in front of the tall glass building, looking up at the gold engraved sign—Tha Hustle Records, Inc. When PitBull went to prison, I thought it would take years for our plans to come together. Then Tony Moreno appeared and, as if by magic, things took a sharp turn in the right direction. That night when Tony and I celebrated our success in the Blue Sea Horizon seemed like yesterday.

Finally, we had accumulated the amount of money we needed. The next day, Tony would meet me at the lawyer's office to sign the paperwork to start the label.

Tha Hustle Records wasn't named to represent a gangsta image, but to represent my struggle to become successful in life. Life itself was a struggle, and in order to survive, one had to understand the hustle and be willing to sacrifice to get ahead. I had done just that, not realizing my work wasn't nearly done.

Tony and I decided to celebrate our success by visiting the Blue Sea Horizon. Not only was the Blue Sea Horizon a bar and nightclub, it was also a strip club. The strippers there were okay—not perfect, but they could rake in a buck or two. Since I was a single man and no one would nag me about the hours I kept; I could indulge a fantasy or two.

Music poured out of the club so loud that people could hear it two blocks away. Chairs were lined around the bar and the men who filled the room strained through the heavy crowd to get a better view of the stage. Tony and I quickly took the two remaining seats near the stage—called the "house specials"— which were in the high spenders' section.

"Gentlemen, what are you drinking tonight?" The bar maid leaned over the counter, her big brown breasts spilling out of a low cut halter. The crowd's attention focused on the long-legged stripper on the stage. The music switched from Ginuwine's "Pony" to Mase's "What You Want."

"Let me get a bottle of Hennessy," I told her, slipping a hundred-dollar bill between her breasts. "This also covers my boy over here."

And so the flirting began. Females loved that shit. No matter how good she had it at home, a woman would always flirt with a brotha if she could get away with it. What pissed me off was when a woman had a good man at home who treated her right, and the minute they argued, she'd give the pussy to someone else she'd known only a few minutes, claiming her need for revenge. And bitches are so sneaky with it, too. She could fuck another man that morning, and then crawl right back in bed with her main man that night. And they call us dogs!

"Two Hennessys coming up," she said sweetly, while putting her index finger in her mouth and sucking it off slowly before turning to walk away.

I took the bait. "Come here."

"Yes?" She turned back, replying in a seductive manner.

"Why are you sucking your fingers like that, boo?" I ran

my fingers between her full breasts. "You wanna ... *taste* something?"

"You have something you want me to *taste*?" she fired back over the loud music.

I gazed at her for a moment. "That could be arranged." A wad of bills flew over her head, hitting the front of the stage.

Big breasts leaned in and whispered, "Meet me after work."

"Done deal."

Tony had his finger up in a blonde stripper on his lap working her as quickly as possible. The musky smell of sex wafted through the air.

"Turn around and let me spank that ass," Tony suggested.

Without hesitation, she did a quick spin and whipped her golden ass toward Tony.

His large hand pulled back and—whack—the sound crackled as it landed, drawing the stares of men nearby. I thought the whole damn club could hear it even though the music was pumping loud enough for folks in New Jersey to shake their behinds.

"I like that, Daddy," she said, grinning. "Do it again."

"Naw, Ma, I need somebody fresh over here," he told her, placing a couple of bills in her thong. She walked away, putting a switch in her hips for Tony's sake.

Hell, if he'd given me that much, I'd be switching for him too. Where the hell would she spend that shit? "Slow down, Tony. You're spending it all in one place."

"It's a'ight, man. I've got it like that."

Reaching into his pocket, I took his wallet, pulled out a few bills, and handed them to him. "That's your limit, man. I'm not letting you throw it all away on women you ain't taking home."

Tony sulked for a moment, and then said, "Good looking out, son."

I made a mental note that when we went out to clubs, taking Tony's wallet would keep him from hitting the poor house within the next month.

Luda's "Fantasy" pumped through the speakers as the first set of strippers left the stage to make way for the next batch.

Sipping on the Hennessy, I paid a bit more attention to the one wearing a pink and blue genie outfit. Something about her eyes was familiar, and I wanted to find out how I knew her. The stripper on the stage gyrated to the upbeat music, but I didn't take my eyes off the little genie.

As she came forward, our eyes made contact. She quickly turned in another direction. I walked over to the bartender across the room and told her to have the "genie" meet me in the VIP room in five minutes.

A private room would be the perfect opportunity to check her out.

Exactly five minutes of waiting in the elaborate, dimly lit comfort of VIP Room Twelve, and Miss Genie strolled in. She froze, immediately averted her gaze, and then held her head down so I couldn't get a good look. She mumbled, "I'm kinda tired, and I don't feel like doing anything tonight. But I could get you someone good. I promise you won't regret it."

I leaned back on the leather sofa, pulling my jacket off, laying it to the side. "I want you. Plus, we don't have to do anything. I just wanna...talk." I was now holding her waist as she stood in front of me with her head still down.

"Okay, but there are plenty other strippers out there who are willing to listen," she said, trying to move away.

I pulled her back to me. "And like I said, I want you, nobody else."

"I guess it won't hurt to talk to you for *five* minutes then," she said after a few moments of silence.

To gain her trust, I kept her out in VIP because the private lounge area was for people who wanted to have sex. VIP was for people who wanted a lap dance. Rather than take her into the private lounge, where action was the natural order of the day, I kept my spot across from her, allowing her to take a seat away from me.

"So tell me, Miss Genie, why would somebody with beautiful eyes like you, hide her whole face?"

"It's a costume, duh." She giggled softly.

I laughed along with her before replying, "So if it's a costume, remove it and let me see that beautiful face."

She backed away. "Nope, you said you wanted to *talk*."

"Well, I'm pretty sure I'm gonna have a hard time hearing you with that thing over your face."

"Then I guess you need to move closer. Then you'll hear me better."

I did move closer, not because I couldn't hear, but because I wanted to lull her into a comfort zone.

"Why is it that somebody as beautiful as you is dancing in a club like this?"

"None of your business," she snapped, squirming in the leather seat a little.

"A'ight, calm down." I patted her thick thighs gently. "I was just wondering."

A moment of silence passed between us.

"Well, if you must know, I plan on attending law school this fall, so I need the cash. Stripping's my only option."

That piqued my interest and did gain her a bit of respect, but now I really wanted to know her identity.

"So don't they give you grants, scholarships, or some type of financial aid? Can't you take out a loan?"

She laughed a sad, bitter sound. "Well let me tell you about college, because obviously you have no experience with the concept. The government supports you in an undergraduate degree if you're not making that much. As soon as you start making one dollar over minimum, they kick your ass off. Then you're on your own unless there are scholarships that cover the whole amount. In my case, there aren't."

I leaned forward, resting my elbows on my knees. "Before I say anything else, maybe you're just running game right now. Someone could've told you that much about college." My gaze locked on hers. "And how do you know I don't know anything about college? Something tells me that you know more about me than you're letting on."

She didn't reply. Her gaze lowered again. I could've kicked myself for saying that.

Miss Genie fumed, but remained silent. "For your information," she began, "I do know about college because I have a bachelor's degree from Albany University in criminal justice, and also a master's in criminal justice. As far as taking out loans, I don't believe in that. I hustled in the street to make enough money to put my ass through school." Her eyes were sad and moist. "Yeah, I took a big risk, not just that, I could get killed. Everybody has to die. But the kind of hustling I did could've put me behind bars. Getting locked up would have prevented me from getting my degrees. Stripping is a safe cash cow. I dance, stay to myself, and don't get caught up in the bullshit. Soon, nothing I've done in the past will matter."

The room was silent, except the thumping bass line from the club's speakers. She placed her hands behind her head, removing the mask. Her dark brown, slanted eyes focused on me.

"Hello, Chin."

I laughed loud and hard. "Chyna, is that you? It's been, what? Seven years since the last time I saw you?"

"Stop it, boy, it ain't been that long. Only three years."

"Come here, girl, and give a nigga a hug or let me feel on that ass, or somethin'."

Her face brightened, and the worry lines eased.

"You look so different," I said, admiring her curvy body. "You put on weight in the right places. Look at that ass." My gaze fell to her breasts. "You got implants, didn't you? I don't remember those being there when PitBull—"

"Yeah, I got some, but everything else is real," she assured me, evidently not wanting to be reminded about her man.

"No implants in that ass?"

She slapped me, laughing hard. "Chin, stop it."

"Well, you know you have to let me suck on 'em."

"When? Right now?" she asked in a low, throaty voice as I wrapped my lips around her engorged nipple. "You still into that freaky shit?" she asked, pulling my head closer to her body.

"Even freakier, baby."

She straddled my thighs. "I'd love to get to know that freakier person."

I ran my tongue over the outside of her lips. "I have no problem showing you. "What time you get off work?"

"In the next hour," she answered in a breathy whisper. Her body arched to give my finger access to her pussy. "Why?"

"Because you're leaving with me."

"I have no problem with that," she said, moving off my lap and disappearing through the smoke-tinted door.

That night, Tony scored a few lap dances from the strippers. I scored much more.

CHAPTER 17

BABYGIRL

The Bronx: March 25, 2004, 11:25 p.m.

My watch read 11:25 p.m. when the crew pulled up at the base. The light leading to the driveway reflected off the neighbor's gate. The sound of a car engine revving up could be heard a block away since the block was so quiet in the first place.

At eleven thirty on the dot, a car came backing out of the driveway onto Seton Avenue where it did a quick reverse, popped a U-turn, and ripped straight down the block, leaving just a trail of smoke behind.

"Okay, he's out." PitBull glanced at both of us. "I'm giving y'all ten minutes to complete the job."

Dimples followed me out of the car to the driveway, carrying the black duffel bag PitBull had shoved in her hands. The garage door stood open, leading directly inside the house. Surprisingly, when we turned the knob, the side door cracked open. All the lights were off except the flickering images from the television in the master bedroom. We slowly crept up to the door, peering into the room. A young lady lay sprawled out in the bed with a blanket spread across her waist. Her legs dangled off the bed as though some man had just broken her off with a good piece of dick. From the door I couldn't tell if she was sleep.

Dimples pulled on my jacket. "Let's search for the drugs and the money so we can get the hell out of here."

"Hell no!" I snapped. "Not without tying her ass up first."

She yanked me away from the door. "We ain't got time, BabyGirl. We've already wasted a whole minute. Now let's go get the drugs and the money and be out," she whispered.

"How the hell we gonna find anything when we don't know where the hell it is?" We backed away from the room, keeping our voices low. "It'll take us all fucking night to find it. I suggest we put the gun to the bitch's head, tie her ass up, and let *her* tell us where the shit is."

"A'ight, I see your point," Dimples said with a frown. "Now let's hurry up. We've already wasted enough time."

Moments later we entered the room.

"Get the fuck up," I yelled while holding the gun to the girl's head.

The girl's eyes fluttered and focused on us. "What's—"

"Wake the fuck up, bitch," Dimples smacked her gun across one of the girl's high cheekbones.

"Where's the drugs and money?" Dimples asked, snatching the blanket off the bed, and then tying the woman's small hands with the phone cord.

"Please, I don't know nothing," she begged, her eyes wide with horror.

"Bitch, you're wasting my time," I warned in the hardest voice I could manage.

She began to cry. "I don't know."

Dimples tapped her hand against the nine-millimeter. "You don't know?"

"Please, don't kill me," she begged, her soft brown eyes moist and sad.

"One last time," Dimples snapped. "The drugs and the money?"

I began to feel a little anxious. We had wasted a whole five minutes on her ass, and still hadn't gotten anywhere.

"Kill her, BabyGirl," Dimples said, turning her back and strolling toward the door.

"Wait," she screamed.

Dimples whirled back to face the bed.

The girl swallowed hard. "In the bathroom down the hallway. Take out the medicine cabinet and you'll find the cocaine. Three tiles up, and two across to the right, the money's under there."

"Go check, BabyGirl," Dimples said, tossing the duffel bag to me, and then pointing her gun toward the girl.

I raced to the bathroom, followed every detail and found a half kilo of cocaine. Seconds later, one hundred fifty thousand dollars in cash fell into my hands.

"Got it," I yelled from the bathroom, quickly checking my watch. "One minute left. Let's get the fuck outta here."

As I ran down the hall, a sudden—BOOM—made me freeze on the tiled floor. I almost dropped the stash. Dimples had killed the girl. Definitely not part of the plan. I forced my feet to move as a sudden wave of nausea came over me.

With thirty seconds to spare, we ran straight to the Tahoe carrying the black duffel bag filled with the goods.

"Found it?" PitBull inquired.

"Yeah," Dimples said, slamming the door. The tires screeched as our ride broke ground at top speed.

I turned to Dimples, asking, "What the fuck happened? She told us what we wanted to know."

"Don't sweat it," PitBull pushed the argument away.

My heart was beating faster than a speeding car racing out of control. Sweat poured down my face, nearly blinding my vision. I didn't have to see where we were going. I knew. But everything had changed. It wasn't the first time I heard gunshots, but when that shit went off, it brought back memories of my parents' deaths as though it had happened just a minute ago.

Dimples leaned over and whispered something to PitBull. He nodded and then turned to me. "If there's one thing you're gonna learn in this game, BabyGirl, it's get rid of eye-witnesses. Never, ever leave someone to tell the tale. Because snitchers will have your ass in court facing football numbers."

Little did PitBull know, for me, facing ten to twenty would be easier than facing the assignment.

The next assignment would consist of someone dying. And I wouldn't be too happy about that either.

CHAPTER 18

CHIN

Chin's Office 42nd Street: May 24, 2004, 10:21 A.M.

Racking my brain trying to figure out who was behind the robberies left me with a throbbing headache. The fact that it might be an inside job had crossed my mind more than once. My thoughts ran first to Tony, but I soon pushed that thought away. Tony had already made it to the top. He had no need to cut me out of things to get ahead.

PitBull may have held a grudge because I'd given Tony a big chunk of the business. Maybe he couldn't understand the move was necessary due to Tony's financial assets and his willingness to trust me with nearly every dime. But PitBull could have yet another reason to hold an even bigger grudge—my involvement with Chyna, his ex-girlfriend. My dick might have gotten me in a world of trouble—again. In the back of my mind, a nagging thought that PitBull knew about my time with Chyna lingered like a crackhead outside the drug house on check day. If he knew, he was smart enough not to step to me. But then again, he was also smart enough to mastermind the current robberies and keep his name out of the details.

That brought me to another thought, one that couldn't

be possible, but then again, it's the impossible that normally happened. Chyna could be behind the robberies. She was intelligent, had street smarts, and no one would expect that someone with such an angelic face and sexy-ass body could do the unthinkable. At times, she popped up in the most unlikely places, so I had to believe that the unthinkable deserved a second and third look. I remembered one incident that distinctly set my nerves on edge.

One day I wanted to surprise Porsha at work, so I stopped by the flower shop to pick up a bunch of red roses and a box of chocolates. Ulterior motives were in play. I wanted her to be on my arm for the grand opening of Exquisite Restaurant, another one of Tony's ventures with me.

Ten minutes before her lunch break, I walked around a bit, riding the elevator up to the twenty-second floor for a quick peek at the view. The sun shined brightly in the sky. The elevator was made totally of glass, offering a view overlooking the water and the Statue of Liberty. I enjoyed looking out at such a beautiful afternoon.

The ping of the elevator arriving and opening at the twenty-second floor broke through my thoughts. Stopping at the oak circular desk several feet from the silver doors, I waited as the receptionist picked up the phone and dialed Porsha.

"Tell him to come to the back," I heard Porsha's sexy, seductive voice say through the blonde-haired woman's headset.

Excited, I put a pep in my step. But then I heard laughter, and a vaguely familiar female voice said, "Porsha, I'm not walking out until I meet the guy you've been so crazy about."

Suddenly, I felt a stab of apprehension. I stepped into the entrance to face my reality. For a brief second I just stood there staring at the woman sitting across from Porsha in a burgundy leather chair with her long legs crossed.

Porsha finally broke the silence by saying, "Is there something going on that I don't know about?" Porsha glanced at me and then glared at Chyna.

My heart began to pump faster, and I swear I could hear the flow of blood rushing through my veins at a racehorse's pace.

"Nothing at all," Chyna said smoothly, uncrossing her legs, then standing next to Porsha who squared her shoulders. "Just shocked to see you dating such a handsome guy."

"I chose the best." Porsha's shoulders visibly relaxed before planting a soft kiss on my lips.

"Are these for me, baby?" she asked, looking down at the roses and the box of chocolates that I had totally forgotten.

"Yeah," I answered, still keeping my focus on Chyna as a sudden rush of bitterness crept into my mouth. I smelled trouble with a capital "T."

"Then stop holding onto 'em and let 'em go!" she exclaimed, trying unsuccessfully to retrieve her gifts from my tight hands.

"Sorry, baby," I said softly.

Porsha turned to Chyna. "This is Chin, the wonderful man I told you about."

"Nice to meet you," Chyna said innocently as she shook my hand firmly. Her eyes never lost sight of me.

"Chin, this is my girl, Chyna. She just started here, but I'm telling you, at the rate she's moving, homegirl's about to reach partner before I do."

Over my dead body, I thought, then paused at Porsha's next words, "She's a good friend."

I nearly choked before stuttering, "A—a good friend?" Sweat gathered at the top of my forehead. Where was Tony Moreno when I needed him?

"Well, I'm not going to keep y'all for long, but it was nice meeting you . . . *Chin*," she said in a soft, sultry voice as she put her back to Porsha. Her tongue snaked out, licking her lips. "I sure hope we meet again." She closed the door securely behind her.

Coming from somebody else that would be a compliment. But the way Chyna licked her lips had me worried. Whatever thoughts rolled through that smart-ass brain of hers couldn't be good for me or Porsha.

Porsha's gaze bore down on me. "Why are you sweating like that?"

"It just a little hot in here," I said, adjusting my shirt, tie, and brain.

"You must be going through menopause at the rate you're sweating." She laughed, popping a piece of chocolate into her mouth.

"It's just a little hot, that's all," I assured her smoothly, trying to put a lid on the can of worms that almost opened. Unfortunately, all sorts of dangerous scenarios played out in my mind. Chyna could cause a major meltdown. I couldn't let that happen.

"So what is it you have planned for me today?" Porsha asked before planting her hips on my lap. Somehow that little act didn't bring me pleasure. The sun peaked through the slats covering the floor-to-ceiling window like it was trying to give away a secret. Porsha's desk was neat and tidy, a far cry from what I felt at the moment. Damn, this was so fucked up.

"What do I have planned for you? This!" I began to pump my dick on her coochie.

"Freak!" she hit me, giggling like a schoolgirl.

"I can show you how freaky I can get."

"Let's get out of here before one of the partners starts looking for me."

Before we walked out of the building, I wanted to find Chyna and say something to her about keeping her mouth shut, but I wasn't sure how I could pull it off without Porsha being suspicious.

"Hey baby, you said that your lawyer friend is new, right?" I asked as I followed her through the marble tiled hallway out to the elevators.

"Yup!"

"Did she get any criminal cases yet?"

Porsha shook her head. "She's real good at corporate litigation, but no one wants to take that chance with her on criminal matters and lose this early in the game."

Porsha smiled up at me as I placed my hand in hers.

"So how about I take one of her business cards in case one of my boys gets in trouble. I'll just put them on to her. You know, like put in a good word so she'll get some experience."

Porsha beamed up at me. "You would do that, baby?"

I shrugged absently. "A friend of yours is a friend of mine."

"Aw," she said, pinching my cheeks. "That's why I knew I made the right choice by picking such a sweetheart like you."

"Don't stroke the ego." I grinned at her compliment to hide my guilt.

"Please, negro. How much bigger can that ego get?"

"It's not just my ego you have to worry about," I snapped playfully, passing her the parking ticket. "Go on and have the valet bring the car around, then wait outside for me. I'm going to let her know what she's in for."

"Okay, I'll see you downstairs." She kissed me on the lips, tightening her hold on the Gucci pocketbook I'd bought for her twenty-seventh birthday.

Chyna's office door was halfway open. Gold-rimmed glasses sat perched on her nose as she scanned the law book in her hand.

I knocked twice before she completely lifted her head and a broad grin spread over her full lips. "Come in. Actually, I was expecting you."

"Do you mind if I close the door?"

"Not at all." She got up from behind her desk and walked around the mahogany desk to face me. "So what can I do for you?"

She slipped her wide hips onto the edge of the desk. Her long, sexy legs were exposed through her coffee colored stockings. The black mini skirt suit wasn't helping at all either.

"Chin!" Her hand flashed across my face to get my attention.

I snapped back to reality. "Um listen." I paced the tan carpet for a moment. "Porsha and I have been dating—"

"Uh huh," she answered absently, while opening the buttons to her jacket revealing the tight blouse underneath, as well as an imprint of her big breasts. The sight made me gulp before I could get another word out. "And I was just—" I tore my gaze away from the breasts overflowing from her white shirt. "Let me get to point. Are you gonna tell her we used to fuck?"

She grinned in such a manner that my heart slammed against my chest. "Hmmm...now let me see."

"How much?"

"How much what?" she snapped, irritation creeping into her tone. She toyed with my zipper, pulling it down to reveal the outline of my dick.

"How much are you charging to keep your big mouth shout?"

"Fuck you, Chin!" She yanked the zipper up, nearly catching my dick in it before backing away. "You think that your little rich ass could come up in here and buy me out?" She laughed heartily. "Naw nigga, I'm sitting on dough, too. May I remind you that I have a Benz parked downstairs and I live on Park Avenue?"

"Your point being?"

She picked up the globe on the end of her desk, rolling it

around in her soft, delicate hands. "My point is I don't *need* your money."

"So what do I have to do to keep your mouth shut?"

"Ain't this a bitch?" She slammed the globe down on the desk causing a few papers to fall to the floor. "When the ball was in your court, you was disrespectful and all sorts of shit. Now the ball's in my court and you want me to work out a deal with you?" She leaned toward me, whispering, "Why Chin? Why should I cover your ass on this one?"

Her phone rang and I prayed to God it wasn't Porsha calling to check on me. Chyna didn't answer it. I swallowed hard, hoping the truth might work in my favor. "Because I love her, and I'm being sincere. I want a chance with her, Chyna." I plopped down in the nearest chair. "What happened between me and you, believe me, I'll never regret it. But I was just not ready for a relationship until Porsha showed up and taught me that relationships actually work."

She turned her face away from me for a minute. Upon turning around, tears began to roll down Chyna's face. She got off the desk and turned quickly to face the ocean view from her window. She had a better view than Porsha's office. Who did she sleep with to get here?

I walked over and kissed her on the neck. "I'm sorry, Chyna. I'm sorry for what I did to you. I can't change it now, but I do realize that I could have done better by you and the baby."

She didn't speak right away. Instead she turned to face me, her eyes gazing into mine. The next thing I knew, her hands wrapped around me as she opened her mouth to kiss me, and I plunged in.

She pulled back suddenly and it felt as though someone had dashed cold water on me.

"Go get your woman, boy." She walked behind the desk and lowered herself into the chair. "Don't worry, I won't tell.

Just don't hurt my friend or it's your head." She ran a single finger across her throat to make her point.

"You sure?"

"Get out before I change my mind."

"A'ight girl," I said, catching another view of her luscious breasts.

"You still haven't changed." She laughed, peeling back her bra to expose her nipples. Drool formed in the corners of my mouth. She smiled as she placed her legs on the edge of the desk; crossing them just enough to allow the mini-skirt to reveal the tip of the small nestle of curls at the top of her thighs. "It's nice to know that I can still have you on lock like that, Chin."

I ran into the door twice before I could get it open. Her harsh laughter followed me down the hall and to the elevator. Some nights, I can still hear it.

Each time Tony explained that we'd been hit again, I heard her laughter and remembered the deadly glint in her dark brown eyes the night I forced her to get the abortion.

CHAPTER 19

PITBULL

Watson Avenue—Bronx: April 3, 2004, 12:19 a.m.

The girls really came through on their first assignment. When we got back to their house, I followed the girls inside, dropped the duffel bag on the kitchen table, and went to check on Sandy, who was still sound asleep.

Dimples tore open the bag, dumping the contents on the table.

"The cocaine is mine." I came back and pulled the bags of white-filled powder toward me. "And we'll split the money six ways."

"Hold up," Dimples said, standing. "What do you mean split six ways?"

A sudden tension filled the small kitchen. Chico looked at Shotta, who looked at BabyGirl, who in turn glanced sheepishly at Dimples.

"The money's split six ways. What's so hard to understand about that?"

Dimples cocked her head. "Well, do you mind telling me who the six people are?"

Her dark skin flushed with color and her dark brown eyes

flashed with anger. *How in the hell was a female telling me how to run my business?* I wondered.

I met her angry glare. "Okay, if you need to know, the money's gonna get split between Chico, Shotta, BabyGirl, Sandy—"

Chico and BabyGirl stole a quick glance at each other as Dimples said, "Hold the fuck up! Sandy?"

"Yes, Sandy," I snapped, wondering what the hell the girl's problem was.

"What the fuck she do? She wasn't out there taking the risk. All she did was lay up in that mothafucking bed complaining about how she got her period."

"Listen, this is teamwork," I argued. Dimples wasn't hearing it.

"Exactly. *Team* work!" Dimples placed her hand over the stash. "And she was *not* a part of the team, so why should she reap any benefits?"

I snatched Dimples' hand off the money and gave it a squeeze. "Let me tell you something, bitch, I call the shots around here. Whatever I say, goes."

Dimples pulled her hand free, rubbing it to ease the pain.

"Now if you wanna have all that female cat fight shit, you take that up somewhere else. Not on my time." I paused long enough to look at BabyGirl, and thoughts of how Chin had betrayed me popped into my mind. "This is a team. Y'all need to learn how to be together. It's just the beginning and we're already arguing over money." My gaze fell on each one of them. "What happens when we start bringing in big money?"

"It doesn't matter, PitBull," BabyGirl dipped in, trying to calm things down. "I told her that I'd have her back, so let's get our $25,000 each, and take our asses to sleep."

"Anyone else have something to get off their chest before I start squaring the money?"

Everyone remained silent. Dimples' face had set in a hard line as though she would explode any moment.

After I handed Dimples her money, she grabbed it and walked off to her room mumbling about how foul the whole set up was. Then she turned to face me and said in a voice that carried across the room, "And when I have my motha-fucking period, things had better go down the same fucking way. No favorites. You expect us to pull the load for your bitch, then it damn well better work both ways. Watch what happens if your game changes."

At that moment, I knew I had made a mistake. Two women on my crew giving me grief was a bad sign. A very bad sign.

CHAPTER 20

BABYGIRL

Fifth Ave, NYC: April 5, 2004, 11:01 a.m.

Twenty-five thousand was a lot of money for someone to be holding. Especially when a few days ago, I didn't know where my next meal was coming from. Dimples, Sandy, and I went on a shopping spree on Fifth Avenue, where stores like Gucci, Fendi, and Elizabeth Arden were all spread out over a few blocks. A stop at Tiffany and Company, the grand finale of that spree, was where we draped our bodies with jewels that cost a fortune. It had been a week since Dragon's release, and I felt bad I didn't get him anything, so I got a pinky ring for him as a welcome home gift.

Elaborate spending made our reserves dwindle down to nothing, and our next assignment was three weeks away. Pit-Bull's crew had been staking out a base in Harlem for three months—even while we committed the first robbery. So far, we had managed to gather enough information to know what time everyone left, what time they got back, what day of the week shipments came in, and what day too many people were there.

"In three weeks we're gonna make this move," PitBull said while rolling out a map with physical pointers on how we would take them down. "Since only one of them is there on Thursday afternoons, Sandy, I'll need you to take the front door and distract the guy." PitBull looked across the table. "Dimples and BabyGirl, I need you to go around the back and slip through the bedroom window. The drugs are in a walk-in closet in two barrels."

Dimples peered at him. "How can you be sure?"

"We bought from this spot a couple of times to get familiar with the surroundings."

"How much time do we have to complete this assignment? And should we grab money if we see it?" I asked, feeling a rush in my veins at the thought of filling my pockets again.

"Fifteen minutes tops, because he's not going to stay out there and talk to Sandy for that long. Just grab as much as you can so that everyone gets a fair share. And yes, BabyGirl, money's always welcome. Just hurry, handle the business, and get the fuck outta there. Chico and Shotta will be waiting in the van down the block."

I clapped my hands, showing I was ready to get things started. "No problem."

"Everyone in agreement?"

"Hell, yeah," Dimples answered, giving me a pound. "Let's do this."

Three weeks later, Sandy dressed as the cable lady and Dimples and I wore ordinary black sweatsuits with our hair tucked into tight buns. As soon as Shotta got in place, Chico, who was just a few feet away pretending as though he'd come from another apartment upstairs, lifted his walkie-talkie and said, "Okay, I got it."

Sandy took one last look in the mirror to make sure her breasts were pushed up to the point that they spilled over. Her shirt was unbuttoned to reveal a good amount of cleavage. We watched from the backseat of the car as she strolled across the street with a clipboard and made her way toward the building.

Four minutes later, Chico gave us the signal that she had made the sale, and we were out of the van, sprinting through the back of the building, then scaling the fire escape. Seconds later, we pried open the bedroom window and ran to the closet. Opening the barrel, we stumbled upon two kilos of cocaine. Placing them in the bag, we fixed the top back on the wooden barrel. Making our way to the living room to signal to Sandy that we were finished, Dimples yanked my top, holding me in place as we froze at the entrance. My mouth fell open. Not only had Sandy managed to sell the man fake cable, but she had also crossed the line and had the man giving her head. Since he was so deep into eating the goods, the two of us wasted no time searching the other rooms. We grabbed three hundred thousand dollars in cash and went out the window. Since we knew that today was collection day, finding that much money wasn't a surprise. And it certainly put a smile on Dimples' face.

We made it back to the van safely and waited for Sandy to finish. Two minutes later Sandy ran out the front door of the building with a big grin on her lips, the same smile she had pasted on her face when we got home.

"What the fuck are you so happy about?" PitBull asked as we piled into the house.

"The bitch had the nigga eating out the coochie up in there," Dimples dipped in before busting up with laughter.

"Say word." PitBull laughed as he watched Dimples fall out on the floor, holding her sides.

"That's the shit I'm talking about," I said, laughing along with Dimples. "Sandy always gets the fun job while Dimples and I are always stuck with the lousy ones."

Chico chuckled, gave me a flirtatious smile, as if to say "I'll eat you," and then elbowed Shotta in the side. I almost fell over when Shotta actually smirked.

"Don't be a hater. Join in bitch, and be a player," Sandy teased, swiveling her hips like a hula dancer.

"Don't be a hater. Join in, and be a player," Dimples mimicked before rolling her eyes.

Although I found it funny, there were other things on my mind. This new money could get me the information I needed to get the ball rolling and find out who had killed my parents.

CHAPTER 21

CHIN

Tha Hustle Records, NYC: April 25, 2004, 11: 33 p.m.

The first day in the studio, Dragon sat in the lobby of Tha Hustle Records waiting for me. Tony and the producers had him spit a rhyme to see if he could get a rap deal.

"Chin will be with you in a few," Tony told him from the door as I clicked back over to the other line to answer a call.

The office was busy yesterday because wannabe artists kept calling for a deal every five seconds. Dragon getting through was pure luck. I was close to hanging up the phone when he just belted out a beautiful love song, and I was forced to listen to every single word.

The boy was multi-talented. Not only could he sing and rap, but he played the piano as well. Not to mention the women would soak his sexy ass right up. He stood no more than five feet, eight inches, with a cool, dark complexion and slanted eyes like mine. He had a deep voice, dressed like a thug, and had a charismatic personality—the type that would make a woman fall for his sweet words not knowing that she had fallen right into a trap.

Rhyming in the hallway caught the attention of Nico, one of the producers who was on his way to the listening booth.

Instead of having Dragon wait a while longer, he immediately called him into the studio so he could start doing his thing.

An hour later, the noise outside the studio pulled me away from the desk. Dragon must have made a good impression on the producers because as soon as he came out, he thanked Nico and said, "When I get my advance, I'm taking you to dinner."

"Don't thank me, boy," Nico said, gripping his hand. "Thank God for giving you such a talent."

"Yeah, I thank him, but if it weren't for you I would never have spoken to Chin and Tony."

"True that," Nico yelled as Dragon stepped into the elevator.

"That's why dinner's on me," he yelled back.

"That boy's gonna make us money!" Tony said, clasping his hands together, and then walking into the office with the last page of Dragon's signed contract.

"I couldn't agree with you more," I said, slipping the papers into a folder. "We can never let a money maker like that slip out of our hands."

While walking back to my office, I couldn't help but smile at our luck. Dragon was someone who labels wished for. A rapper and a singer—how much better could it get? Most artists can make or break a label. I invested a lot of money in Dragon. I wondered if he would make or break Tha Hustle Records, but that was a risk I was willing to take. Closing the door to my office, I poured a glass of Hypnotic to celebrate in my own way.

CHAPTER 22

BABYGIRL

145th Street, Harlem: April 26, 2004, 7:08 a.m.

One thing I have never liked, and still don't like to this day, is the police. After seeing the ass whoppings they put on my father when they arrested him several times, their fate with me was sealed. When I heard that PitBull was joining forces with two of them for our next assignment, it made me wonder if I still wanted to be a part of the team.

As Sandy, Chico, Shotta, and two new guys sat around the table, I leaned over to PitBull and said, "I'm not feeling this."

"What's your problem, BabyGirl?"

"How do we know we can trust these mothafuckas?" I whispered so the two pigs couldn't hear. "What if they turn on us and lock us up after they get paid?"

"Do you have another way of getting police uniforms, police cars, or police radios?"

"No," I whispered cautiously, as he tipped me off to the real deal.

"Then I suggest you shut your fucking mouth and go along with the plan."

"Whatever," I shot back. "But when they take you down,

don't say I didn't warn you." I left the table to join Dimples at the window.

PitBull thought he could do whatever he wanted, but I was gonna make sure I protected myself after this robbery shit went down.

I nudged Dimples.

"What?" She asked in an agitated tone, shooing me away. Wondering what was so interesting, I leaned forward to peek out the window. Somehow I had interrupted her view of a nigga in a green Range Rover who had pulled up in front.

"Listen, I have a plan," I said.

"Go on girl, spit it out," she spoke without once letting her eyes leave the man downstairs.

"How about we take down the two cops after the robbery's complete?"

"Yeah, I'm down for whatever," she answered while hastily grabbing her purse off the couch and running to the stairs.

"Where are you going?" I ran behind her like a two-year-old after its mother.

"To go get my man."

I stopped short at the edge of the stairs. "Excuse me, what man—"

"The nigga downstairs. You know, the one in the green Range."

"When? I—"

"Don't sweat it, girl. Good looking niggas like him you never let get away. Especially when they look like they're rolling in some deep dough."

"But listen," I shouted as her foot hit the stairs.

"I'll listen when I get back." She turned around and disappeared without saying another word.

With nothing else to do, I had no other choice but go back in the other room and listen to PitBull talk to his police *friends* about his plans. I could never understand that shit. Dimples and I did all the nasty and dangerous work around here, and everybody else got fucking paid off us. *Not for long.* It was time for a female to step up her game and let these bitch ass niggas know that a woman can take charge.

I watched PitBull from the entrance. Where the fuck did he get this philosophy that the police and criminals are friends? Never in my life have I heard of such bullshit. That was like mixing oil with water. Didn't PitBull know that police were the biggest snitches, especially when Internal Affairs caught them with their hands dirty? Well, that shit would not go down over my dead body, much less while I was living.

PitBull extended his hands to the two men and didn't hear me say, "You wait, PitBull. I'm gonna teach you how this game is really played, not how you *think* it should be played."

Yes sir, after we finished with the assignment, I planned on putting their white, desperate asses to sleep.

CHAPTER 23

CHIN

Tha Hustle Records NYC: April 26, 2004, 8:49 a.m.

The situation with Chyna being so close to Porsha was getting to me. The more I thought about it, the more I couldn't go another day without consulting Tony.

"What the fuck is wrong with you?" He looked up at me while biting on a slice of pizza as I entered his office.

"Problems, man," I replied. "Or should I say problemos, as you put it?"

"From the look on your face, I smell female bullshit."

"Check this out, Tony," I said before sitting on the sofa. "A while back I went to Porsha's job, right?"

"And?"

"There was another female in the office whose voice sounded familiar."

Tony leaned forward, resting his elbows on his knees. "This shit ain't sounding too good, kid."

"Trust me, it ain't."

Tony put the slice of pizza down on the wrapper.

"Anyway, I went to the door and Chyna was there."

"*The* Chyna," he said before retrieving a napkin to wipe the grease from his lips. "Chyna you fucked back in the day?

PitBull's wifey? The same one you took to the hotel after picking her up in the strip joint?"

"Yeah, *that* Chyna," I said, wishing my appetite was as good as Tony's.

"What the hell she do to get in jail?"

"That's the problem, man, she wasn't a client."

"Then what is . . ." His eyebrows drew in. "Aww, shit!" He slapped his hand on the desk. "Don't tell me she's an attorney?"

"Yup, homegirl's a lawyer at the firm and happens to be a good friend of Porsha's."

He now got up from behind his desk to turn off the demo he had playing in the stereo.

With a shake of his head and a little chuckle, he said, "Man, you're in some deep shit."

"You don't think I know that, Tony?"

He shrugged. "Okay, so Porsha and Chyna work together. What's the problem?"

"What the hell am I gonna do?"

"Ain't shit you *can* do, nigga. Unless you gonna hit Chyna off to keep her mouth shut."

I slipped back into Tony's gray sofa. "Tried that already. She ain't having it."

"What did she say?"

"She just said she ain't working out no deal. Then she changed her mind and said that it's okay and she wouldn't talk."

Laughter burst from Tony, and for some reason when he laughed I knew I was in big trouble.

"Let me ask you this, Chin." He sat back in his leather chair and clasped his thick hands together as though saying a prayer. "You believe the puta?"

"Hell, naw!"

"Oh, because I was just about to tell you that you're being played and don't know it."

"So what do you think, Tony?"

I felt confident that Tony would have some great advice. He was a married man, a little older than me, and way more experienced with getting out of female games. So any advice from an elder would be appreciated, especially now.

"Okay, let me tell you," he said between bites, as he resumed eating the last piece of pizza. "She refused the money; therefore, this shit's personal. As far as her not telling Porsha, why would she? She wants you and going to Porsha with a secret like that will not only put distance between their friendship—which she probably doesn't give a fuck about—but it will also make you hate her, which is not her goal."

Now what could I say to that?

"She wants you back, or worse, she wants revenge, Chin. And when a female wants something, she's like a lion after her prey, but in a much sneakier way."

"So what's she going to do?"

"Seduce you, maybe, but prepare for harassment when she can't get what she wants. Because from back then 'til now, if a female wants you, there are no such words as 'I'm going to let you go' in her dictionary."

Running my fingers through my freshly braided hair, I sighed and said, "I sense trouble, Tony."

"No mi amigo-*my friend*, I sense desastre- *disaster*," he teased, using an old-fashioned Italian mobster voice.

"Wow." I blew out a long, slow breath and slid back into the sofa.

"Look, Chin, fuck that! If she wants the dick, I say fuck the puta if you have to. Lay it on her ass. That will keep her mouth shut for now until we can think of something."

"Isn't that like playing with fire?"

"Either you're gonna have to play with fire, or you're gonna experience a major disaster."

"I want neither."

"Suit yourself, man. Now, put all female problems aside. It's business time." He wiped his hands on the napkin then fixed his tie. "I need a date on dropping the fashion line, and a date Dragon can come in to sign the last of the paperwork. Last, but not least, the guy who handles our shipments needs to know the amount of supplies you want him to ship."

"I'll get back to you later on those dates." I rose from the chair, heading toward my office. "As for the UPS man, hold off. That nigga's getting pulled over and having my supplies seized by the Feds too much. So let me check out his story, and then I'll let you know."

"Take it easy, man," Tony said in a solemn tone. "And never underestimate your opponent."

"Who, Chyna?"

"I'm talking about everybody in general. Chyna and Pit-Bull. I smell disaster, and you're not listening to me on the PitBull issue. I can only pull your ear to some things, but it's up to you to act." Tony switched the stereo on, and the demo he had on earlier resumed play. "You know we're partners, so it's a definite that I have your back." Tony now turned his head toward me. "Yeah, so don't worry about me. I'm loyal to the end."

CHAPTER 24

BABYGIRL

Watson Avenue.: April 27, 2004, 1:17 a.m.

"Dimples," I shouted, walking from the bathroom with a towel wrapped around my waist.

"What's up?" she answered, leaning back in her bed and watching television. Her maroon blanket lay crumpled across her waist.

"What happened with stud?"

"Mr. Green Range Rover? Or better yet, Mr. Marquis?" She muted the television. "He made himself too vulnerable, too quick. He likes to play games, but his skills ain't up to par yet, so I'll have to school the player on how it's done."

What I was about to say to Dimples was very important, so I moved over her blanket, sat on the edge of the bed, and waited until she finished bragging.

"What did you want to tell me earlier?" Dimples asked.

"Nothing," I said quickly, having second thoughts about telling her anything. Dimples had her own thing going on, and she was real quick to side with PitBull sometimes. Maybe telling her my plans wasn't a smart thing.

She peered at me, trying to make eye contact. "Do I sense an attitude?"

"Bitch, I said it was nothing."

She grinned. "Let me find out you one of 'em bitches that's a cock blocker."

"Cock blocker? Bitch, please! With the amount of dick that's available on the streets, ain't no need for me to block you from getting a damn thing."

"You sure 'bout that?" She looked me square in the eye. "Because I ain't seen you with no man."

"Fuck you, Dimples,"

"See, I knew you were gay!" She laughed, nearly rolling off the bed. "Why the hell you would say 'fuck me'?"

"Get the fuck outta my face, punk." I laughed back, remembering all the times that people had accused us of being that way because we were so close.

"Seriously though, what did you want to holler at me about earlier?"

"PitBull, man. He's moving foul." I lifted one of my legs off the floor and placed it on the bed. "How the hell he gonna have us working with police?"

"I ain't feeling that shit either," Dimples said before letting out a soft sigh.

"And then to top it off, when I said something earlier the nigga's gonna suggest that I keep my fucking mouth shut and go along with the flow."

"So what do you want us to do?"

"I say we kill 'em when it's over."

"Kill 'em!" She jerked up. "You don't think that's a little too extreme? They're cops, not drug dealers nobody'll look for. Somebody *will* miss 'em, and the next thing you know, the FBI will be on our asses."

"I never thought of that." I said, seeing my plans take a nosedive. "So, what are we gonna do?"

"Just go along with the plan, man," Dimples suggested.

"No, I don't trust crooked cops. We gotta take them down. It's just a matter of how."

"Whenever you come up with a plan, let me know." She turned up the volume on the television. "But right about now, a sister's gonna get some beauty rest."

3:34 a.m.

I woke up in a cold sweat after another nightmare. This nightmare was about Dimples being killed. And if that wasn't enough, I was accused of killing her. It was definitely a sure sign that something would go wrong real soon.

"I can't let those pigs just walk away when we're done," I whispered, pacing back and forth in my bedroom.

The thought of being questioned by the police or the FBI wasn't really a problem, but being sentenced to life without the possibility of parole—or death—was a different story. My mind became bombarded with so many different thoughts that I turned on the television to ease the images running through my head. As I flipped the channels finding nothing to hold my interest, I finally stopped at HBO, hoping I could catch an early morning run of *The Wire*. Shows like that always gave me good ideas. However, that night, it came up short, because before I knew it, I felt drowsy.

My eyes were burning, not only because I was tired and wanted to sleep, but because I was fighting sleep. I couldn't say why. Deciding not to torture myself anymore, I lifted the remote to put it on mute when something on *The Wire* caught my eye.

I sprung out of bed with my eyes glued to the television. "This is the mothafucka right here." I turned up the volume as one of the characters said, "This is how we're going to take these police down without drawing suspicion to ourselves."

I sat glued to the television until the end of the show. As soon as the credits began to roll, I checked the clock. It was four in the morning. I got up, walked through the hallway, and called out, "Dimples."

CHAPTER 25

PORSHA

Red Lobster—42nd Street: April 27, 2004, 2:00 p.m.

"So tell me, girl, where did you meet him?" Chyna asked, looking up at me while sipping on her glass of Coca-Cola.

"In a cab. He accidentally dropped his business card on the seat next to me."

Chyna's eyebrow shot up. "Yeah, right. Nobody *accidentally* drops their card. You fell for one of the oldest tricks in the book." She placed another piece of fish in her mouth and shook her head disdainfully.

"Well, it worked in my favor," I said, laughing. "Now he's got me and I've got him, so what's the problem?"

Chyna wiped her mouth with the napkin, and took up her glass to take another sip. "You like him?"

"No, I love him, and if he continues with all this good treatment, he might make me step the wedding date up."

Liquid came spraying out of Chyna's mouth, covering her plate and part of mine. "You are gonna step the date up earlier?"

"Is there something wrong with that?"

CHAPTER 26

BABYGIRL

NYC April 26, 2004, 1:22 p.m.

This time we were hoping to score one hundred thousand dollars each. Two days before the robbery was scheduled, a meeting in Sandy's dining room with the three officers was well underway. PitBull addressed the team with details, but my mind wandered off, knowing the plan I had come up with had met Dimples' approval. We wouldn't share it with Sandy. She definitely couldn't be trusted. A quick look out the kitchen window showed that the weather tonight would remain perfectly clear.

"BabyGirl." PitBull pulled me out of my thoughts. "Is there something on your mind you'd like to share with the rest of us?"

Sitting up straight in the chair, my eyes gave him a deadlock stare, "Why would you ask me something like that?"

"Because your facial expressions says there's something you wanna get off your chest."

"No, not at all," I said, shrugging. "I'm just listening and trying to absorb the information."

The three officers stood, explaining police procedure so

our movements during the robbery wouldn't look suspicious.

The tall, dirty blonde officer with the thick mustache spoke first. "If any complications should arise, that's when Brad, another officer, will come in."

Dimples sat up. "Hold up. Your friend, Brad?" She looked at me, then to PitBull. "Who's this Brad person?"

Matt, the second officer, said, "He's a third party."

"Hold the fuck up, PitBull," I said, feeling Dimples' concern. "When were you gonna tell us that a *third party* was involved?"

"Is there a problem here?" Matt, sporting a crew cut and a gut, glared at me. "Because I'm sensing disagreement. And the last time I checked, you were the boss, PitBull, but we are the head of this operation." He whirled to face PitBull, who was standing between Chico and Shotta. "And it was stipulated that we would do it our way since we're helping *you* guys out."

PitBull whipped around to Dimples. "Dimples, what I tell you the other day about your mouth?" He said, poking her in the chest with a single finger. "The next time you open your mouth about some fucking shit, I'm gonna take your ass off the assignment, without pay."

My eyes dimmed and my blood was boiling. I wanted to take care of those smart-ass cops right then and there. Fuck the FBI and the police. Charlie, the dark-haired policeman, had a big grin on his face because PitBull had put us in our places.

Strolling away from the table, I mumbled under my breath. "Let's see how long that grin's gonna last when my ass shoves a glock down your mouth."

After their little meeting, everyone but me went to T.G.I. Friday's for dinner. I was so upset about how PitBull put us down in front of everybody, that I didn't go with them. Instead, I went to my room and absorbed the quiet atmos-

phere, thinking over my plans while being grateful that the
three studs didn't have us all in jail cells somewhere. I couldn't
understand PitBull's logic. Hopefully, when those two bodies
dropped, he'd understand mine. Personally, I thought he
made a mistake testing me the day he asked me to sleep with
him. After he gave in so easily when I turned him down, he
showed a side that told me if you knew the right words to say,
or the right things to do, he would back down easily. With no
loyal family to my name, I had nothing to lose. Nothing at
all.

CHAPTER 27

PITBULL

T.G.I. Friday's, 50th Street NYC: April 26, 2004, 7:14 p.m.

I was still pissed that BabyGirl had decided not to come to dinner, but I kept silent as the rest of the crew chatted away. How dare she get angry about pulling Matt and Charlie into my next plan? Where did she get off having an opinion? And I wasn't too happy either about how Chico and BabyGirl had been getting a little close.

When I first saw BabyGirl, she was more special in my heart than Sandy or Dimples because she reminded me of Chyna. The only difference was, Chyna had been more obedient—well, at least she was before that stint in jail. BabyGirl had too many sparks to her flame, which I would have to cool down in due time. And I would cool her ass down the moment I found a way to tap that ass. At that moment, I wasn't above taking what I wanted. Sometimes a little dick is all it took to break a bitch down.

As the waitress took the orders, my mind left the surroundings of Friday's, and I thought about how I had met Chyna. I cursed myself for not seeing the first signs of her betrayal.

*   *   *

Chinetta Sway was born in Trenton, New Jersey, but moved to White Plains, New York when she was five years old. At the time she lived with both parents, strict Pentecostals who tried like hell to keep her in check. Of course, with her hot ass that didn't always work.

I met her at Jimmy's Café off Fordham Road in the Bronx, where my boy Chin was throwing a birthday party for Trae-Black—one of the crew members. Chyna and a couple of her girlfriends had walked in, and I couldn't take my eyes off her five feet, five inch, 140-pound frame. Her hair was cut in layers and ended just at her shoulders. She had a tan complexion, and looked as if she had just come off the beach in the Bahamas or some other tropical place. Her thighs were thick and firm, and her breasts were not big, but good enough to satisfy. I elbowed Chin in the side and pointed toward her to get his opinion.

"Shorty's fine," I stared at her, nearly drooling as I licked my lips.

I instantly wished I hadn't said anything. "I'm gonna holla."

"Do your thing, boy," Chin said, without taking his eyes off the woman.

As she made her way through the thick crowd, I held on to her hands and would not let go. Turning to see who it was, she took a quick glance, and gave me a flirtatious smile.

"Come here for a minute, shorty," I said over the loud music.

"I'm a little thirsty, so I'm trying to get to the bar and get back to my girlfriends. Maybe next time." She tried to wheel out of my hold.

"So I'll walk with you to the bar," I offered.

I could tell that she was thinking about it because of the

one-minute pause, but then she disappointed me. "It's okay, I can go by myself."

"So what's your name?" I asked still pushing for conversation.

"Chinetta, but you can call me Chyna."

"Nice to meet you Chinetta or Chyna," I said, laughing, but still holding onto her soft hand. She relaxed some. "And yours?"

"PitBull."

"I know you've got a real name," she said, leveling her dark brown eyes at me. "Your mama didn't name you that."

"Marvin," I replied sheepishly.

"Nice to meet you . . . *Marvin.*"

"So Chyna, can I buy you something from the bar?"

"No, because when you guys buy a female drink, y'all be thinking that y'all own us for the night. Or a drink equals the telephone number."

"Sweetie, let me tell you this—the amount of dollars that's floating around in my pocket, a bottle of Belvedere ain't shit. I'm gonna ask for your number because I like you, not because I bought you a drink."

"Well . . . I was going to get a bottle of water since I'm not old enough to drink."

"Ain't nobody gonna know. I'll get you something."

"Aight," she answered softly.

"Let me get a glass of Henny and a glass of Belvedere," I told the bartender.

"One Henny and one Belvedere coming up," the bartender replied.

"Shorty, you look good. Can I get a number or something, 'cause I would sure love to get to know you."

"Hmmm . . . how about you give me *your* number?"

"A'ight, when we get outside I can walk you to your car and I'll give you the number."

"No problem." Then she swiveled her hips in a sexy way. "So can I at least get one dance?"

"Well, that won't hurt," she responded as the DJ put on the next cut and Naughty by Nature's "OPP" blared through the speakers.

After the dance, two couples having an argument in the club broke into my thoughts, but I immediately shifted my attention from them and back to the matter at hand—walking Chyna to her car.

Chin had just walked out of the club, so I signaled him over. "Chin, this is Chyna. Chyna this is Chin."

"Pleasure is all mine," Chyna said, staring openly at Chin. Her soft pink tongue snaked out, licking her lips seductively. Chin smiled down at her, forgetting that I was even around.

"Ready, dawg?" I asked, without taking my eyes off Chin, who still stared openly at Chyna.

"Yeah," he answered, but leaned over to say something to Chyna and she responded. The word fuck came out of Chyna's mouth and Chin just smiled, making me immediately pull Chyna away.

"Sir, here's your food." The waitress at Friday's pulled me back to the present.

"Thanks." I looked up at her, then down at my plate, and suddenly lost my appetite.

As I looked down at the Orange Peel Shrimp with Jasmine Rice on my plate, it occurred to me, all the signs had been right there out in the open. And I had a feeling that my new plan would fail if I put BabyGirl on an assignment that included close contact with Chin. I could see my heart breaking all over again. But I couldn't pull off this final piece of the plan by using Sandy or Dimples. They weren't intelligent enough. Dimples didn't have a good verbal game. Sandy would be on her back giving up that ass in a matter of seconds. BabyGirl was just right, but I'd be damned if I'd serve up another piece to Chin without sampling that ass first.

"That bitch," PitBull growled before slamming his hands on the restaurant table. Dimples and Sandy jumped. I was pissed that BabyGirl didn't want to fuck me, and now she was giving me grief—as though she didn't trust me. I hated that she was getting so hip to the game. I hated that Chyna had chosen Chin over me.

After a good fuck, BabyGirl had an ass whipping coming for almost blowing this upcoming assignment. It was time to show that little bitch exactly who was boss.

I'll be damned if I let another female try to get over on me, I thought.

I would have to deal with BabyGirl sooner than expected.

CHAPTER 28

BABYGIRL

I-95 South—N.Y.: April 28, 2004, 9:15 a.m.

The sun beamed bright and hot on I-95 as we drove South to Westchester Avenue. PitBull, Dimples, and everyone else were all in position waiting for the UPS truck to reach its destination. As much as I hated the police, I had to give them credit. The uniform looked real good on me.

"Everyone ready?" PitBull crackled over the radio.

"Yup," Matt, the blonde officer, answered.

I was sitting back listening to the radio when Matt said, "Show time." Sirens went off, and two police cars and a black van chased the dark brown truck. "Pull over to the shoulder." Charlie spoke over the microphone, so it echoed through the bullhorn.

The driver pulled over, extending his hands out the window.

"Step out and away from the truck," Matt yelled while Charlie got out and walked over to the dark brown van.

"Anything illegal in here?" he asked the truck driver as he held the gun out in front of him.

"Now how would I know that? These are sealed packages from customers using the service," the driver responded.

Sweat formed on his forehead. "Sir, would you mind telling me why I'm being pulled over?"

"We've been observing you for a while, and if I search this truck and find something illegal, you're going in," Charlie informed him. He opened the driver's door.

"Away from the truck, sir," I yelled. My gun stayed up and pointed.

Dimples, with flashlight in hand, followed Sandy as she searched the truck.

"Do you have a search warrant?" the driver asked. "You can't hold me responsible for other people's packages."

PitBull flipped open a thin official looking sheet of paper. These motherfuckers really were prepared! Sweat on the driver's face poured down like last week's thunderstorm, soaking his shirt.

"Let me holler at you," I told the Hispanic driver who looked like he was in his early forties. I glanced at his left hand and made a quick decision. "I know you got a wife and kids at home. And I know the last thing you want to do is go to jail right about now, right?"

"Believe me, that's the last thing I want, officer," he confided in me, wiping his forehead with the back of his hand.

"Give me a minute." I turned to the rest of the crew and said, "Hey, Matt and Charlie, he says that some of that shit isn't real. Since ya'll know the good stuff from the bad, make sure you taste each one so we're taking the good shit. *If* you can find it."

Matt glared at me, probably a little pissed off that I used his real name. "We've got it covered."

Now, the Hispanic man had said no such thing, but this was part of my plan.

"They've got you on camera." I said to the driver. "All you have to do is tell them you have the drugs, where you were dropping the packages, and they'll take it from there. The men out here," I said, pointing to PitBull, Chico, Shotta, and the two male officers, all clad in uniforms, "they're like slaughter machines if you fuck around with them, so just make it easy and tell me where the drugs are. Give me the information, and we'll let you go free."

"Free, no charges?" he inquired, sweat beginning to dry a little.

"Free, no charges."

"It's in the back inside the big boxes. I was delivering to a warehouse in Hunt's Point."

"Name of the warehouse?"

He handed me a piece of paper with all the information I needed.

"Check the back, boys," I yelled. "It's in the large boxes with a Hunt's Point address."

"Come with me, sir," Chico remarked dryly.

The man whirled to me. "I thought you said I wasn't going to be arrested."

"You're not going to be arrested, but you ain't getting off a free man," Chico told him. "I'm gonna write your ass a big fat summons."

"For what?" The man's voice rose an octave.

"You'll see when you get it."

"Good job, BabyGirl," PitBull patted me on the back. I didn't respond, thinking of how dumb Shotta was to hand over his fingerprints. "That was never a part of the plan. The way you handled that? I'm proud of you, girl."

Yeah, right.

After everything was removed, the driver received what he thought was an official summons for court. As Matt and Charlie were in the back tasting the last of the packages, putting even more drugs into their systems, Dimples and I relieved them of their packages, and tossed them to the fellas.

Then Dimples stood next to me as we lifted our guns, aimed, and fired.

* * *

That day when PitBull had nearly forced me to sleep with him to keep a roof over my head, I knew that I would have to kill sooner or later. No matter how much I was against it, it was part of the game. Little did I know, my next kill wouldn't be in self-defense. It wouldn't even be something that was part of an assignment. But the act itself would ride cold into my soul as though ice had been poured into my veins instead of blood.

Three weeks after our third robbery, the next assignment had taken form. This one was a little different, but sounded a lot easier to pull off than the last one.

All we had to do was count a bunch of money PitBull had brought over in a leather bag. Apart from counting the money, we had to make sure the amount was accurate and then deliver the money to where he instructed.

I opened the bag and found a whole bunch of one-dollar bills. At first I laughed, thinking that shit was a joke or some-thing. But realization hit me, wiping the grin off my face. Counting single dollars could be a problem. A problem I could do without. If the money wasn't right, there'd be hell to pay.

Almost two hours later, I still hadn't finished counting the money. I was sweating like a whore in church. If anyone asked why it took so long, I couldn't say. But being one dol-lar off could mean my ass, and I certainly felt the pressure.

After the last dollar had been tucked away, I rejoined the group in the living room where I sat patiently listening to Pit-Bull's detailed instructions. He wanted just the girls to travel to Philadelphia and drop off the money I'd just counted.

Dimples and I would handle the money. Sandy, on the other hand, was going with us, but she didn't have to go to the place where we'd drop the money. All she had to do was make the phone call to set up the meeting. Maybe the fact that she had been in the business for a long time meant she wasn't required to do much. Dimples and I were rookies, but I suddenly began to see things Dimples' way. The set-up was unfair. Each time we did the dirty work, Sandy got a cut without lifting a finger or taking any risks. Some changes were definitely in order. Dimples had plans and I would back her up.

The next morning, rain pelted the house like bullets, coming down so hard that I was sure a flood would come. Lightning and thunder racked my already stressed nerves, constantly making me jump every time the crackling sound hit the air. I tried to focus on getting into my clothes.

"BabyGirl, you ready?" Sandy shouted from her room.

"Almost. I should be done in five minutes."

I checked my image in the mirror again, making sure the money strapped to my body didn't bulge, making it obvious that I carried the stash.

Outside, the cab waited to take us to the Port Authority bus terminal. After placing our suitcases in the trunk, I tapped the glass and said to the driver, "Go straight for the Cross Bronx Expressway," leaving little time for the cab driver to start a conversation.

We arrived at the bus station forty-five minutes early, so I grabbed some breakfast and sat in the waiting area with Dimples and Sandy until loading time. After eating, I felt sluggish and wanted to close my eyes for a minute. Suddenly, I remembered the money strapped to my body and knew that I couldn't sleep a wink until business was done.

A few minutes after they called for the bus to load, we settled into the seats near the back of the bus. The rain had let up, but the thunder remained loud and unsettling. A girl close to my age filled the empty seat next to me. Sweat had pasted her hair to the sides of her face. She fumbled in the seat uncomfortably, eyeing everyone suspiciously as though she, too, was smuggling something she didn't care to have.

"Such a nasty day!" she noted in a thick Jamaican accent.

"Yes, it's quite disgusting," I answered, eyeing her cautiously.

"Hey, at least I have a friend on the long journey to Philly with me." She grinned and patted my thigh softly.

Instead of responding, I gave her a smile, one that said, *listen, bitch, leave me the fuck alone. I'm not in the mood for no long conversations.*

Unfortunately, Ms. Jamaica didn't get the hint. She had to be new to the game. There was no fucking way a pro would talk so damn much, especially when doing something illegal. If she didn't get busted one way or another just because of her mouth, then God must be on her side.

Three hours later, I leaned over to look out the window of the bus like everyone else and thought, *damn, I must've put some bad luck on her.* No sooner had we arrived in Philly, then the bus was pulled over and Ms. Jamaica was greeted by two white guys with walkie-talkies. They cuffed her ass and carted her off like a lamb to the slaughterhouse. A nervous tremor flooded my body. The three of us moved swiftly off the bus and out of the bus terminal into the car that awaited us.

Sandy made the phone call as soon as we hit the hotel. Two minutes after she made the call, the phone rang, informing us that someone was waiting for us downstairs. Two beefy looking guys met the two of us in the lobby and quickly escorted us to a black Escalade parked in front of the hotel.

The truck slowed down and came to a stop in front of a nice two-story family home half an hour later. Stepping out of the truck, the two guys led us into the house where a tall, Spanish man opened the door then led us to the living room.

"Murdera's waiting to see you guys," he said five minutes later. *Murdera? What kind of name was that?* As we walked down through the living room, past the kitchen and the bathroom, we soon passed another room all the way in the back of the house. Loud screams came from a room just across the hall. Although I didn't see a soul, I could tell by the wavering voice that a woman was crying, begging for her life. Our "tour guide" turned to face me. I picked up the pace and kept moving. The woman's situation wasn't my business.

Our guide led us into a room where a thick guy with a caramel complexion, bald head, and full lips sat behind a black desk, making it difficult to get a full view of him. But the scowl on his face said, "If you fuck with me, I'll kill you without thinking twice."

I think the screaming lady had already found that out.

"Strip!" he demanded without blinking an eye.

I glanced at Dimples, then at him, stuttering, "Ex . . . ex . . . excuse me?"

"You heard me, I said *strip*. Get naked. We have to make sure y'all are not wired."

My eyes darted around the room, then at Dimples who began taking off her clothes without asking questions. Two guys sat to my left each holding a gun. To my right, one guy in the corner held another gun. I couldn't believe this man wanted me to strip in front of all these men.

"Could you ask these guys to leave, so I can take my clothes off?" I asked, not bothering to move an inch.

Murdera looked at each one of the guys, then at me, and bellowed with laughter.

For a minute, I forgot where I was and my assignment as I snapped, "What's the problem, I'm sure you speak English, so could you please ask these guys to leave?"

Instead of answering, one of the guys who had been sitting in the corner of the room, got up off the sofa, walked over to me, and pointed a gun to my head, shouting, "Strip, bitch! And stop playing fucking games. If your trifling ass wants to leave out of here alive, you'd better take them fucking clothes off, and make sure the money is correct."

"Just take your clothes off, BabyGirl," Dimples pleaded

softly with me, hoping that I didn't do anything stupid to get us both killed.

The sound of the man's voice, with him holding the gun to me, made my knees shake, but I managed to say, "Our business is with him." I pointed to Murdera. "If I have to strip in front of him, that's business. The other guys don't get a free show or a free ride."

"What part of strip don't you understand, bitch?" the man repeated, pressing the gun further into my skull.

"If you kill us, you'll get the money, but this is the first and last time you'll deal with PitBull." I said, looking at Murdera. "Maybe you can afford the loss. Maybe you can't. Is allowing these studs to see me naked worth that chance?"

Murdera glanced at the other two guys in the room and gestured to the door. He pointed to the guy with the gun and gestured for him to switch places with the short guy on my left.

"I respect your point, but one of them has to stay," Murdera said, grinning at me. "That is *not* negotiable."

A small victory, but I was so nervous, I skipped over buttons without being aware of it. I took off every piece of clothing except for my panties and bra.

Murdera grimaced, and I obliged, taking off everything before placing the money on the table and standing in front of him butt naked as the cold air whipped against my ass. Some stud had left the window open and I was too afraid to ask anyone to close it. As I shivered next to Dimples, Murdera signaled for the dark-skinned man to close the window. I whispered my thanks.

It took them thirty minutes to count the money, and I had to stand there stock still as they eyeballed my figure.

"Not too bad," Murdera stated, licking his lips as he looked me up and down. "You have a pretty little pussy there," he added, chuckling.

I didn't know whether to say "thank you" or keep my mouth shut, so I chose to keep my mouth shut. He put in a quick call to PitBull, but I couldn't hear what they discussed.

"The money's okay. You can both get dressed now," Murdera said, leaning back in the tall leather chair.

Scooping my clothes off the floor, I got dressed as fast as possible. My eyes caught the nine millimeter sitting on his table, and I moved closer, trying not to get caught while inspecting it.

"I see you like guns," Murdera caught me off guard speaking this time with a Spanish accent I hadn't noticed before.

I continued getting dressed so we could get the hell out of there.

"Since you were playing so difficult earlier," he said, tapping the handle of the gun, "I'm going to test you to see how much of a tough person you are!" He laughed as his cronies walked back into the room and joined in.

"Oh, shit," Dimples mumbled, holding her head down, while pulling up her zipper.

Murdera stood and walked from behind the desk, picked up the piece, and inserted bullets in the gun.

"Follow me," he instructed.

My heart slammed against my chest. Without hesitation, we both followed him into the room next door.

For a second, I thought I would vomit at the overpowering stench of piss and shit. Dimples swayed and hit the floor in a faint, but quickly woke up when one of the guys kicked her in the side.

A young girl with a dark complexion, around five feet, six inches and weighing no more than 125 pounds, lay butt naked on the floor tied up with an electrical cord. Burn marks covered her entire body. Blood splattered the floor, trickling from her thighs. The guys had raped her repeatedly. She lay half dead on the ground, but her sad eyes focused on mine. They screamed a silent cry for help. My heart went out to her. I wanted so badly to help, but how could I? At the moment, I couldn't help myself.

"You see, this drug game is a serious business," Murdera lectured as though we were in a college classroom. "And when you cross people you end up one of three ways: badly beaten, dead, or both."

I couldn't take my eyes off the young, tortured girl. "Okay, so what am I supposed to do?"

"I was gonna kill her, but I didn't have the time," he said as I looked up just in time to see a grin part his thick lips. "And now that you're here, you'll just take it on for me."

This nigga must think I'm stupid or something, because no way could I believe that his fat ass didn't find time to kill someone who crossed him.

Murdera slapped the gun into my hand. It was a trap, a nasty, dirty trap, and I smelled PitBull all over it. He probably wanted to get back at me for not sleeping with him.

"You want me to kill her?"

Murdera laughed, a hard bitter sound. "I don't see anybody else around here who looks like they could use it," he said, looking at his soldiers. They all let out an ugly peal of laughter.

"Please! Please! I'm begging you, don't kill me." The girl's weak voice echoed in the room. "I did it for my son, he was sick. I had to use the money to pay for his medical bills." Her sobs tore through the air and straight through my heart.

"Shut the fuck up, bitch," one of the guys said before hitting her across the face with the end of the gun.

"Kill her!" Murdera shouted angrily, glaring at the girl, then at me. "What are you waiting for?"

"Please, it was for my son," the girl shrieked, eyes wide with horror.

"Could I at least hear her side of the story?" I asked softly, turning to Murdera.

The laughter on his lips came to an instant halt, replaced by a look laced with anger and frustration.

"Gimme this fucking shit," he demanded while grabbing the nine out of my hand. "Now, listen to me. You said you wanted to get in the game. Who the fuck told you that being in the game was as simple as A, B, and C?" His face was only inches from mine. "I'm giving you a taste of how the game really is. So what's it gonna be, mi amiga?"

He held out the gun. I didn't take it.

"Puta, you'd better make up your mind."

"Make my mind up about not killing her?" I challenged, knowing that in my heart I couldn't kill someone who hadn't done anything to me. Now the mothafucka who had killed my parents was a different story. Him I could do blindfolded.

"Make up your mind," Murdera growled.

I felt a sudden sting of pain as the back of his hand smashed across my face.

"Now quit being a fucking punk and shoot her."

Dimples stood in the corner of the room shivering. Seeing the strong, almighty Dimples about to pass out again didn't put me in a better mood. I couldn't believe this bitch. When I needed her advice, she's helpless, just nodding her head telling me to kill the girl.

"I know I said I wanted to join the game, but it's about the money. I never wanted to kill anybody," I explained in the strongest voice I could manage.

"Oh, isn't that so sweet," Murdera teased. "You hear that boys? She never *wanted to kill anybody*," he mimicked, then turned to me and yelled. "What the fuck you think would keep you in the game, your pretty looks or the fact that you're in it for the easy dinero?" He paced in front of me. "Because if it's looks, there's always prostitution or escorting. And if it's money you'd better be willing to put some work into it to earn your money."

I began to wonder if this was a test of my loyalty. No matter what, I wasn't down for killing anyone.

Glancing at the girl, then to him, I didn't take the gun from his hand. "I can't do it. I'm sorry, Murdera, but I can't."

"Okay, you can't do it," he said with a weary sigh. "Well here are the choices you have: you can either kill her, watch me kill her then I kill you, or you can let me kill you first, then I kill her after." His gaze bore a hole into me. "Choose. I don't have all day either. You are so fucking lucky. A lot of people don't get a second chance, and here I am feeling sorry for your ass and giving you choices. You have balls, girl. I'll give you that."

I looked at him and began to wonder if the man was out of his fucking mind. How the hell could Murdera say he had given me a choice, when there was no choice to begin with?

"Oh, you're having second thoughts." He took the gun, placing it at my head. "So let me do this my way. One— Two—"

CHAPTER 29

CHIN

Tha Hustle Records NYC: April 30th 2004, 1:56 p.m.

An uneasy feeling settled in my stomach as I thought of PitBull. Tony might have a point. Before he went away, he was supposed to be the one running this empire with me. But since fate had its own plans, the game had changed and I had to do whatever it took to stay on top.

After PitBull got locked up, I didn't have enough money to do everything, and I knew that in only a matter of time I would fade away completely and have to start again. Having Tony Moreno sit down next to me one day when I stopped to have a drink in downtown Manhattan was a stroke of luck. Over a few glasses of Vodka I found out that Tony had just earned millions in a lawsuit and wanted to open a business, but he didn't know how to go about it. Lawsuit money. *Legitimate* money! Things were definitely looking up.

I explained to him that opening a business was on my mind, too, and I just needed a partner. We exchanged information and I told him that we'd talk soon. I needed time to check him out. All I had to do was give a brief description: Tony Moreno, Puerto Rican and Dominican with a Caesar haircut, a connected fade, and Chinese tattoos on his arms. He was about six feet, two inches tall and weighed 225 pounds, most of it menacing muscle.

Word on the street was that people called him "Big Tone" and he had a ruthless edge to him, but didn't use it often. After all the reports were in, I chose Tony as my partner because I liked his approach. My sources told me that when it came to business, he knew when to let shit slide and when to put someone's lights out. From there, things took off and we became inseparable.

PitBull was put on the backburner, and his share of the money, which was made before he landed in Marion, sat in a safe deposit box waiting for his return. I only tapped that source once, when I gave Chyna the money to pay for three years of law school. I wanted her to stop stripping for a living, and I didn't think PitBull would mind.

But now I could feel the strange vibes from PitBull, and sooner or later, I would have to deal with him. Tony was a different story. I felt strange mistrusting him after all this time. The fact that he'd put almost his entire fortune in my hands should have said plenty. Maybe my focus should stay on Pit-Bull and Chyna.

Now Chyna was a real piece of work.

When a man's locked up, some females wait, but many decide to do their own thing. In addition to the money I gave her for school, I would give her a little dough from my own pocket every now and then while still holding down my man PitBull. She chose to show her gratitude on her back. Who was I to turn down some good pussy?

To PitBull, Chyna was his wifey. But to me she was just another "ordinary fuck around the block" type of chick. To be honest, I never meant to sleep with her after PitBull's incarceration. In the beginning, the sex was "no strings attached." Unfortunately, things didn't stay that way, and I constantly went back to her for more. Then she hit me with the news, "Chin, I'm pregnant."

I didn't deny shit because I rode her a few times without a condom. But I also knew prison visits could include a little sex, too, so either me or PitBull could have been the father.

"You can't have it, Chyna," I said, knowing that it was the best decision. "I can't take on a responsibility like that, not when I'm trying to get myself together."

"So what are you suggesting?" she asked, her eyes dark and moist.

"I'm suggesting that you have an abortion. Don't worry about the money. I got it covered, along with any other medical expenses," I assured her.

"When the fuck do you get to decide this baby's fate? I'm not killing my baby, so you'll have to get used to that."

"Okay, do whatever you want, but I'm not being a part of that. Remember you're fucking PitBull too, so it could be his baby."

I shifted my attention away from the sad look on her face to the basketball game, hoping she would take what I said into consideration.

"So tell me, Chyna, you want to have this baby, hoping that I'm the daddy, so I could take care of it? I can knock you down with some cash, love. That's no problem, but you're on your own for everything else. I don't want to be involved." I still didn't face her as I said, "Or it turns out to be PitBull's and he's locked down and you gonna have it hard, boo, because he can't give you a fucking dime. It's your choice. Either way, you're gonna be fucked."

The room became completely silent. For two hours we didn't exchange a word. Then she stood, crying uncontrollably, and said, "I'll have a price for you tomorrow."

"No doubt," I responded without taking my eyes off the

Detroit Pistons, who were giving the L.A. Lakers a serious problem.

After the abortion, I saw her one more time and then gave her enough money to keep her straight until PitBull got out of prison.

Seeing her in Porsha's office was a shock, but my dick said that memories last forever.

CHAPTER 30

BABYGIRL

Philadelphia: April 30th 2004, 11:05 a.m.

Murdera stood over me with the gun. I swallowed hard as the nine millimeter clicked.

I held my hands up in surrender.

"A'ight, A'ight," I said. "I'll do it."

Murdera's grin made me sick. "I knew you would see it my way."

I took back the gun and looked at the poor girl on the floor. How the hell could I kill somebody's mother? Thoughts of my father and mother began flashing in my head. I thought of how my father begged for his life, just as the girl was begging for hers.

"Shoot," Murdera commanded, making me wince.

Closing my eyes, I blocked out the girl's cries and pleas, aimed the gun at her, and fired.

The sound of the gunshot in the small room sounded more like the end of the world to me.

I slowly opened my eyes and relief surged through me. Again she pleaded, with more tears streaming down her face, as a pool of blood formed near the gunshot wound in her shoulder. I couldn't bear looking at her, so I closed my eyes, shot again, and missed. My aim had definitely been better in other circumstances. Actually, I could shoot all day and not hit any major places. But then, I would only be prolonging the inevitable. The girl would die anyway, and if I didn't take care of it, Murdera and his crew would continue raping her and torturing her before they killed her.

Her soft brown eyes were glazed with pain as I pushed away any thoughts of prolonging her death, and aimed. This time the bullet sliced through her head, killing her instantly.

I wiped my fingerprints from the gun and dropped it to the ground. I ran to the front of the house, crying.

Murdera came into the room behind me. I had curled up into a corner on the floor. "Get up," he demanded. "There is something I need to tell you, *mi amiga.*"

This mothafucka had the nerve to call me his *friend* twice in one day. But slowly I pushed the guilt and pain aside and sat up.

"BabyGirl, a majority of the people who enter this game don't know the rules. They know that flashy cars, flashy clothes, and money are a part of the game, not realizing that the game's about the survival of the fittest. One has to follow the rules in order to survive. If they mess up, there are consequences. Nobody should be blamed for their actions because nobody forced them into it. No one forced you in. You had other choices. I know you're angry right now, but you cannot hate the players, you have to hate the game itself."

I backed away from him, understanding his words, but still hating him for including me in his issues.

"Before you go," he said, ignoring my angry glare. "Let me leave you with this advice: this game consists of winners and losers. The side you're on doesn't depend on you, but on how well you play the game."

I thought about what he said as the truck pulled away from Murdera's place. I glanced back at him. He stood at the window and blew a kiss at me. I flashed him the finger. His body rocked back and forth as he laughed.

He had a point, but soon, very soon, I would change the game and make my own rules. First, the people who killed my parents would pay. I remembered them as though the incident had happened just a few minutes ago. One of them had a mocha complexion, but his mentality was far from sweet chocolate. He stood six feet, was well built with braided hair, clean shaven, and had slanted eyes. The tattoo on his neck displayed half-eaten strawberries and juice dripping from the fruit, with the words "lick me" written underneath. This man had it coming.

And today, besides PitBull, there were now five other people I'd just added to my list.

The bus ride back from Philly was extremely quiet and long, with the incident replaying in my head. Being forced to kill that way had wrecked my nerves. Every now and then, a tear fell from my eyes. I prayed for that woman's soul. I prayed for her child. I got so exhausted from crying and praying, that I don't remember falling asleep. I jolted awake as the bus pulled into the 42nd Street bus terminal.

Dimples came over and sat beside me. "Hey, you okay?"

"Yeah, I'm fine." I shrugged. "It's life, you know."

"Don't even sweat it because I had to do the same thing. The good thing is that you passed the test, because let me tell you this," she whispered in my ear, "I heard them talking. PitBull told him to make sure you killed the lady in the room."

"And you didn't tell me this?" I asked, as a sudden anger filled me.

"I couldn't." She said, reaching for me. "I knew you'd back out and we'd pay for it the hard way."

"Ain't this a bitch." I sighed, slumping into the bus seat feeling lost and betrayed.

"Just forget all of this and remember the real reason you joined the game."

With that, she smiled, gave me a hug, and I prepared to leave the bus and start making plans to avenge my parents' deaths. PitBull? I'd deal with him later.

Since I didn't want to squander my money this time, I went out and bought a small safe to hide in the bottom of my closet. I put in fifty thousand dollars inside, along with an additional ten thousand dollars from the last robbery. If I had learned anything from my father, it was that you can't be stupid in this game. You make sure money is stashed away in case a situation pops up.

No doubt some of the cash was for bail money, along with money for the future. I also knew after the Murdera incident that funeral expenses might come as part of the deal. Sixty thousand ain't that much, but it was a good start.

"Wait till you see the outfits I got!" Sandy walked into my bedroom, breaking my concentration.

"Girl, how much more clothing are you gonna put in that closet of yours?"

"Fuck you, BabyGirl," she said in an aggravated tone. "You wanna see the clothes or not?"

"Of course, but let me ask you this—is your bail money for your future intact?"

With her hands on her hips, she sighed in a frustration, saying, "Money? Girl, please, what you think PitBull is here for?"

"You must be outta your fucking mind if you're depending on PitBull. Listen to me, he gets us jobs. *Hello!* Robbing drug dealers. What, you expecting him to take care of your responsibilities with his money after he gave you ways to make your own money and you blew it away?"

"Hell, yeah!"

"Then you're dumber than I thought."

"No bitch, don't be mad that I have more pimp juice than you," she said bobbing her neck and snapping her fingers.

"Whatever." I shook my head at how dumb she could be at times. "Just show me the stuff you bought."

On the floor beside Sandy stood fifteen shopping bags making me wonder if she had bought out the whole damn shopping district. Her bags ranged from our favorite expensive stores, to local ones like Macy's, Bloomingdale's, and H&M.

"Fuck! Does Manhattan still have clothes, shoes, or pocketbooks left?" I asked, unable to keep my sarcastic tone at bay.

She laughed in such a way it set my nerves on edge. "They're lucky I ain't bought out the whole damn Tri-State area."

"How much do you have left?"

She put an outfit up to her body and shimmied in the mirror. "One hundred."

"One hundred dollars! You expect that to last you 'til the next assignment?"

"No, but pussy's for sale. Fucking niggas for dough is the game."

I tried to keep from laughing. "Word?"

"Ya best believe it. I keep telling you pussy ain't free. God blessed us with a gold mine between our legs, and he expects us to use it."

I swung my legs off the bed and stood. "Your life is sad." With that, I left her preening in the mirror and went outside to analyze my own sad life.

CHAPTER 31

PORSHA

Leland and Mitchell Law Firm, Manhattan: May 27, 2004, 3:12 p.m.

"So what's new with you and Chin?" Chyna asked, sitting down on the chair in the far right corner of my office.

Chyna's curiosity about my relationship with Chin was starting to get on my nerves. Chin got edgy whenever I mentioned Chyna's name. Something was up with those two. I just couldn't put my finger on it. After a little research, I found out from a male co-worker that my friend had once worked at the Blue Sea Horizon. Chin went to strip clubs on a regular basis, no matter how pissed off I was about it. So there was a chance that he had known the woman and both of them were keeping it a secret.

"Why are you so interested in my relationship?" I took off my thin glasses and stared directly at Chyna.

Chyna crossed her left leg over her right. "Can't a best friend check in to see what's going on? That's what friends are supposed to do."

"You sure are a friend, Chyna," I said in a sarcastic tone, but not enough to make the petite woman aware that I had suspicions.

"So are you gonna spill the beans or what?" Chyna said before crossing her legs in the other direction and placing her elbows on the desk—all ears.

"Nope." And that's all I would say. I remembered the last time I made the mistake of sharing too much information with a close friend. Nikki and Tyrone ended up in bed after I had poured out all the juicy details about how marvelous he was in bed. That bitch sucked up everything I said, but with some stroke of luck, I found some underwear with which I could expose the truth. I was with Nikki when she bought the pair, and Nikki had left them on purpose, just to set Tyrone up. Those two were made for each other.

Chyna huffed and got up out of the chair. She turned and headed toward the door. "A'ight Porsha, keep it a secret."

"I'm sorry, Chyna, but some things shouldn't be shared between friends. What goes on in my bedroom is at the top of my list."

Her lips spread into a fake grin as she said, "Suit yourself," Then she closed the door.

I knew that the situation was far from over. I would just keep my eyes and ears open. If Chyna didn't give it away, Chin would slip up sooner or later. Men always did.

CHAPTER 32

BABYGIRL

Dominican Base, Harlem: July 12, 2004, 9:08 p.m.

The hours turned into days. Days turned into weeks. By the time we looked up, the next assignment had been planned. Every single night for the past two weeks, the men had staked out this Dominican base. Many had tried robbing that base and failed, so for females to take it down would be pure luck.

One Hundred Fifty-Fifth Street wasn't as lively as it was supposed to be. Few people were in front of the building where the base was located. Maybe it was because of the block party that was being held down the street. The whole situation was weird, but I chose to ignore it. I didn't want my girls to think I was chicken. The robbery should be as easy as one, two, three. Good planning could do that.

Still, we didn't want to take any chances, so I loaded the gun while Sandy made a U-turn and dropped us out front. We didn't have a key to the apartment building, so we buzzed a bell for a tenant who lived on the other side of the complex, away from the spot we planned to hit.

"Who is it?" The scratchy voice echoed from the intercom.

I held my nose, disguising my voice. "Could you open the door? I left my keys and my baby's diaper bag upstairs."

A noisy click followed the buzz as the locks opened. Seconds later we were inside the building creeping toward the stairway. With a ten-minute timeline, the elevator would have only slowed us down.

We made our way to the fifth floor in less than two minutes. Now all we had to do was pick the lock, and if we had no trouble with that, we would be inside in less than a minute.

"I got it," Dimples whispered softly.

Although we had staked out the place for a while, finding the stash wasn't as easy as PitBull said. We dug out every room, and even removed the medicine cabinet in the bathroom, but came up empty-handed.

"Sandy," I whispered into the phone, "We can't find anything. They're never out of here for more than five minutes. I think we should go."

"Naw, don't worry about it. I'm in front of the building. If they come through, I'll call y'all back and let y'all know. Keep looking."

"Let's go, Dimples," I whispered, tearing through a bedroom closet.

"I found it!" Dimples jumped for joy.

"You found the stash?"

"Yup. I'll need the pliers out of the bag"

Although I was anxious to get the hell out of there, I didn't mind staying an extra five minutes so we didn't have to hear PitBull's big mouth about failing a mission.

As I ran from the bedroom, I stopped cold at the front door when I heard a man with a Dominican accent say, "I told you that shit wasn't locked, Ecaudo."

"So lock it now."

Now, any professional would not just lock the door without checking to see if everything was okay inside the base. But I didn't hear a thing and wondered why the hell Sandy didn't let us know those studs were back.

I ran back to the bedroom and whispered to Dimples, "Hurry, the fuck up, we— "

"Bitch, what the fuck is your problem?" she snapped, yanking the pliers from me. "Make yourself useful and stop nagging my ass, then maybe we could finish and be out of here already."

She started to pry open the furnace with the pliers. Not wanting to spend another moment in the house, I quickly grabbed the bag, stuffing packages of cocaine and the money in the bag as she tossed them to me.

The last batch of cocaine was taken out of thefurnace, and Dimples and I began to make our way back to the living room so we could take the fire escape.

A sudden click from the living room made me freeze in place. Holding a single finger to my lips, I gestured to Dimples that we had company. I flattened my body against the wall as they pushed open the door.

"You hear that, Danny?"

"Hear what?" Ecaudo asked.

"Voices! I heard voices. Someone's inside the house."

Suddenly, everything went quiet, but I heard the click of a gun as they prepared to search the house. Both of us were in a vulnerable position. Dimples shifted to hide in the closet. A big mistake.

BOOM! BOOM! BOOM! Shots rang out in the house as a blur of something whizzed past me. Both my arm and chest began to burn, and blood gushed out just above my elbow.

"Fuck, I got shot," I whispered to Dimples.

"Stop worrying about your fucking arm, and start shooting back if you want to make it out of here alive," Dimples growled, holding her gun steady.

We were trapped. The taller guy had blocked the entrance

and the only way for us to leave was to take him out. No problem.

Dimples nodded her head to the left, and the next minute we were diving behind the sofa. The living room window was our only choice for safety.

Luckily, the bullet didn't hit my shooting arm. With the pain I felt, I was not about to leave the house without taking somebody down. As Dimples scampered to the window, I continued shooting to distract them. I was still angry at the nigga blocking the door. He was the one who had shot me. Before going through the window, I aimed my gun just like my father, pointed it at his forehead, and fired a single shot. The man's body spun around in slow motion and hit the floor. What a waste! The man was a cutie.

Sandy was still outside in the car, and by this time my feet were dragging like dead weights.

"Come on!" Dimples screamed at me, while hauling her ass across the concrete to the car.

"I can't make it!" I yelled back. "You go on. "

"Hell no! We got in this together," she said, turning back to lift me up. "And you're damn right we gonna get out together. Remember, it's just like Spades. We're partners."

As we ran through an alley, shots fired from the apartment window. When they stopped, I knew someone was coming downstairs to finish the job.

A handsome muscular man standing near the car door scurried off as Dimples banged on the passenger window. "Open the door, Sandy!"

"What the fuck happened?" Sandy asked, looking stupid. Not much of a stretch for her.

"No time to explain! Just *drive*," Dimples demanded, glaring at Sandy, as we both understood why Sandy hadn't been able to warn us. Flirting on the fucking job almost got us killed.

Sandy stepped on the gas. The tires screeched in response

as the remaining Dominican came running down the street firing at the car. Dimples put her head out the window and returned fire while Sandy made her way off the block.

We were tearing down Adam Clayton Powell Boulevard when Sandy asked, "How the hell did BabyGirl get shot?"

Dimples whirled to face her. "I don't think you should be asking a fucking question like that. Your fucking job was to watch the front and tell us they were coming."

"But I was," Sandy snapped.

"Bullshit! You would've seen those niggas before they slipped up on us," Dimples shot back.

"If your ass wasn't flirting with that guy," I added, "You would've seen them come through the side. You were parked right out front and couldn't handle something as simple as keeping your eyes open. You stupid bitch!"

Sandy didn't say a word as she barely managed to keep the car on all four wheels. Her driving skills couldn't be doubted. Her brain was another story altogether.

"So what do you want to do with her?" Sandy asked cautiously, eyeing me in the mirror.

"With—" Dimples began.

"Naw, Dimples, I got this one," I said, lifting up from the seat a little. Pain shot through me. I glowered at the blonde-haired woman through the rearview mirror. "What the fuck do you mean what are you supposed to do with me?" I mimicked her flat voice. "Bitch, you better take me to a fucking hospital. That's what you're supposed to do."

"What is y'all's problem? Why ya'll jumping on me?"

"Because you lost fucking focus." Dimples popped her fingers on Sandy's head, treating her like a third-grader. "You need to think with your fucking brain instead of your pussy."

Sandy yanked the steering wheel, pulling the car off the road. She glared back at Dimples. "If you touch me one more fucking time, it's gonna be on up in this mothafucka!"

"What the fuck you gonna do, huh?" Dimples got up in Sandy's face. "Let me tell you something, you trifling ass ho—"

"Ho?" Sandy's neck almost popped out of joint. "Did you just call me a ho?"

"Helloooo, I'm in pain back here," I managed in a weak voice. They ignored me.

"Yeah, you heard me right," Dimples shouted at the top of her lungs. "You never should've been on this project from day one. If we ain't careful, your trifling ass will sell us out. You damn near got us killed."

Sandy pulled out her gun. "Get the fuck out before you make me hurt you."

"Hurt me? Go ahead, bitch, I dare you." Dimples' lips spread into an evil smile as she too whipped out her gun. "So don't start shit you can't finish because you *will* become my next victim."

A crowd had formed outside the car. I could see that both women were angry enough to kill each other. Then what would happen to me?

"Will somebody please drive my black ass to the hospital?" I shouted in the loudest voice I could manage. "I just got shot, remember? And I'm bleeding."

Sandy glanced at the back seat, then to Dimples. "You're lucky I have to take BabyGirl to the hospital, or else . . ."

"Or else what, bitch?"

"Nothing," she said, putting her gun back into her waistband and taking the wheel.

"You damn right, nothing."

"Y'all need to stop this shit," I snapped. Talking was taking what was left of my strength. "We agree that Sandy messed up, but arguing about it is not going to help the situation. It certainly isn't helping me. So let's go."

I was expecting one of them to answer. No such luck. Dimples folded her arms across her chest and stared out the window at the crowd. Sandy pulled the car onto the road. The ride to Harlem Hospital was cold and silent.

Dimples helped me out of the car and ushered me inside the emergency room. "Could someone help her please?"

"Grab a stretcher," one of the nurses yelled, running toward me. "We have a gunshot victim coming in."

"Miss, can we ask you how she got shot?" a tall, blue-eyed doctor asked Dimples moments later.

"I'm sorry. I don't know," Dimples answered quickly, helping me onto the stretcher. "You'll have to ask her what happened. I left the baby out in the car, and I'm double parked. I have to go."

Dimples ran through the hospital's sliding doors without another glance back as they wheeled me in.

A few hours after I was released from the hospital, the three of us were laid low at a hotel outside of Queens. We couldn't go back to Sandy's place for a while. From my point of view, eating takeout every day and having housekeeping pick up after Sandy's lazy ass was a definite step up from her little shack.

As the three of us watched Maury on the television, the phone rang. Sandy didn't move a muscle. Only fate had kept her alive at this point because every time my arm or chest hurt, I wanted to take her ass out.

"Here," Dimples handed me the phone.

"Who is it?" I asked, without tearing my eyes away from television.

"PitBull," she whispered before plopping back down on the bed.

"What the hell does he want now?"

She didn't bother to answer. Dimples had barely said two words to either of us since she had gotten into another argument with the stupid one.

"Hello!"

"BabyGirl, you a'ight?"

"Yeah, my arm's just aching right now. Thanks to your girl."

"Dimples pulled my ear to that. I'll take care of it."

"I'm sure you will," I said, doubting every word he said.

"Okay, I don't want you going to the clubs tonight. I want you to recuperate fast because I have another assignment just for you."

"For me?" I glanced at Sandy who finally turned to look at me. I lowered my voice. "What about the other girls?"

"Well they're involved too, but you're the main star for this assignment. This one I think you'll like better."

Fluffing my pillow so I could sit up right, I waited for his next statement.

"And trust me, if you play your cards right this should be an easy assignment. Plus you'll make enough money that you won't have to work for a while."

I took a long, slow breath. "First of all, I hate when you use the word *easy*, and second, I wanna know what this assignment's about."

"Have you ever heard the saying *the phone is your worst enemy*?"

"Nope."

"Well learn that, and always remember that. What I need from you is to get well so you can stop by to get the details. I'm sure y'all will enjoy the Lexus when you get back to Sandy's."

"I'd enjoy it even more if I had my own."

"That can be arranged, *if* you complete this next assignment."

Without saying another word, he hung the phone. Dimples sat at the edge of my bed.

"So I guess no party tonight," she said with a frown.

"Nope, special instructions from PitBull."

"I wonder why he wouldn't want you to go to the club tonight."

"I get the impression that he doesn't want me to ruin something."

She rolled over on the bed to face me. "Hmm . . . I wonder what it is."

"I don't know, but whatever it is, it must be real serious."

"I feel you girl, but I just can't fight the feeling that I smell Sandy all over it," Dimples whispered in my ear. "All I have to say is be careful what you say to her and around her."

"No doubt."

CHAPTER 33

PORSHA

Manhattan Court House: July 29, 2004, 10:09 a.m.

The judge dismissed my motion for change of venue, so trial was set to begin and the proceedings in court would be long and tedious. The defendant was not making it any easier for me to defend him. He was charged with murder, but all he had to do was give up the name of the person who actually did the shooting and he could at least get a plea. The buzz of conversation around the courthouse gave me the perfect cover to talk with him.

"Why are you so stubborn?" I whispered. "All you have to do is hand me somebody else so I can give their name to the DA, and *boom* you're doing less time."

Mr. Collin Wright, my client, was about five feet, seven inches, with a low Caesar hair cut. His file stated that he was no more than twenty-two years old, but because of his rough street life, the man looked as if he had just hit his late thirties. He wore a tailored black suit, and although he was warned against it, his neck and fingers were adorned with jewels—a big no-no in a courthouse.

The man's cold eyes focused on me. "So if I give a name, can you guarantee my freedom or my life?"

"I can't guarantee they'll let you walk right now. You *were* involved, but I am going to try to get them to consider you for the witness protection program, and drop all charges if what you're giving is worth their while."

"Did you hear what you just said—worth *their* while?" he challenged.

"Well, what do you want me to say, Mr. Wright? I'm being up-front with you. You're paying me to represent you, and I'm pointing out the only options available to you."

"Still can't do."

"Why not?" I asked, my irritation beginning to creep through.

"Too many lives will be ruined."

"So what do you care about other people's lives being ru- ined? What you need to worry about is you. You're the one facing hard time. Just give them a name."

"You think it's that easy, huh?"

"I *know* it's that easy."

Mr. Wright's steady gaze unnerved me as he managed to crack a smile despite the stressful situation. "Miss Hilton, if you only knew."

"Knew what?"

"Whose life would be ruined."

Ignoring the people scurrying around them, I leaned for- ward. "What are you talking about?"

"Let's put it this way, you know more than you think you know. But eventually it will all play out."

"I'm sorry, you lost me."

"Oh no, Miss Hilton, I didn't lose you, I just happened to find you. You see, this situation is like Pandora's Box. Once it's opened, all the secrets are gonna come out—puff—all in people's faces," he gestured with his hands to make his point.

"Well court's about to start," I snapped. "So let's save this vague discussion for later."

"Yeah, let's do that. I'm sure Andre Chin will thank you for it."

My heart slammed against my chest when he said Chin's name. What the hell had I gotten into? Did someone at my firm actually know what I was doing to help him? Before I could question him, I heard the words, "All rise."

The court officer waited for everyone to stand.

"The Honorable Judge Scheinberg is now presiding."

Once the judge took his seat, I sat down and took one last look at my client, thinking, *Either it's me, or my clients are getting weirder by the moment. And what the hell does this man's situation have to do with Chin?*

CHAPTER 34

CHIN

Tha Hustle Recording Studio: July 29, 2004, 11:47 a.m.

Mixing Dragon's album was pure joy. His shit sounded hot. As Tony bobbed his head along with me, my cell phone rang. The number that popped up wasn't familiar. I let it go straight to voicemail.

Soon the phone rang again displaying the same number. Excusing myself from the studio, I answered. A female voice cried hysterically on the other end.

"Who is this?"

"Chin, it's me Chyna!"

A sudden dread filled my heart. "What's wrong with you, girl? Why are you crying?"

"I'm going through a lot. Can I talk to you?"

I turned to look through the glass and saw Tony looking back at me. "Hold up, let me holla at Tony for a minute."

"Okay," she answered softly.

Covering the mouth piece, I stepped back inside, signaling to Tony who shook his head.

Damn, no break for me. We had a deadline to make. "Umm . . . Chyna, can I call you back on this number? I'm in the middle of production."

"Yes," she sniffled on the other end.

Walking back in the studio, we finished the last track and I went over to Tony and told him, "I'll be in the office for a few."

"Handle your business, bro, I'll be right here making sure everything goes down right."

"Cool."

Chyna answered the phone on the first ring. Through my entire stroll of the hallway, she cried.

Swiveling in the office chair, I took a long breath before asking, "Chyna, what's wrong?"

"I'm in love with you, Chin." I stopped swiveling for a minute and pulled up closer to my desk as I listened. "I thought it would be easy for me to get over it, but it's hard."

I was speechless. It's not like I had never been in this situation before, but I made sure things went smoothly. This case was different. Not only did Chyna work at my woman's office, to top things off she was very emotional right now. Choosing my words carefully was an absolute must.

"Chin, you heard me?" she sobbed into the phone.

"Yeah . . . ah . . . ah, could you hold on one second?"

Putting her on hold, I raced back over to the studio and tapped Tony on the shoulder. Before he could respond, I pulled him out of the room and explained the situation.

He shook his head, barely holding in his laughter. "She's good. Better than I thought."

"I know, man."

"Plan two is in effect," he laughed heartily, his golden skin flushed red.

"It's a stunt, right?"

"Yup!"

"I figured that. Let me go deal with it."

Moments later, I said, "Chyna, sorry about that. I had to go in the studio to make sure the mixing was going down correctly."

"Okay."

Leaning forward on the desk, I grabbed the picture of Porsha. "I care for you, but I can't love you like you would want me to."

"I know," she replied softly.

Tracing the outline of my woman's perfect face, I said, "I love Porsha. That's why I proposed to her."

Maybe I pressed the wrong button, but the tears and sniffles dried up as the claws came out real quick. "Here I am telling you that I'm in love with you, and that's all you can say? Fuck you, Chin! I don't even know why I wasted my time pouring my heart out to you."

"See, listen to you!" I snapped, grateful she had stopped with the emotional shit. "You played yourself, showing me that your call was a bunch of bullshit. You don't want me. You just don't want Porsha to have me."

She cursed before slamming the phone down in my ear.

Everyone except Dragon had left the studio by the time I came back. Dragon wanted to add one more song to the album before it went through the final phase. I hesitated at first, but after he pleaded, telling me how much this song meant to him, I allowed him to lay down the track.

> *The clock struck midnight, you didn't call*
> *Girl, don't you know that I was tight.*
> *If you never wanted me, that's all you had to say*
> *So I wouldn't have to be in pain today.*
> *Hurting because I loved you with all my heart*
> *You promised me we would never be apart.*
> *Here I am sitting all alone,*
> *Wondering if you ever gonna come back home.*
> *And if this love note just happens to reach you before*
>   *I do,*
> *Remember that I had, and always will love you.*

Chorus: Baby I'm in pain
Sitting here crying in the rain.
The way I felt for you
I never felt for anyone else
I wish I could stop living in this hell.
Sitting here baby I'm in pain
Now I know that loving you was in vain

As I listened to Dragon crooning out the tune, my mind drifted off, relating the words to his life story. I remembered the details perfectly.

After a session in the studio when he recorded a song called "Blood on My Hands," the lyrics were so violent they had me concerned that women would be turned off by the song. The words were so strong that I felt as though someone had sent a bolt of lightening straight through me. I asked him about the song. He leaned back in the chair and looked at me for a moment.

"My life wasn't perfect, and to be honest, it still ain't," he said while rolling a fat blunt in the studio. "First, my father abandoned my family when I was three years old. I remember that as though it was yesterday. He told me to pack my bags, 'cause he was taking me to Disney World. I believed the nigga, yo, and like a fool, I packed my bag."

Placing the blunt on his lap, he picked up the glass of vodka and orange juice and took a sip.

"Night came and went, and still no sign of my father. I fell asleep in my clothes and woke up from time to time. My father still wasn't there. I eventually put on my pajamas, but I still had my bags packed hoping that one day he would return for me."

"My mother didn't know how to take his leaving us, so she turned to drinking," Dragon told me. "And as if that wasn't enough, she started doing crack. Street hustling was never my thing because for one thing I hated how drugs destroyed my mother. And second, I always wanted to be a rapper. But knowing my dream was miles away, eventually I had no other choice but to turn to the streets. I started to sell nickel and dime bags for this man named Anthony Smith. He taught me a lot. It was cool until some nigga smoked him and his wife. For a while I took care of their young daughter. I actually had a thing for her, and she loved me, too. I promised that I wouldn't touch her until she turned eighteen. But through some stupid shit, I ended up in jail and she had to fend for herself until I got out. If I ever find the nigga who killed her parents, I'm gonna smoke him before she does."

Dragon now held his head down, shook it, and sighed, placing the rolled up blunt in his pocket.

I remember I felt his pain deeply that day, because no one should ever have to experience that, but it also made me aware that I had to be careful what I said around Dragon.

CHAPTER 35

BABYGIRL

Harlem, NYC: July 29 2004, 10: 42 a.m.

The meeting with PitBull finally came. My arm was fully healed, but I wasn't ready for this assignment. I couldn't say why.

Anything that had me thinking too much and second-guessing myself, I wanted no part of. But for now, whatever PitBull said, went. And whatever he wanted me to do, I had to do. This time, I was gonna make enough to get out of the game in a big way.

"I'm still not feeling this assignment," I whispered to the empty room, while plopping down on the bed. Every other assignment was easy, but this time, I thought I was taking on more than I could handle. PitBull was up to something. I couldn't say what it was, but I just couldn't fight the feeling that shit was not going to turn out the way it should.

The last things left for me to do before meeting PitBull were to put on my shoes and call the cab. Somehow this sudden cloud of darkness had me procrastinating so long that I would end up being late for my appointment. I came up with a better idea, picked up the phone, and dialed.

"Hello, Linear one," the dispatcher said on the other line.

"Can I get a cab at 2365 Watson Avenue?"

"Where are you going?"

"Harlem, 145th and St. Nick."

"Come outside in five minutes."

A money green cab with tinted windows sat in front of my building. As I got inside and made myself comfortable, I had to remind myself that when I joined the game it was for the money. I wanted to make myself stable because of my parents' deaths and Dragon being put away. Money in the game was not handed out like welfare checks, which would be much easier to collect, but I still had to follow somebody's rules to keep the benefits. Nope, this game was about constantly proving oneself over and over again. Once I thought I'd established that certain level of trust, PitBull wanted me to prove myself again. That's why I couldn't wait for the *plan* Dragon and I had to take this empire down to come through.

The 3rd Avenue Bridge going into Harlem was backed up. Frustrated sounds of car horns and angry drivers cursing could be heard from a mile away. As the cab driver waited for the light to turn green, I slipped into my own little world, trying to figure out what the assignment might be. If there were any more killings, it would be only a matter of time before the Feds caught on and started putting two and two together. Next thing I knew, I'd be behind bars doing life in prison, which was definitely not a part of my plans.

"Miss, we're here," the driver said, breaking my concentration. "Your fare is seventeen dollars."

"Oh, I'm sorry. Here it goes." I handed him the money while making my way out of the cab to join PitBull. He stood right in front of the building. A wide, evil grin crossed his lips the moment I stepped out of the cab.

Now I really wanted to turn tail and run.

CHAPTER 36

PORSHA

Manhattan Court House: July 29, 2004, 4:14 p.m.

Four hours passed and the jurors were still deliberating with no signs indicating that they would come out anytime soon.

"You might get lucky today," I whispered in my client's ear.

Mr. Collin Wright didn't bother to make eye contact. "You think so?"

"No, I *hope* so."

We sat on one of the benches in the courthouse lobby watching people scuttle in and out of the rooms. "I thought I paid you to make sure my ass stays out of jail."

"Sometimes justice doesn't play on the side of the defense, you know," I reminded him softly, still keeping my questions about Chin to myself.

Looking directly in my face, he said, "Justice does not play on the side of the defense. Give me a break with all that justice bullshit. There's no such thing as justice. And if there is, who receives justice?" he challenged as his voice now rose from a low tone to a point that people stared at him as they walked past.

"Keep your voice down," I informed him. "Do you know

that our court system is one of the best court systems in the world?"

"And did you forget it's one of the most corrupt in the world, too? Things work in your favor. All you need is money and a little power." His voice was now angry enough to make me concerned. "So save the bullshit story for one of your clueless clients."

"First of all, no need for you to get rude with me," I said, matching his tone. "I was just letting you know and trying to comfort you, because from my point of view, you look pretty clueless yourself."

He whirled on his Stacy Adams to face me. "I'm helpless? Please woman, I think you need to check yourself about the helpless bullshit. And as far as comforting me, save that shit," he spat. "Your family will be needing it when they have to pick out your casket."

"What the fuck!" I yelled, totally forgetting my surroundings. "Listen, you'd better stop with this bullshit, or else I'm gonna—"

"Gonna do what? Tell them to lock me up?" He was now toe-toe with me. "Because frankly, I don't care. I'm going to spend the rest of my life behind bars, so another life sentence won't matter."

"I think this has gone too far, and as soon as—"

"The judge comes back, what? You're gonna ask him to re-move you from my case? Now, why would you want to do that? We're basically at the end, so what's the point?" He followed behind me as I walked briskly toward the courtroom. "I asked for Chyna and she told them you would do better on my case. Let her tell the story, you were some hotshot at-torney. So why are you running when the heat is on?"

Instead of answering him, I shook my head. "I think we should wait for the verdict because I will not entertain this sort of argument anymore."

Silence expanded between us like a balloon filling with air.

"I'm just fucking with you," he said, laughing at the solemn expression on my face.

Stopping in front of the door to the courtroom, I looked at him. "You're not serious?"

"Woman, how the hell am I supposed to be serious? It's not like I've got connections to kill you. I'm *helpless*, remember? I'm behind bars," he teased. "I was serious about people with power and connections. Tell Chin that if I go down, I'll go down singing."

"I'll talk to him," I replied absently, trying not to look too nervous, although internally, I was shitting bricks. I couldn't understand the man's tactics, but I could somehow feel all of my hard work with Chin was slipping away. I burned to ask Colin about Chin, but I was afraid to find out more than I could handle.

CHAPTER 37

CHIN

Tha Hustle Records NYC: July 29 2004, 4:40 p.m.

Although I let the situation about Danny's killing slide for the moment, it would only be a matter of time before things started leaking out. Once people knew that there was a million dollar hit on the women's heads, tongues would start wagging.

I did manage to get a hold of Lou, and he brought the tapes. One of the robbers forgot to tuck in her ponytail properly. I still couldn't believe that women were the source of the problem. The day I got my hands on those little females, not even the Feds and DEA would take on the case. Law enforcement would have to come larger than that, because when I was through, they'd be lucky if they had dental records to identify those bitches.

"Come in," I responded to a solid knock on my door.

"Dawg, can you believe this shit?" Tony asked while giving me a pound. "Business is booming since the Columbians gave us that fresh batch of supplies."

I couldn't help but grin. "And the funniest thing is that I knew it would sell. Remember we estimated three days? That shit's been selling out in one. I think this calls for a celebration."

I took out a bottle of Hennessy and poured Tony a drink.

Tony tapped his glass to mine. "How about it, man? Big Tymers tonight, VIP style."

"I'm down for whatever," I said, laughing. "To show how happy my ass is, I'm willing to get on the dance floor for a change. And you know me, I don't dance or get up from a VIP table for shit."

"True that, true that." Tony shook his head as he sipped on the Henny. "So, you gonna forget you're damn near married and hang loose?"

"What the fuck I look like? Shoot, I might grab me a woman and hit her doggie style in the bathroom. Porsha won't even enter my mind."

Tony laughed hard. "Oh, a nigga's getting gully on my ass."

"Naw man, just keeping it real."

"I'm gonna hold you to that," he cackled, taking another sip. "You better be on the dance floor, getting down for real."

"And I will. But how about it? There's no time like a banging ending. What about hitting Freaks Strip Joint after? I heard the strippers are off the hook, doing all kind of acrobatic movements and shit. Because *that*, I don't mind. A private lap dance, some good head, a bitch can be flipped upside down and suck my dick. I don't give a damn. As long as I'm getting my money's worth, it's all good."

"Oh shit." Tony's wide grin was a sight to see. "I can really see that a nigga's extremely happy. I've never seen you like this before."

"Tony, this shit's about to be on. I mean, I love Porsha because she's my wifey, and she knows she's my wifey. But sometimes, I can't help the fact there are other asses out there I wouldn't mind tapping."

"I feel the same way too. Strippers can fill the void. I mean, you're not married to Porsha, but I'm married to Maribel with two fucking kids." Tony took a long sip from his glass. "When we first got married the sex was off the hook, but after she spit out the two babies everything changed. To this day I think she regrets marrying me. Her father had a heart attack and died when he found out."

"I've tried to make it up to her," Tony said. "I make enough fucking dough, for God's sake. If she wants a Bentley, that shit could be in her driveway tomorrow. I'm willing to spend to make her happy, but she just . . . I don't know man, I think she's cheating. She doesn't treat me the way she used to. I'm trying to save my marriage, but it seems like I'm trying in vain. That's why I spend less time at home and more time at the studio and the strip club."

I swiveled to the window and allowed the warm rays to touch my skin. The tables really had turned. Now I felt like giving Tony advice. "Well, have you tried telling her how you feel? Have you told her you're not enjoying the sex? Ask her if there's someone else. By the way, what makes you think she's cheating?"

Tony laughed, a hard bitter sound. "I think you're not hearing me right. Let me tell you this much, not even foreplay is a part of our lovemaking when there is sex. It's just strictly sex. It's almost like sleeping with a prostitute. A high paid one at that. As far as the cheating, she is always leaving the kids with her mother and dressing up to go out with friends.

"I don't know what to say to that, but tonight is Porsha's night for a while, if you know what I mean."

"Ahhhhh, you gonna hit it up tonight, huh?"

"Of course, you know how females can get when they haven't had it in a while. I have to make sure I leave her in a happy mood tonight, so when I'm gone later there should be no complaints. She should be reminiscing about what I did to her earlier."

"I hear that, man. At least you got your love life sorted out," Tony said, letting out a deep sigh.

Maribel was stupid. The man actually loved her and probably wouldn't stray if she just gave him what he needed.

"I still have Chyna to worry about. But if Porsha starts complaining when I come back in the morning, then round two will soften her ass out."

"You're crazy, son."

"Naw, it's only true, and you should know that passionate sex, blended with a little roughness, is the key to soften a woman's heart. It makes her weak to the point where even if she doesn't love you, you have her screaming that she does."

My speech must have surprised Tony. The only thing he did was clap his hands and laugh.

"Trust me, I got Porsha on lock like that."

"I hear that." He emptied the last of his glass. "I'm glad to see that a female ain't got *you* on lock."

"Never that. I whip pussy. Never, under any circumstances, has pussy whipped me."

Tony roared with laughter. "Trust me, son. There's a female out there who's got your number, just like Maribel had mine."

The thing I like about my relationship with Tony is that we are able to easily move from personal issues, to business, to being ghetto-ass thugs. And when it's time for us to step down and become cold ass killers, it still isn't a problem. And that would definitely come in handy when we found those bitches.

CHAPTER 38

PITBULL

Harlem NYC: July 29th 2004, 5:19 p.m.

"This bitch better not fuck this assignment up or it's gonna be her head," I thought to myself as I paced the floor of the Harlem base.

I had worked too long and hard for anybody to ruin it, especially since I was a breath away from having what I wanted most. But there might be a problem. Word on the street was that Dragon Bentley was asking around for information about the night of the murder of Anthony Smith. It would only be a matter of time before the man would land on my doorstep and there would be hell to pay. I wondered if Dragon was asleep to the fact that Chin was in on the deal. He had to know something. He was in the man's studio working on that album everyday.

Then to make matters worse, BabyGirl disappeared at times and wouldn't tell Sandy or Dimples anything about her movements. Definitely not a good sign. I would have to get that girl on lock before I put her onto this next assignment. I knew BabyGirl was still a virgin, and I really wanted to fuck her before I put her onto Chin. Women always became attached to their first piece of dick, and I definitely wanted her attached to me. Just like Dimples. BabyGirl was loyal to a point, but her fire had the girl pulling in the wrong direction.

I crossed the room, picked up the phone, and dialed. Tracey, the receptionist, picked up on the second ring and spoke smoothly on the other end. "Good Afternoon, Tha Hustle Records. How may I transfer your call?"

"Hey baby, what's up? What you been up to?"

Tracey sighed wearily and whispered. "Playing two sides of the coin is wearing me out. I'm about to get out of here and get some rest."

"Can I join you?" I asked, thinking of the lunch date that had turned into so much more.

Tracey was on her way out of the building one afternoon, when I saw her and jumped on the opportunity to join her. I soon learned enough to pull her into my plans for Chin. The promise of more money could make even the most loyal employee turn the other cheek. Besides, she was in love with Chin and he wouldn't give her the time of day. I would love to give her so much more. She wasn't having that, either. Tracey had set her goals a little higher.

Born and raised in Castle Hill Projects in the Bronx, Tracey's mother had been on welfare for a short period of time before she finally landed a job that would meet their needs. Word on the street was Tracey's dad was nothing but a "hit and run" and left her mother to take care of a child on her own. Being tired of the cards life dealt her, Tracey fell hard for a high profile drug dealer.

After a few dates, she found out she was pregnant. Surprisingly, he claimed responsibility for the child even though he had a wife and another daughter. Things were going fine, visits were regular, and they still dated. But her Cinderella story didn't last long. Tragedy struck when her daughter, Brianna, was only four. Anthony Smith was killed in a drug robbery.

I didn't make much of the story until I started to put all the pieces together. Then it hit me—Anthony Smith was Natalie Smith's, aka BabyGirl's, father. Brianna was BabyGirl's little sister. I wondered what that little piece of information would do for me in the future. And I also wondered how I could use it to my advantage without bringing up the fact that I had something to do with Anthony Smith's death.

"Hell naw, nigga," Tracey responded, laughing at his invitation. "Man, who the fuck do you want, Chin or Tony? Tony's still here but Chin left for the day."

"A'ight, since your little feisty ass don't wanna holler at me, put me on to Tony then."

"Dream on, nigga," she teased. "You will *never* tap this ass."

I could always hope, but the info she gave me from time to time paid off in a big way. The phone clicked off, and for a moment I thought she had hung up on me.

"Tony speaking."

"What's up, dawg?"

"Just here finishing up some paperwork and Dragon's promotional flyers for his album release so I don't have to do it tomorrow."

"Oh yeah? When does his album drop?"

"November 15th."

"Word, I heard it's hot. I gotta add it to my collection."

"I think this boy's gonna go platinum. And you know you don't have to wait 'til it hits stores. Just come up here and get your copy."

"Now that's what's up." I then smoothly slipped into the real reason for my call. "So, what's up for tonight?"

"Big Tymers, but Chin wants us to hit Freaks right after."

"For real? That's what's up."

"Hell, yeah."

"That's funny. A friend of mine was telling me about that joint. I said one of these days when I got some time I was gonna check it out."

"Yeah? Well no need to wait," Tony said, as papers rustled in the background. "And you know when we party it's nothing but VIP style."

"No doubt, so I'll catch up with you later because I can hear you have work to do."

"A'ight."

"Bye."

I smiled, knowing that things were falling into place according to my plan. The next call put an even wider smile on my face.

CHAPTER 39

PORSHA

Manhattan Court House: July 29, 2004, 5:03 p.m.

After waiting for five full hours, the jury finally came back with a verdict. I waited with bated breath.

The foreman stood, his dark brown hair plastered to his pale skin. "We the jurors find the defendant *not guilty.*"

The verdict was music to Collin Wright's ears, but to the victim's family it was cause for outrage.

"Is this your idea of *justice*!" The angry voice of the victim's father carried across the courtroom.

"Order in the court," the judge demanded while banging his gravel. He signaled to the sheriff, who had already moved to the center of the courtroom.

"We don't need order, we need justice!" The man's wife stood in a calm manner, rubbing his shoulder, but her head nodded with his every word.

"Another outburst like that and I will hold you in contempt," the judge warned.

"Yeah that's right, hold me in contempt," the portly man shot back, breaking away from his wife's hold. "Because I don't have money to buy your ass like the defendant did."

The judge's face turned bright red. "Officers, take him away."

I stood, watching as the officers placed handcuffs on the man. Situations like these made me question my line of work. I wasn't even supposed to take this case, but somehow Chyna had set this up. Some friend!

"Thank you for helping to free this monster," the father spat at the jury who stood watching him closely as the officers pulled him away. Then his angry glare landed on me. "So he could continue to hurt other people's kids."

"I'm sorry for your pain, sir, but I was just doing my job," I reminded the angry man.

"Lord have mercy on your soul if this happens to you. You might end up like my son—dead. And I hope you'll remember that the same people who you help today can harm you later. And it doesn't matter if you were *just doing your job.*"

"Okay, that's enough," the court officer said, dragging the father down the aisle.

I turned to Collin, who beamed like a light bulb.

He leaned in, whispering, "Remember that information I promised to tell you?"

"I don't want anything from you. I don't want to know how Chin helped you."

"I'll keep my promise anyway." He tucked his shirt in his suit. "And you just may want to hear about this."

I stuffed the last paper in the file, ignoring him completely.

"Your boy Chin used to kick it with that bitch in your office."

Now that made the hairs rise on my arms. "You can't be right about that."

"So you don't know that she used to strip at Blue Horizon Bar and Lounge?"

"Yes, but that has nothing to do with Chin."

"Trust me, my sources never lie. He forced her to abort his baby."

I stood shock-still as the rest of the information poured from Mr. Wright. He held the door for me as we proceeded out of the courtroom. "Well, I hope that I've given you as much as you've given me."

"Probably even more."

As I watched Collin's tall frame disappear down the hall, I whipped out my cell phone and called the office.

"Your fiancé called," My secretary said softly.

"Okay, thanks. I won't be stopping back at the office. I'll see you tomorrow."

I disconnected with my secretary and dialed Chin's personal line.

When he answered, I said, "Hey, baby."

"Hey, honey, what's up? Why you sound like that?"

"Hard day at work today," I said, masking my anger.

"What happened? Did you lose the case?"

"Naw, we won."

"So what's the matter? This calls for a celebration."

"You're not listening to me, Chin, *sweetheart.*"

"Baby, all you have to do is get off the phone, come home, and I am all yours." His seductive voice would normally put a smile on my face. Unfortunately, too many questions rattled in my brain to lift the corners of my mouth this time.

"You promise?"

"Have I ever gone back on my promise before?"

I hesitated a moment before saying, "No."

"Aight, so come on home."

I ended the call. Going home was the last thing on my mind, but as my mind formulated a plan, I knew that pussy was the last thing Chin would get from me tonight.

CHAPTER 40

PITBULL

Harlem: July 29, 2004, 5:45 p.m.

A single call to Tony, and he explained Chin's plans, which kicked my plans into high gear. This couldn't be a better opportunity. Everything was playing right into my hands. *BabyGirl better not tell me that she ain't got any clothes to wear. Fucking females! Everything gotta be perfect before they could leave to go anywhere.*

"BabyGirl," I said in the phone.

"Yeah."

"Think you could be ready in the next five hours?"

"For what?"

"To go to the club tonight!"

She sighed softly. "I had plans. I thought the plan was jumping off for now?"

"Naw, plans changed, ma, so I'd appreciate it if you and the other girls could be ready in a few hours."

"They got names, you know."

"Fuck that! I know they do, but my main concern is for you to be ready."

"Okay. Luckily I got my hair, nails, and toes done already. I was going out tonight."

"Yeah, yeah. Just be ready. Now let me talk to Sandy."

"Watch her, and watch her closely," I told Sandy after filling her in on the most recent developments, and adding a little twist to the plans.

"No doubt. You know we always have our little *girl talks*, so as soon as something weird comes up, or she's acting kinda shady, trust me PitBull, you'll be the first to know," she assured me.

"That's why you've always been my favorite. I know that I can always count on you."

"Thank you. Glad to be of good service," she said smoothly. "But before I go, one more question."

"What's that?"

"How much is my time worth?"

Inwardly, I cringed. "Sandy, I got you. And besides, that issue is not to be discussed over the telephone."

I hung up, fuming, thinking female crews were definitely not worth the headache.

CHAPTER 41

BABYGIRL

Watson Avenue: July 29, 2004—Time, 8:00 p.m.

Finding something to wear at the spur of the moment was easy since Dragon had already asked me about meeting him at Big Tymers tonight. PitBull was willing to issue major bucks for this assignment, so it had to be of some importance to him. Everything had to be right in order for my strategy to work. Not only did the clothes have to be right, but the conversation had to be off the hook, too.

"Oh well," I sighed getting off the bed, and walking over to the closet.

Fifteen minutes later, I came up with the perfect outfit.

Sandy came barging into my room. "What are you gonna wear tonight?"

"Don't you know how to fucking knock?"

"Please, this is my house," she flashed me off, sucking her teeth at the same time. "So, what are you wearing?"

"Well since you want to be nosey, I'm wearing my all white Chanel catsuit with the big crystal belt around the waist. I guess my white, low-cut, high-heel, Prada boots with the silver buckle on the side will do to go wear with it."

"Bitch, what hot date you got tonight?" Dimples laughed, strolling through the door. "Or better yet, who the fuck you plan on pimping being that you're all whited out?"

I laughed. "Be easy girl, and stop stressing a pimp."

"What the fuck's up with all this pimping?" Dimples asked as the towel wrapped around her waist slipped down, and water dripped all over my new white carpet.

"First of all, you need to dry your ass off, and stop wetting up my expensive rug." I snapped.

"What, this piece of shit that you paid no more than a Benjamin for?" Dimples said, her voice dripping with sarcasm.

"So! *You* didn't buy it."

"Whatever." She rolled her eyes, turning to Sandy. "So, what's this pimping shit all about?"

"Since BabyGirl ain't filling you in," Sandy said, "she has a hot date."

"What . . ." Dimples leaned her head back for a better view of 174th Street through my window since a hot car drove past.

Shrugging them off, I said, "It's not even that kind of party."

"Nobody ain't saying all of that, but you sure are going the extra mile to make sure whoever he is can't take his eyes off you." Sandy's eyes traveled over my body.

I turned to face her. "And is there a problem with that?"

"Nope, no problem," she responded quickly. Something I couldn't quite name flashed in her eyes.

"A'ight then." I opened the bedroom door. "So both of y'all get the hell out of my room and get dressed."

"Oh please, keep acting up, Miss Hot Stuff," Dimples teased as she closed my bedroom door.

"Fucking nosey-ass bitches," I cackled to myself. Then all laughter disappeared as I realized that Sandy knew more than she was letting on. Something about her whole approach made it seem as though she was checking me out, rather than just being plain nosey. I filed that piece of information away for future use. PitBull was playing some serious games. And I didn't trust Sandy as far as I could spit or shit.

CHAPTER 42

CHIN

Staten Island: July 29, 2004, 9:21 p.m.

I sat in the warm water sipping on Cristal as I listened to Porsha's heels hit the pavement leading to the pool.

"What is all of this?" she asked.

"I thought I would do something special for you," I answered, making my way out of the pool to help Porsha undress. The things I loved about Porsha were her beautiful face and her educated ass. Damn, nothing turned me on more than a female who could hold down a decent conversation and could ride me like a jockey in bed.

Unfortunately, educated ass or not, she backed away. Definitely not a smart move.

"Baby, my day at work was horrible today," she said.

"Yeah, tell daddy all about it," I walked forward, kissing her on her neck.

"First my client, he's so fucking stubborn and—"

"Uh huh . . ." I responded, biting on her earlobe and not wanting to hear anymore about Colin's stupid ass. I'd already set Tony on taking care of him—permanently.

She pushed me away. "Baby, you're not listening to me."

"I am, baby. I listen with my ears, not with my tongue, you know." I continued teasing down her neck.

"Well, I need your full attention," she demanded, pushing me away again.

I pushed my body to hers. "I *am* giving you my attention, with a little affection."

"Chin, stop. I'm dead-ass serious," she expressed in a solemn tone.

I sighed wearily, pouring her a glass of Cristal. "A'ight, ma. You got my full attention."

"I had the worst client, the one I told you about before. First he didn't want to cooperate, and then the jurors came back with a not guilty verdict, then to top it off, the victim's family started to curse, and then the judge ordered the victim's father to be held in contempt."

"I'm so sorry you had to experience all of that. He's someone who used to work with me and PitBull when we were just getting started. Somebody as fine as you should never have to go through that," I said, stroking her ego, hoping that soon I would get to stroke something else.

"You mean that, baby?" she asked, blushing.

"Of course. Why would I tell my wifey shit I don't mean?" I assured her while climbing onto the beach chair and straddling her chocolate thighs.

The dims lights, along with the candles in the dark night, set the romantic scene for Babyface to bellow his songs from the speakers. The running water could be heard from the hot tub outside. The cool breeze completed a perfect romantic setting.

Placing the wine glass on the floor beside the chair, my tongue gently parted her lips. At first, I slipped my tongue in her mouth, then I removed it, and rolled it around in a circular motion while dipping one of my hands down her blouse to play with her nipples. For some reason, they didn't get hard. Something was wrong.

"And did I forget to mention that my client threatened me?" she said, pushing me away once more.

"Don't worry about it. I told you your man is going to take your mind off things." I tried to hold on to those luscious lips.

"I know, but I can't help but wonder whether I'm doing the right thing by helping your friend get off."

My dick instantly went soft. Didn't this bitch know that talking is a turn off for a horny man? I was trying to make love to her, and she was yapping away like a fucking CNN reporter.

"What's wrong, sweetie?" She asked in a soft voice. "Why are you putting on your robe?"

I glared at her, trying hard to hold in my anger. "I just remembered that Dragon's album is about to be released soon. We need to finish working on the promotional flyers at the office," I said toweling off. "So, I thought I'd just run down there for a minute."

"Hold the fuck up," she snapped. "You don't expect me to buy that shit? You told me over the phone that tonight I would be all yours. Then in the middle of a conversation your ass is gonna get up and leave? What kinda bullshit is that, Chin?"

"Listen, I ain't expecting you to believe shit." I looked down into her icy glare. "If you want to believe it, fine. If you don't, then that's your fucking business." Wrapping the robe around my body, I turned to her. "I'm telling you what I have to do so that the mothafucking bills can be paid and those fine ass clothes can stay on your back."

She jumped off the lawn chair and roared, "Fine ass clothes on my back? Nigga, you're acting like I'm some trifling bitch sitting around waiting for your drug money to flow in." She grabbed the wet towel from my hand, and followed me through the kitchen. "I'm the one that's trying to pull your shit from criminal to legit. I work a legitimate job; therefore, I can hold down my own. Remember that."

I got up in her face, and could feel the blood pounding in my head. "Yeah, but you don't be complaining when that drug money is spent on your ass."

"Fuck you, Chin,"

"Maybe if you were doing that, I wouldn't need to rush to the office."

"Oh, so it's like that, huh?" She flung her hands up in the air and snapped back her head. "Well, let's see how you do *without* some pussy."

She stormed behind me toward the bedroom, and then trailed me to the garage. I pushed my head outside the car window. "Girl, please. I got my...hands." Damn, I almost slipped up. "They never fail me."

"That's right, do what you do best—jerk off."

"Don't worry about it."

"Or maybe you're going to fuck Chyna again," she yelled down the driveway.

I stomped on the brakes. The car came to a screeching halt just before the gate. Leaning my head out of the window, I looked back at her. "What the fuck did you say?"

"You heard me, nigga."

"Bitch, you tripping."

"I've got your bitch right here," she said, pointing to her pussy. "And I've got your bitch back there in my office, too."

With that I tore out down the street, realizing that a whole new set of problems had just opened up. Porsha could put a serious dent in my plans, especially if she decided to tip off the Feds.

Damn!

CHAPTER 43

BABYGIRL

Big Tymers Nightclub—Manhattan: July 29, 2004, 11:22 p.m.

The music was pumping so loud in the club, we could hear L.L. Cool J's "Headsprung" across the street in the parking lot. A crowd of people wrapped around the club and up the street.

"Where's PitBull?" Sandy asked, folding her arms over her tiny breasts.

"That's the same thing I'm asking," Dimples said, tapping her feet on the concrete. "Because I know his ass don't expect us to stand in a mothafuckin' line like that."

"Stand in line? Please!" I said, my hands firmly on my hips. "Girl, you see how we're dressed. There's no need for us to wait."

Dimples was dressed in a white halter top with the long strings dropping to the center of her back and one of those mini-skirts that made her ass cheeks pop out slightly if she bent over. A white Gucci pocketbook and thigh-high Dante Jeans boots matched the outfit.

Sandy had to be the extreme hoochie. Hell, I don't even know how to describe it because frankly, she had nothing on. A tiny baby blue halter with four little feathers covering those little knobs she called titties. Batty rider shorts, all covered in feathers, and with laces up the sides, exposed the fact that the child didn't have on a lick of underwear. And everything matched her feather high heeled slippers.

"Damn, don't this bitch think she overdosed on the feathers?" I chuckled to Dimples, who laughed hard.

Sandy turned and glared at me. "You just wish your ass could look this good."

Actually, I did look good. But I kept it simple with my white Chanel catsuit that had lace exposing my skin on the sides. I kept the zipper halfway unzipped too. I had to make sure my 38Cs and my cleavage greeted the world with a sexy smile. The crystal belt, sunglasses, and pocketbook completed the look and shouted, "money." My hair was laid with a fourteen inch deep hair weave that reached the middle of my back. The little wisps of hair at the front were combed to perfection to blend in with the curly hair, making me look like a Puerto Rican.

"Sorry to have you *ladies* waiting so long," PitBull apologized, checking us out.

Dimples elbowed him in the side. "About time your black ass showed up."

"A'ight ma, be easy with your little sexy self."

"Thank you." Dimples blushed. "You like it?"

People passed by us as they went to the end of the line. Cars were circling the block looking for parking space. I wished them good luck with that one.

"Hell yeah, y'all are off the hook tonight!" PitBull rubbed his hands together, licked his lips, and stared all three of us up and down. "Damn, I sure—"

"Stop it right there." I cut him off dead ass in his track. "Just get us inside."

"Feisty, huh!"

"PitBull!"

"A'ight, BabyGirl, let's go."

As we made our way past the other patrons in line, guys stared with their mouths wide open as if their jaws were about to drop off. Bitches were kicking us down with envious looks as if to say "I know these trifling hoes didn't come out here looking like *that*." But instead of rolling our eyes or giving them the time of day, we just stuck our asses out more, and swung that shit like we've never swung it before. Unlike them, we didn't have to stand in line.

Dimples glared at everyone around her. "Shoot, these bitches and niggas better realize who the real females around here are."

The club had four different rooms. One room was for hip-hop, one for reggae, one for salsa and meringue, and the other was a strip room. The club was situated in a way people in VIP could look down on the dance floor, but sometimes people on the dance floor could see people in VIP depending on where they were seated. The DJ onstage spun hip-hop, and bartenders worked their asses off, trying to get everyone's order without missing anyone. The air conditioning was at full blast, which would hopefully prevent me from smelling anyone's funky armpits.

"Well, here y'all are mamitas, just order whatever y'all want and put it on my tab."

"Now you know you don't have to repeat that twice," Sandy said.

I slipped onto a bar stool.

The music blared, thumping up my spine.

"PitBull," I said, pulling him to side.

"What's up, ma?"

"Where's the person that I'm supposed to meet?"

"Turn the other way, so you can face VIP. Then pretend— or better yet, play as if I'm trying to holler at you."

"Okay."

I immediately switched positions with PitBull, resting my elbow on the gray and white marbled counter.

"You see the guy up there with the red, white, and blue jersey?"

I scanned left, then right, before I said, "Yeah."

"That's your target right there."

"Him?"

"What's that supposed to mean?"

"I mean, he's fine as hell." I continued staring at the man. "But for someone with money, I thought he would've been all decked out."

"Don't let simple dressing fool you," he whispered in my ear. "That nigga's sitting on dough."

As PitBull continued on about the man across the room, for some reason the man's eyes glanced down to the bar and caught me staring.

Dragon walked up to stand next to that man, patting him on the shoulder, then he turned around and gave me a wink. I sent one back. Both men stared at me from across the room.

"PitBull, he's staring at me now."

"Well, start doing your job, ma." He grabbed my ass and gave it a squeeze. "One of these days you gotta let me tap that booty," he whispered, leaning close enough for his cologne to make me dizzy.

Smacking his hand away, I glared at him. "Not a chance."

"A'ight! But I hope you remember that when you're getting down with Chin."

CHAPTER 44

CHIN

Big Tymers NYC: July 29, 2004, 11:43 p.m.

I had just told Tony about Porsha's outburst concerning Chyna. He assured me that in order for her to say something, she had to *know* something. Now I was wondering what the hell Chyna'd been up to, and if I should put my foot up her ass. As I tried to push my troubles away, I glanced out toward the dance floor and found instant excitement.

"Who's that?" I asked.

"Who is who?" Tony inquired, eyes scanning the dance floor area.

"The girl PitBull's talking with."

"I don't know," Tony replied gazing down on her. "Maybe some girl he's trying to get with. Why?" Tony asked, eyeing me suspiciously.

"She's looking sexy as hell."

"Well, he got to her first, so try somebody else. Look, she got two more girlfriends on the floor, so why not holler at one of them?"

"Naw, I want *her*." Suddenly the taste of Belvedere didn't appeal to me anymore.

"Well, PitBull got to her first, so feast your eyes on some-body else."

Tony pointed at the other two women at the bar.

"You know why I wouldn't holler at the other two?"

Tony shrugged.

"Look at the one in the feathers. What kind of woman does she look like to you?"

"A ho and a gold digger," he replied.

"Exactly. Just watch how she acts on the floor, pushing her-self up on every nigga she sees. I bet she doesn't turn down a drink from any nigga who buys. "

"A'ight, what about the one in the mini-skirt? She's stick-ing to herself."

"Yeah, she's cool, but her ass is high-priced maintenance. Look at the guys she rejects, and the ones she exchanges a few words with."

"So?"

"Let's put it this way, she's a fucking headache. Something I don't need on top of Porsha."

"And the one you're after?"

"Something about her sparks my fire."

"Well, as I said, she's taken. PitBull's got her on lock."

"Wrong!" I pulled back my chair. "He's walking away and he did not get the digits."

"What makes you think you're gonna do any better?"

"How am I supposed to know if I don't go down there and try?"

"You're sick, man," Tony said, shaking his head in disap-proval. "You really have a thing for the women PitBull likes."

"No, PitBull and I just happen to have the same taste in women."

By the time Tony and I finished debating, PitBull, Chico, Dragon, and Shotta joined Tony at the table.

"No luck, man?" I asked, grinning at PitBull as he slipped into the booth.

"Naw, shorty's frontin' on me, dawg."

"You mind if I try?" I asked, ignoring Tony's hard glare.

"Be my guest, but I doubt you're gonna do any better," he warned, glancing at the woman then back to me.

"Nothing beats a failure but a try," I assured him, patting him on the shoulder on my way to the bar.

PitBull laughed. "I think she's gonna give you a run for your money."

"I certainly agree with that," Dragon added, peering at me from underneath hooded eyes.

CHAPTER 45

PORSHA

Staten Island

I can't believe Chin just walked out on me like that, I thought to myself as I put out the candles around the pool area. I was steaming mad. He promised me he would be mine all night.

The house phone rang, interrupting my angry interlude. I sprinted to the kitchen and yanked the phone off the cradle. "Hello!"

"What's up, girl?" Chyna said in a cheerful tone, irritating the hell out of me.

"Nothing, just here cleaning up the pool area."

"What's wrong with you?" Chyna snapped. Then her voice became solemn. "Before you say a word, let me guess— Chin."

"Mmm- hmm."

"What'd his trifling ass do now?"

"After he said he wanted to spend time with me, the nigga got up and walked out because I wasn't giving him the pussy at the time he wanted it."

"Fucking men!" she shouted. "Please, that's all they think about . . . pussy."

"You're telling me." I sighed, slumping down on the patio chair.

"So what you gonna do? Just sit at home all night and sob about it?" Chyna inquired evenly.

"What am I supposed to do?" I asked, hoping that I might get an opportunity to pluck a little information from my lying friend.

"Get dressed and hit Big Tymers with me tonight."

I thought it over for a moment. "I should, and let that nigga come home and see that two can play this game."

"There you go, girl. Don't let no man walk over your ass."

"A'ight. Give me thirty minutes."

"See you then."

CHAPTER 46

BABYGIRL

Big Tymers

"Can I buy you something to drink?" A deep, sexy, masculine voice asked over my shoulder.

"No, thank you. I got it." I shrugged, eyeing him suspiciously. "Besides, what I drink might be too much for your pocket."

"I didn't ask you the *price* of the drink," he fired back. "I asked you if you *wanted* something to drink."

"And I told you," I said, lifting my glass. "I got it."

"A'ight, I hear you," he said looking intently at the glass, before turning to the bartender. "Let me get a glass of Dom Perignon for the lady, and a Thug Passion for myself."

"I see that you have fine taste in liquor." I couldn't keep the grin off my face. "And why are you so stubborn?"

"Naw, I'm just determined, especially when I see something good and I want it." He moved closer to me. "I don't bow out that easily. And like you said, I have fine taste. So are you here with somebody?" He asked.

I gently rocked my shoulders to the beat. "Nope," I replied simply.

"You left him at home, huh?"

"No sweetie, I'm as single as they come."

His sexy lips spread into a satisfied smile. "Word? Somebody as fine as you single? How come?"

"Because it's hard to find a decent man these days."

"Maybe you're not looking in the right place."

My gaze focused on him. "Trust me, I have. And they're all full of shit."

The bubbles from the Dom tickled my tongue.

"It's like that, ma?" He laughed heartily.

"I don't need any of them." I settled the glass on the bar. "I take care of myself, both financially and sexually."

"So how do you take care of yourself . . . sexually?"

"Why are you in my business?"

"You put it out there. Just asking a question."

"Well, they don't make vibrators just to sit on the shelf, you know."

He burst out laughing. "You're one of those females who's on that electronic bullshit?"

"It works perfectly. Stops when I tell it to stop, no disease, no pregnancy, and it doesn't need Viagra to keep it up."

"Damn, ma," he said, laughing so hard he almost spit out his drink.

"Damn what?"

"You have me rolling out here tonight."

"Hey, that's me. A sense of humor's a good thing." Peering at Sandy on the dance floor, I sent up a silent prayer, hoping she wouldn't make a fool of herself this time.

"So, what is it you're looking for in a man, being that none of them seem to impress you?

He caught me off guard with that question as my head bobbed to Sean Paul's "Gimme the Light."

"Why should I make your job easy, and myself vulnerable? Why don't you tell me the qualities you possess as a man? And then *maybe* I will inform you if that's what I'm looking for."

"First you have to tell me your name."

"What's your name?" I fired back.

The scent of his Tommy Hilfiger swirled around me.

"Chin. Andre Chin."

"Well, Chin," I said, my right hand extended to him, "meet Jane Doe."

"So you're not gonna give me a name?"

"Nope, because I'm not trying to get with you, so there's no need for you to know my name."

"But I'm trying to get with you, Miss Doe."

Sliding off the barstool, I moved closer to him. "So you want to know my name, huh?"

"That would be nice."

"If you want to know me that bad, how about I leave it up to you to figure things out?"

"Why are you making it so difficult?" He asked, grabbing for my hand. "Who am I supposed to ask?"

"I'm sure you'll find a way."

Before he could say anything else, R. Kelly's "Feeling on Your Booty" came on. I immediately made my way to the dance floor and began moving my hips to the rhythm of the music. I watched as Chin sat on the bar stool, his eyes tracing the curves of my body every time I moved my hips. Wanting to tease him a little more, I strolled to him and leaned over to place a gentle kiss on his neck. Suddenly my whole body went ice cold. Chin had a tattoo on his neck. Two strawberries with bite marks, the juice dripping, and the words "lick me" underneath, brought all the bad memories flooding back.

PitBull would have keeled over and died if he could read my mind at the moment. Seduce Chin for five hundred thousand dollars?

Hell, I thought as rage filled my body. *I'd kill his ass for free.*

"Hmm," I moaned loudly, a plan forming in my mind. Since the tattoo said "lick me," I wasted no time using my tongue to trace around the strawberries in a slow sensual way, making the strawberries wet. His glass of Thug Passion nearly fell out of his hand. I slipped in two fingers, took out a piece of ice, let the ice cold water drip along his neck, and licked it up once more.

"Hmm . . ." His moan echoed just under the beat of the music. A group of men nearby pointed to us as they watched the scene.

"You like that?" I whispered.

"Uh-huh," he groaned.

Using my other hand to explore him, his eyes became thick with lust. Not only was homeboy hard, but his dick was packing enough to fill up even the most well-used pussy. The man had what Dimples called a "hurt me dick."

"Join me on the dance floor," I whispered in his ear, while flicking his diamond earring with my tongue.

Without a moment's hesitation, he got up off the stool, held me around the waist, and followed me to the dance floor. My back was turned to him, which was a good thing. Now I could really grind my ass on his dick.

"Feeling on your Booty" continued playing, and slowly I moved my waist round and round, pushing my ass back on that dick.

"You getting me hard," he whispered.

"Really?"

"Hell, yeah!"

"Then I *know* I'm doing a good job."

I bent over slightly, positioning myself at a doggie style angle, placed his hands on my thighs, and moved my ass up and down along his dick. By this time the blood was pumping through his dick at a speed as if it was about to bust out of his pants. I could feel it throbbing.

I wanted so bad to see the expression on his face, so I turned around, but this time I sucked on his neck a little.

"Why do you enjoy licking my neck so much?" He asked, his voice heavy with anticipation.

Instead of giving him a direct answer, I placed my fingers on his lips and replied, "That's my specialty."

By now his puzzled expression was replaced with a sexy ass smile exposing perfectly straight, white teeth. "So what part of your body do you want me to lick?" He asked.

"Wouldn't you like to know, huh?"

"Oh, yeah!"

"Find me, get to know me, then you can lick me." I teased with a big grin.

"So . . ."

I didn't give him a chance to finish his statement before I signaled to Sandy and Dimples, left the dance floor, snatched my pocketbook off the bar counter, and sprinted for the exit along with my girls.

"Hey, hold up," I could hear him yelling through the crowd, but I continued walking away without a backward glance.

CHAPTER 47

PITBULL

Big Tymers NYC

"Damn, a nigga doing good," I said. "He got shorty on the dance floor grinding all over him."

Tony nudged my side. "I know," he replied, "but are my eyes really seeing what I am seeing?"

Shotta's head spun around. "What's that?"

"Porsha and Chyna are checking in at the door."

"Damn, Chyna's one sexy bitch," Shotta said, while the boy's mouth began to drool over her fine ass. Why did everyone seem to want my girls? First BabyGirl, now Chyna, again.

"Nigga, you're not getting the whole point." I got up from behind the table to head for the bar. "Chin's about to be busted in a big way."

"Oh, shit." Chico jumped up.

I followed.

Tony was right behind us.

CHAPTER 48

PORSHA

Big Tymers

"This shit's kinda crowded in here tonight," I yelled to Chyna.

"Girl, don't even worry about that. Just have yourself a good time tonight. Flirt a little if you can with a few of these niggas, and then hop your merry ass back on home."

"You're right, but I sure do miss Chin." I eyed Chyna closely. "Poor baby, he's probably hard at work right now, and I'm not even there to bring him dinner at the office."

Chyna whirled around to face me. "Fuck him! If he was a real man, he would've been beside you listening to you instead of running off. And who knows if he's at work anyway? He's probably shaking his ass with some hoochie."

"You know, I think he may have been digging some bitch for a minute, but it had better be over now 'cause I'll beat a bitch down over my man." I eyed Chyna again. "I'd better not find out he's cheating. I'd kill him *and* her." Then I grinned. "Since we have that understanding in our relationship, I trust him."

"Understanding my ass, but don't come running to me when that nigga breaks your heart."

"Whatever." I placed a single hand in Chyna's face, making it clear that I wasn't in for the bullshit.

"Hey, Porsha." PitBull walked up, hugging me, and giving me a kiss on the cheek, while rolling his eyes at Chyna.

"Hey, baby, what's up?" I planted my arms around his back. "What honey did you bring here tonight?"

"Naw, no honey tonight," he said, blocking her view of the dance floor. "I just came here to chill and see if I could pick me up a shorty," he said with a wink.

"Boy, you and your wild self. When are you gonna settle down and find a wifey?"

"She ain't *found* me yet," he whispered to her, before showing his teeth. "So I'm still gonna get down til she come running."

"Shut up, you dog," I said, laughing.

"Oh, yes." He laughed along with me. "And the females love the dog in me or else they would've stopped hollering."

"Them bitches must be blind because even if I was desperate, I would never come running to your ass," Chyna said, throwing in her two cents.

"Shut up. It ain't my fault no nigga wanna fuck you cuz you a ho."

"Ho? Let me tell you some—"

"A'ight, cut this shit," I said, standing between the two of them. My gut feeling told me that they knew each other better than they were letting on, but I was just gonna play along. "We here to have fun, and that's what I'm about to do." I said, eyeing them closely.

My eyes locked on Chin just as some girl walked away from him. Now Chin and I stared at each other across the crowded dance floor.

"Girl, I told you he wasn't fucking working," Chyna said with a hard glare in her eyes.

"Andre Chin!" I yelled, causing several heads to turn. I pushed my way through the angry dancers to get to him. "What the fuck are you doing here?"

CHAPTER 49

CHIN

Big Tymers NYC

"Me? I'd like to ask you the same question," I said, while still trying to get a last glimpse at Miss Doe.

"Nigga, don't fuck with me." She shoved me—hard.

"Be easy, ma." I held on to her hands.

"Get the fuck off me, you no good whore."

"Girl, quit tripping on him," Chyna said, glaring at me with a mischievous glint in her eyes. "You can get him later. Let's find the bitch he's been with and fuck *her* up."

"Why the fuck are you always up in everybody's business?" I asked angrily, stepping into Chyna's face. "Don't you have a dick to go suck on or something to keep your mouth shut?"

"Fuck you! I wasn't over there with some bitch all up in my grill." Chyna's neck almost rolled off her shoulders with each word. "I told Porsha to stop fucking with these ghetto-ass niggas, but naw, she wants a thug." Chyna's slender body turned to Porsha, who was glaring at me so hard that her eyes nearly popped out of their sockets.

"Porsha, thugs are headaches, fucking headaches. You hear that? What you need to do is find yourself a *real* man," Chyna said, taunting me. "Not these ghetto-ass thugs. Someone who's at your level, and knows nothing about being ghetto."

"Well maybe if you stopped fucking homosexuals," PitBull dipped in, "and started fucking real niggas, you wouldn't even have time to be up in everybody's business."

"Ooh." Chyna simmered with anger. "One more mothafuckin' word from you, and I swear a bottle's gonna connect with your big-ass head," she warned, hands tightening into fists.

"Chin," Porsha said, "you still ain't answered my question. What are you doing here?"

"Don't ask him to explain shit, Porsha." Chyna grabbed Porsha's hand, dragging her away. "You came here to have fun, so why even bother with him? Let's go find some other niggas up in here," she said, looking over her shoulder at me and grinning.

Running to catch them, I yanked Porsha's hand from Chyna's hard grip. "I know your bitch ass ain't telling my *wifey* to go feel up on another nigga! If you know what's best, you'll sit your ass down somewhere." I took a long breath, hoping to calm myself and them down. "VIP area, Belvedere's on me."

Porsha shrugged me off. "Oh, it's not okay for me to dance with other niggas, but it's cool for you to bump and grind on other females?"

"And how did you know I drank . . . Belvedere?" Chyna asked with an evil grin. "Not a common drink, you know."

The music around them switched to a fast beat. No one in the group moved.

Bitch! Lowering my gaze to Chyna, I couldn't form a quick answer.

"Yeah, how did you know her special drink, Chin?"

Porsha's hands folded over her busty chest. Waiting.

Tony and PitBull slipped in between the trio before Chin could respond.

"Chin was at work with Tony," PitBull said. "They've been working so long on Dragon's project, I called them up and asked if they wanted to hang with me and my boys. So if you want to blame anybody, blame me."

PitBull lied so smoothly even I started to believe him.

Porsha looked at me, then to PitBull and Tony, and then back to me. Her eyes flickered with indecision. She softened a bit, and I felt my heart beating again.

"Baby, I'm sorry," she said, hugging me.

Chyna groaned loudly. PitBull turned to her, gesturing for her to shut up.

"That's a'ight, ma." I returned her hug, flipping the middle finger at Chyna. "When you got trifling hos in your life who don't want to see us together because they're envious, that's what always happens."

Chyna stood her ground. "I can't believe you bought that shit."

"Hush your mouth and hop your ass up to VIP. Maybe you can mingle with real niggas and find your own man. Drinks are on me."

"C'mon, girl. Let's go sit in style," Porsha said, smiling first at Chyna, then at me.

As Porsha and Chyna made their way up to the VIP section, I turned to my boys.

"Good looking out," I said before glancing at the exit door. I missed Miss Doe already.

CHAPTER 50

PITBULL

Big Tymers

"Let me speak to you for a moment," Chin said, blocking the path to VIP.

"What's on your mind, dawg?" I asked.

"Who was that?" Chin asked, keeping his voice low.

"Who was who?"

"The girl I was dancing with earlier."

My shoulders visibly relaxed. "Oh, you mean BabyGirl!"

"That's her name?"

I laughed. "You mean to tell me all that time you were dancing, shorty didn't even give you her name? Damn, your game's weak."

"What do you think I have you for?"

"I know she's from the Bronx."

"What else?"

I shrugged. "I don't know anything else about her."

Chin dipped in his pocket and took out a coil of money.

"I'm willing to pay two grand to find her. Here's a grand up front," Chin whispered. "When you find her, the other grand will be delivered."

"Man I don't know, I mean I have to—"

"I'll make the deal three grand. Here's another five hundred. Now find her!"

"A'ight, I could get some information for you by next week."

"Naw, not next week. *Tomorrow night.*"

Tony walked up, patting Chin on the shoulder. "Damn, you want her that bad?"

"Trust me, that bad."

Tony doubled over with laughter. "The great Andre Chin is pussy whipped. What happened to all the big talk about pussy never whipped you, huh?"

"Man, she ain't got me whipped, so just be easy."

"She ain't got you whipped?" I laughed with Tony. "You coulda fooled me! What do you call forking out three grand to find one woman? You damn right that ain't pussy whipped. That's showing she got you on pussy *lock.*"

Tony and I roared with laughter at Chin's expense.

Tony clapped Chin on the back. "I just hope for your sake the pussy's good for how much dough you're willing to fork over."

Chin tipped the bartender, took his glass off the bar counter, and pushed past his boys.

Laughter followed him all the way to Porsha in the VIP room.

CHAPTER 51

CHIN

Central Park West

Maybe Porsha felt bad because she wasn't trying to work with me earlier after all the trouble I went through to plan a romantic evening for her. Now, homegirl had put on some sexy lingerie and was teasing me.

"You like the way I'm bending over for you, baby?" she asked in a soft, sultry voice.

"Yeah, you know I love whatever you do." She would kill me if she knew that I was picturing Miss Doe, aka BabyGirl, dancing for me instead.

She continued with her striptease and kisses, but for some reason my dick wouldn't stand up.

After a minute, she slowed down to a halt. "What the fuck's your problem, nigga?" she asked, pointing to my soft dick.

"I don't know, baby. Maybe you need to give me some head," I suggested, just waiting for her to start tripping so I could put an end to this bullshit.

She hesitated for a moment and something flashed in her eyes, before she said, "That's what you want?"

"I wouldn't ask for it, baby, if I didn't know it would work."

She grabbed my dick with one hand, and soon swallowed my entire dick like a good little wifey.

"Hmm . . ." Closing my eyes, I blocked Porsha's face out of my head replacing her with BabyGirl. I was so excited that I forgot that my dick wasn't in a pussy, and I began fucking her face as if I was backed up for months.

"Calm down, Chin," Porsha said, removing her lips from my dick.

Instead of answering, I pushed her head back onto my dick and kept pumping.

Soon her angry voice interrupted my orgasm.

"What the fuck did you just do?" Porsha yelled before running away from me.

"I'm sorry." I got up off the bed and ran after her. She washed her face and mouth before I continued. "I was so caught up in the moment that I didn't even realize that shit went in your face."

She pushed me away. "Naw, Chin, I can deal with that. I'm talking about the fact that you just called me BabyGirl."

Damn, how the hell would I get out of this one?

"What, you don't like that name?"

"You've never called me that before, Chin." She stood trembling with anger, one hand on her full hips. "Maybe you're confusing me with one of your other hoes."

"C'mon, ma, it's just like you would call me baby boy. It's not like I'm calling you fucking Susie, Nikki, or Keisha. I said baby girl. You're my wifey; therefore, *you are* my baby girl."

"Whatever," she hissed through her teeth and rolled her eyes heavenward.

"I'm telling you, you need to cut this bullshit out. Lately every little thing upsets you and that shit's a turn off. It'll drive a nigga into another woman's arms."

"Into another woman's arms," she whispered, then ran to the bathroom and washed her mouth again.

"Fuck! Here we go with this bullshit again." Wiping off my dick, I slipped my boxers back on.

"What the hell's your problem, Chin?" She was all up in my face. "My attitude's never bothered you before, especially since I was flossing your paperwork. So, why is it now?"

"Because it's fucking annoying, Porsha. And that little scene you created at the club wasn't cute either. You need to learn to trust your man, and not your friends—especially ones like Chyna."

"I know enough not to trust you and Chyna in the same bedroom. Or have you been there before, too?"

Snatching the comforter off the bed, I turned from her.

"Where are you going, nigga? I'm talking to you!"

"I'm sleeping in the guest room tonight. I can't deal with this shit."

CHAPTER 52

BABYGIRL

Watson Avenue

PitBull hadn't even completely walked through the door before he informed me that Chin paid out a lot of dough just to get the 411 about "that chick BabyGirl." After I held out my hand and got my cut of PitBull's fifteen hundred dollars, I grabbed a pen to write down his address. "What's the address to his office?"

"495 W. 42nd Street."

"Maybe I should pay him a surprise visit. I'll get to his office before lunchtime."

Midmorning was bleak, and by the look of the gray clouds, a horrible thunderstorm was on the way. Weather like this only set the mood, putting things in perspective. On the television, highlights of a local drug dealer's death were told with a straight face and animated voice.

"Hello?" I answered my cell, while grabbing the house keys off the coffee table.

"BabyGirl, I just wanted you to gear up for the assignment."

"Okay, I guess we'll discuss that later in person, right?"

"Yeah, just worry about giving the boy a good impression, and don't fuck up the assignment."

"I know my job, PitBull. Have him fall in love with me."

He let out a deep breath. "I hope you remember that."

"If you didn't think I was capable, you wouldn't have given me the job, right?"

"True, but I just want to make sure everything runs smoothly."

"And it will." I turned over in my bed. "I'll be creative if I find myself in a jam. I'll make up something along the way."

"A'ight."

"You know what you have to do after that?" PitBull asked in a *don't play yourself* manner.

"I remember everything perfectly."

Surprised at the fact that it was late in the morning and midtown was still crowded with businesspeople getting their asses to work, I could understand why they called it the city that never sleeps. Stepping out of the cab and standing in front of the building, I checked my notes to make sure the address was correct.

"Yup, this is it." Pulling my mini skirt down a little bit, I noticed a few men staring as they walked past me.

The entrance door was made of rotary glass with a gold strip down the center.

"Tha Hustle Records. Very impressive."

A quick check in the directory gave me the correct destination before I strolled to the elevator.

Excitement and nervousness competed as I wondered if Chin would have forgotten our time together in the club. Maybe he had too many drinks and his game was tight. What would a sober mind bring?

"Fifteenth floor," the programmed elevator spoke before the doors opened.

I expected to walk through another door, but the office space was a bright, wide-open area, with different doors leading down a long hallway. A secretary sat behind a circular desk situated just under a sign that said, Tha Hustle Records.

"Good afternoon. I'm here to see Andre Chin." I spoke in my most proper voice as the golden-skinned, dark-haired woman pursed her lips in disapproval.

The bitch didn't even answer right away. Instead, she gave me a nasty who-the-fuck-this-bitch-thinks-she-is-walking-up-in-here-looking-like-a-hoochie look. After staring at her for a moment, I recognized her face. Of all people for me to run into, the last person I would expect was the bitch that my father got pregnant while he was married to my mom. Since this was my first time meeting Chin on his turf, I didn't want Chin to think badly of me. I decided to play it calm and professional and find another opportunity to give this bitch what she deserved.

"Excuse me," I said. "I'm here to see Mr. Andre Chin."

"Can I have a name?" She responded, while rolling her eyes at me.

"BabyGirl."

"I need a first *and* a last name," she fired back, glaring at me as though I had stolen her typewriter.

"And I just gave you a first and last name—*Baby Girl.*"

"These ghetto-ass girls," she mumbled under her breath.

Professionalism went out the window.

Leaning over so I was just inches from her face, I said, "I know your trifling ass did not just call me ghetto."

"Listen, this is a place where we conduct *professional* business," she hissed. "And if you continue with that nasty attitude I might just ask you to leave."

"Try it, bitch," I said through clenched teeth. "Now stop running your fucking mouth and let Mr. Chin know I'm here." I leaned in closer. "You were fucking my father. I didn't get the chance to bust your ass for my mother's sake. Don't let me have to do it right here."

She got up and moved in to where we were only three inches apart. "Try it!"

The commotion brought Chin out of his office. "Tracey, are you okay?"

"Yeah I am, but this—"

She didn't get a chance to finish. When his eyes caught mine, his lips spread into a huge smile.

I gave him one right back.

"Sorry to surprise you like this," I said.

"Naw, it's okay. Come in." He extended his hands for me to come into the office. "Give me a second to wrap up this deal and we'll talk."

Without saying anything else, I strolled by Tracey's desk, *accidentally* bumping into her name plaque.

"Oops, I'm sorry." Trying like hell to hide a smile, I shrugged. "I guess I'm a bit clumsy today."

Tracey parted her lips to speak, but Chin beat her to it. "That's okay. Tracey got it."

A gasp made us both turn to her, but she had straightened her face by that time.

I turned to follow him into the office. I had to fight the urge to flip her the finger before closing the door.

"So, have a seat."

Strolling to his desk, I removed the folders off the edge and calmly planted my ass on the desk, then crossed my legs.

He was now on the phone, but he swallowed hard as he stared at my ass and the breasts spilling out of my top.

"Okay, uh . . . thanks. . . . uh . . . for calling, and I'll definitely get back to you," he told the person before hanging up the phone.

"Like I said, sorry to surprise you."

"Oh no, don't be sorry," he said as his eyes trailed the length of my legs. "I *love* surprises."

"You do, huh?" I spoke in my most seductive tones, while

using my foot to push back his chair so he could get a perfect glimpse of my thong.

"Yeah, I do."

"Don't be acting all nice on me." I ran my finger down his chest. "Because one thing I love is a thug."

"Is that right?"

"Can you manage to say more than three words, here?" I crossed my right leg over my left.

He grinned, but didn't say a word.

"But to answer your question, yes, I like a man who isn't scared to venture, or do whatever he wants."

"Glad to know that because I'm about to get thuggish on you right now."

I thought Chin was about to whip out his dick and smack my face with it or something. Instead, he got up from his chair and walked over to the mini bar that was situated in the far right corner of his office.

"Would you like something to drink?" he asked.

"Alizé Red Passion."

The expensive and lavish furniture in his office shouted, "big bucks." Not only was he a man with expensive taste, but the neat stacks of paper, the perfectly lined up pencils, and the cherry wood desk with only the bare necessities on top meant that he was also a neat freak. Over in the corner, he had a big, money-green couch which perfectly matched the carpet and his leather desk chair. "Here's your drink," he said, holding a crystal goblet out to me.

"Thank you."

"So I see you decided to come to me," Chin said.

"The last time I checked, somebody shelled out quite a few bucks to find me." I laughed over the rim of my shades.

"Hey you weren't supposed to know that." He smiled back.

I winked at him. "You've got your connections, and I've got mine. You have some sexy eyes and lips," I told him.

"Thank you. And you've got some sexy lips yourself," he said, staring at them intently.

"Wanna *taste* them?"

"Which ones?" he teased, a slight twinkle in his eyes.

Lifting the glass to my lips, I took a sip and didn't answer. By this time, he had placed his glass on the desk, leaned forward, and said, "Which ones do you want me to taste?"

"Both, but let's just go with these lips for now," I said as I pointed to my mouth.

Without delay, his index finger lifted my chin and he kissed me passionately, his lips covering mine before his tongue moved softly into the moist areas of my mouth. The man was an excellent kisser. Things had reached the point where I wanted him so badly that containing myself became impossible. Almost.

My kiss must have impressed him because after he removed his lips from mine, he asked, "Are you busy this evening?"

"Not at all," was my quick response.

"So can I invite you to have dinner with me tonight?"

"Come on, Chin. I'm not dressed to go anywhere tonight. And, if anything, I'd like to invite you to dinner—not the other way around."

"Now I don't have to wonder why you don't have a man," he snapped.

Bristling at his harsh tone, I took a calming sip of liquid. "What the fuck does me not having a man have to do with this conversation?"

"Because you're too fucking independent!" He scowled at me, his cheeks flushed with anger. "Why can't you just relax and let someone treat you to the finer things in life?"

"Hold up." I got up off his desk. "First of all, it's a good thing for a woman to be independent. Second," I leaned in at almost a kissing distance. "I was used to the finer things in life way before the sun, moon, and stars had intentions of bringing us together. So you need to calm yourself down, sweetie." I moved closer to him.

He reached out for me, placing his hand on my thighs.

The game had begun. And I had every intention of playing it—my way.

CHAPTER 53

CHIN

Tha Hustle Records NYC

This conversation reminded me of Porsha, but for some reason I liked the feistiness in this girl.

"So, I'm gonna ask you again," I said before placing a gentle kiss on her the neck. "Would you join me for dinner?"

"And I'm gonna tell you again, I'm not dressed for the occasion."

"Would it make you feel better if I got you something to wear?"

Placing my hands under her chin and looking directly into her eyes, I kissed her again.

"I can afford—" she began, but quickly stopped as I lowered my gaze.

She grimaced and then threw her head back haughtily. "Well, even if you did buy me something, I still have to get home and take a shower."

"You can shower where I'm taking you." My hands slipped down to that ass. "And anything you need, I'll make sure you have it."

"Sounds like a plan to me," she said, after only a slight hesitation. She moved her body just out of my reach.

With that, I reached into the tiny safe in my desk and pulled out the cash, placing it directly into her purse as she watched.

"A'ight. I'm gonna hit the five train and go downtown to start my shopping."

"Did you just say you're going on the *train?*"

BabyGirl bristled with irritation. "Are you deaf or something?"

"As long as you're with me, there'll be no train action. I'll have one of my drivers take you wherever you need to go."

Dialing a cell number, I waited a moment, and then said, "Dave, I want you to pull up to the front of the office. There'll be a young lady in a sexy pink mini skirt waiting." I then turned to the young woman staring at me intently. "My driver will pick you up in fifteen."

"I'll wait here for a few minutes until he comes."

As she sat on the money green leather sofa, she crossed her caramel legs, with the top one swinging in a slight rhythm. If shorty would just let me get a chance to lick those, I'd have her begging for more. I stared so hard that she caught me, and she continued her little charade just to tease me.

"Ooh, my thighs hurt so much, right here," she moaned, uncrossing her right leg and exposing her light pink thong for a brief second, as she rubbed her thighs gently. By this time, not only was my dick hard, but my mouth began to drool at the thought of how she would taste. *God, I would love to taste her.*

"Oh, poor baby," I said. "Do you want me to rub them?"

"Yeah," she replied in a soft voice, her sly grin nearly making me smile in return.

Seconds later, I sat beside her on the sofa. "Does this feel better?" I asked, while slowly and passionately sinking my fingers into her thighs.

Her hands reached out and her fingers ran through my hair. "Maybe if you kissed it, it would feel a little better."

I placed my lips on her ankle and kissed from her leg up to her thigh.

"Umm," she let out a slight moan, and her small hands wrapped around my head, egging me on.

I took this as an invitation that my hands or tongue could venture further. Continuing to lick her legs, I used my other hand to part her soft thighs, running my index finger along the center of her thin underwear. She felt warm. I couldn't help but place my finger in just to see if she wanted me as badly as I wanted her.

"Damn, baby. You're mad wet."

"Yeah baby, and guess what?"

My eyes closed, enjoying the soft wetness of her, but I managed to ask, "What?"

She stood up abruptly, pushing my hands out of the way. "That's as far as you're gonna go. So move out of my way before your driver leaves me."

Before I had a chance to answer, Tracey knocked on the door and came right in. "I have some paperwork that needs your immediate attention."

While signing the papers, a quick glance up at Tracey and BabyGirl let me know that something was wrong. An old-style stare-down had started right there in my office. Signing the papers quickly, I held them out to Tracey so she could leave. She did, but not without throwing an ugly glance at BabyGirl. Damn, what had happened out there in the lobby?

I reached for BabyGirl. "My driver can wait."

She moved out of my reach again. "And if he can wait, so can you," she replied softly.

"Damn, you're sexy, mama," I said as I watched her hips swing from left to right as she walked to the door. "You got away twice, but don't think you will be so lucky the next time."

She turned, smiled, and closed the door behind her. Her soft laugh lingered along with the sweet scent of her perfume.

CHAPTER 54

BABYGIRL

Tha Hustle Records

After closing the door behind me, I strolled past Tracey's desk while attempting to button my shirt.

"Bitch," she mumbled under her breath, and then rolled her eyes at me again. I smiled sweetly, leaned over her desk, and said, "I am a bitch because I am *b*eautiful, *i*ntelligent, *t*alented, *c*harming, and *h*ot-stuff. And you definitely don't want to mess with a bitch like me."

"I'm gonna get you," she replied through clenched teeth.

"Is that supposed to be a joke?"

The door to Chin's office yanked open before he strolled down the hall with a folder in his hand.

"You still here?"

Tracey turned away and pretended to type on the computer.

"I was just wishing Tracey . . . a wonderful day."

"Okay, you did already," he said, turning my body to face the elevator. "Now go handle business." Then he gave me a swift pat on the ass to make his point.

I punched the down button, but turned to face him. "Later, baby."

He smiled at me. "Later, sweetheart."

Taking one last look at the both of them, I sent a quick glare to Tracey and a smile to Chin, knowing both of their days were numbered.

I didn't like the clothes Roberto Cavalli had to offer, so I had the driver take me to Valentino. As soon as I hit the door, fate had already made the choice for me—a multicolored halter dress with a deep split on each side. A draped opening in the back and front would expose a little cleavage and the smooth curve of my back. To top it off, the material was sheer. No bra with this one! The red, orange, yellow, pink, baby blue, and white colors complemented my skin and would bring out my jet-black hair.

"I definitely want this dress," I said, while looking at the price tag which almost blew me away. But then I remembered that I wasn't the one paying for it! So, I asked the salesgirl to get the dress in my size so I could try it on.

"Now, to find the shoes to match." I sighed, knowing there wasn't much money left.

"Excuse me, Miss, but I couldn't help overhearing you. We do have matching shoes," the short, red-headed, salesgirl informed me.

"Let me have a look."

Five minutes later the she handed me a pair of size seven shoes. The shoes only picked up two colors from the dress, but they worked in a way that I knew would make Chin's mouth drool when he saw me.

"I'll take both."

She grinned, a slight flush tinting her pale cheeks. "Might I suggest a pocketbook?"

"No, that's it." I said handing over several bills. I already had my eyes set on a Fendi pocketbook I had seen earlier. No sense spending it all in one place.

The traffic on Fifth Avenue seemed to be at a standstill,

and to top it off, the rain that threatened earlier began to pour down heavily. As people ran to the nearest place for shelter, I looked at my image in the tinted windows of the Denali. *You're good girl. No pussy, and you've got this nigga spending already.*

Then I glanced down, gave the pussy a little pat, and said, "You're going to get even more if he hits this."

Chin was an easy target, and PitBull made it seem so difficult. Please, the way this nigga was spreading dough, a crackhead could probably have him shelling out cash.

The plans were going quite well.

CHAPTER 55

CHIN

Chin's Office—42nd Street

"Hello?" I answered the phone on the third ring.

"Baby, I miss you."

"I miss you, too, Porsha," I lied, groaning inwardly that Tracey hadn't announced her call.

"So, since we both miss each other, what do you think we should do about it?" Was that irritation in her voice? What did she have to be pissed about?

I had to think carefully before I answered this question, because the wrong answer could get Porsha upset and also get me busted with BabyGirl. When Porsha thought something was going on, she had a habit of showing up where she definitely wasn't wanted.

"Ah, listen, I have to go finish a meeting tonight about Dragon's deal—"

"Fuck," she shouted, almost busting my eardrum. "Chin, why is it that when I ask you for some time you always come up with some bullshit?"

"Would you let me finish, sweetheart?"

She sighed loudly on the other end. "Sorry baby," she

apologized, but I could imagine she had folded her arms across her chest.

"As I was saying, I have the meeting at nine tonight. How about you pick up something on the way over here, and come chill with me from five 'til eight? That way I can kill two birds with one stone," I suggested, patting myself on the back for pulling it together so quickly.

"Are you gonna make it worth my while?" she inquired in a seductive tone.

"Don't I always make it worth your time?"

"Hmm!"

"Don't start, woman. Get off the phone and finish up at the firm so you can get your fine ass over here."

"A'ight, baby," she said, giggling like a five-year-old when her parent promises her candy for being good.

"I love you, baby."

"I love you, too, Chin" were her last words before she hung up the phone.

I had to hold on to Porsha—at least until the paperwork was finished. Then I could change the game and put her in check.

CHAPTER 56

BABYGIRL

Manhattan

After my mini-shopping spree, Chin's driver dropped me off at the hotel of all hotels—Trump Tower. Its gold plated metal siding made the entrance glow like the threshold to heaven. It had ceilings high enough for one to catch a nose bleed if you were on the top looking down. The spacious lobby consisted of three glass elevators. The sparkling of chandeliers showed that this place definitely catered to people with money. The front desk was clean enough to eat off of with a shine that would make you think it was used for a Pledge commercial. The majority of my time was spent shopping, so by the time I got back to the hotel I only had enough time to bathe, fix my hair, put on my make-up, and get dressed.

Around nine, a slight knock on the door pulled me to my feet.

"Are you ready, ma'am?" the driver asked politely.

"Give me a minute."

As I walked over to the coffee table to pick up my pocketbook, I took one last approving look in the mirror at the colorful dress that hung so beautifully on my curves. I then closed the hotel door and swiped the card through the slot to lock it.

Chin stood at the limo door, smiling as I strolled through the glass doors. "You look very beautiful tonight," he praised without removing his eyes from my chest.

"Thank you. You're not looking too bad yourself."

To be honest, he looked stunning. So stunning that the man would have any bitch drooling. He was decked out in a Versace cashmere suit, black tie, black Mephisto shoes, and an iced-out watch. His hair was braided in a Sprewell design, exposing the damaging tattoo on his neck. I had never seen this polished side of him before, and it made me want him even more. If things had been different, maybe, just maybe, I could have fallen for him. He was making my job of seducing him easy because it was more like he was seducing me.

We pulled up at a restaurant near the FDR, overlooking the water, around nine thirty.

"This is nice," I said simply, trying not to show my anxiety.

He winked. "I treat my dates to the best."

The tables were covered with white linen and plush oriental carpeting cushioned my footsteps. The lights from glass chandeliers that hung from the ceiling sparkled as they reflected off the wall-to-wall mirrors. Soft jazz music filtered through the air. Not long after we stepped inside, the hostess came up to us, addressing Chin as "Mr. Chin," and with a simple nod she ushered us to our seats in a secluded area.

Scanning the menu, I asked, "I take it you're a regular customer here?"

"Are we a little jealous?" he teased, licking his sexy lips.

I shrugged. "Naw, but—"

"But, nothing," he shot back. "You're just trying to be like every other female wanting to find out who I've brought here." I put the menu down and glowered at him, ready to say something. He didn't give me a chance. "Well, for your information, BabyGirl, I *own* this restaurant."

"Oh, impressive." I shrugged, trying not to act too excited.

"So, what are we having for dinner?" he inquired, "because a nigga's starving."

"Why are you so ghetto, baby?"

"I thought you liked thugs?" Flashing me a sexy-ass smile, he said. "Girl, I'm not about to put on a show for your ass."

"I wasn't asking you to. I want you to be yourself."

"Ok, so since you want me to be myself, are you gonna let me taste your pussy?"

People turned to face us as I busted out laughing. "Oh no, you did not go there."

"Go where? You didn't let me go there yet. I'm just wondering if a brotha can taste, to see if all this investment is worth it."

"You'll taste in due time."

"Well, I'm not gonna wait 'til *due time*," he said, lowering to his knees and disappearing under the table.

"What are you doing?" I whispered in a high voice. I lifted the tablecloth to look at him.

"Open your legs." He tried to spread them apart on his own. "Baby, open your legs, and stop making things so difficult. The faster you open them, the quicker we can get done here."

"Aren't you gonna eat dinner since you're so hungry?"

"Naw, dinner can wait." He tried parting my legs again. "I want dessert."

Slowly, I opened my thighs, and he rested them over his shoulders. Little did he know that I had a little surprise for him.

"You freak," he said, grinning.

"Hey, I expected you would try something, so I made it easy for you by not wearing any underwear."

His index finger tickled my clit. I almost slid out of the damn chair.

"Umm," I moaned. I pressed my legs together. Chin gripped my thighs.

"Open your legs," he demanded.

Instead of fighting him, I complied. This time he used his tongue, stroking it against my clit. First he started off slowly, but then he began to move faster, licking the clit and sticking his tongue in and out of my wet pussy. At times, he would use his index finger to fuck me whenever his tongue wasn't there. A first time for me—my world exploded. I knew that pleasure like this could make a woman do anything. I would have to get with Dragon tomorrow. The way this man was teasing me, I would give up the pussy just on general principle. But I still wanted my first time to be with Dragon.

"Baby, don't stop. I'm cumming," I whispered, knocking the champagne glass off the table. He didn't say a word as I pulled on the tablecloth, literally ripping it off. Though I didn't have anything to use as a comparison, I knew that homeboy wasn't just good, he was great.

Ten minutes later, Chin stood, smiled, then excused himself and disappeared. I could only guess that he was on his way to the bathroom, since his face was all sticky with my juices.

"Is everything all right here?" the waiter asked, staring at the glasses, flowers, silverware, and tablecloth all spread out on the floor.

I grinned, trying to pull myself together. "Um, I accidentally pulled on the table cloth, and everything else fell off."

"Is there a problem, Jeffery?" Chin asked while fixing his tie.

"No sir, I was just about to get the crew to clean up this mess," he said, scurrying away, hiding a smile behind a cough.

"So, was it worth your investment?" I asked softly.

"Hell, yeah. And you better expect that I'm going to be eating that for a while, knowing how good you taste."

Instead of responding, I looked at him and smiled, knowing my groundwork was complete and all I had to do now was start building him up.

"What are we having?" He asked, as the crew put the table back together in record time. Some of them grinned at each other, but they didn't say a word.

"I think I'm going to order the Ultimate Delight," I said.

The Ultimate Delight consisted of steamed lobster tails dipped in butter, curried shrimp, steamed fish, garlic mashed potatoes, and a Caesar salad.

"And yourself?" I asked.

"I'll just order A Taste of Home. Curried goat, fried chicken, jerk chicken, macaroni and cheese, and white rice."

Forty-five minutes after we finished eating, he stood, pulled out my chair, and I followed him to the back of the restaurant.

"Where are you taking me?"

"Would you relax and enjoy the night?" He massaged my shoulders gently. "Loosen up and let me treat you like the princess you are."

We stopped at a balcony overlooking the FDR. As the full moon beamed brightly in the dark blue sky, the boats that were docked in the dark waters sailed the East River slowly.

"You have a beautiful smile," he said, before kissing me on the lips.

"Thank you," I said, blushing even though I tried not to.

"Don't get shy on me now." He lifted my chin to peer into my eyes. "Now, baby, I brought you out here so we could get to know each other."

Being a perfect gentleman, he took my hand, leading me to the lounge chair. We lay down, facing each other.

"So Chin, do you have a woman?"

He lay there for a moment before answering the question. I could tell he was plotting, so before I gave him a chance to answer, I got up from the lounge chair.

"Why are you leaving?"

"Because I see that you're about to come up with some bullshit. I don't play games."

"Calm down, ma. I was only admiring your beauty," he said, sighing wearily. "To answer your question, yes, I have a woman."

"So why do you want me?"

"Sweetheart, I don't *want* you, I *need* you. So could you please come back over here and let me finish?"

Wanting to hear his reasoning, I obliged his plea and strolled back over to him.

"Like I said, I have a woman, but right now we're going through some difficulties. Our relationship is on the edge."

"So you need me to . . . *fill in* 'til she comes back to her senses?"

"God! Why are you making this difficult?" He threw his hands in the air out of frustration. "I'm trying to be up front with you."

"I'm not making anything difficult. You're complicating things to a point where you're about to tie yourself up, and I don't wanna be a part of that."

Leaning toward me, he said, "I do have a woman. We've been together for a while."

"OK, so that's wifey then?"

"If you want to call her that."

"So if she's wifey, what am I?"

"What do you want to be?"

Turning a little more on the lounge chair, my eyes connected with his. "You can't flip my question. Give me a direct answer."

"How can I give you a direct answer if you don't tell me what you want to be? That's like walking into a company and telling the manager you need a job and nothing else. Now how is he supposed to figure out what position you want, if you don't say what you wanted in the first place?"

This motherfucker's good, but he ain't better than me. "First off, I did not walk into a place of employment looking for a job. The last time I checked, the manager came running after me." I now stared him directly in the face. "And, might I add, that he did pay a few bucks to find me, so that truly sums up the situation. So after saying that, let me ask you, what position are you planning on hiring me for?"

At first he laughed. "Different positions apply to different people. So, what are you looking for?"

"I see that we're not going anywhere with this issue, so let's move on to something else."

A single hand traced the outline of my face.

"What do you do for a living?" he questioned.

"I'm self-employed. I design clothing for my friends and a few small companies." Would he buy it?

"Oh, really interesting. You have an album or portfolio of clothing you design?"

I leaned up off the chair, and my eyes connected with his. "Are you doubting my skills?"

"Naw, but a brotha can't see a sista's talent?" he asked with a smile.

"Ain't nothing wrong with that. I'll show you sometime, okay? No need for me to ask what you do for a living since I already know. But there's something I do want to ask."

"Go ahead."

"How did you get to this level of the business?"

"I was always interested in music, so I would hang out at my friend's cousin's studio whenever I got a chance. At first, I wanted to be a rapper until I noticed the ones behind the scenes were the money-makers. Well, one day some luck came my way, and from that luck, I built my empire." He was lying. I knew that was nowhere near the story.

"Interesting. That must've been some luck for your company to take off from there," I responded with a little sarcasm, since I kinda had an idea of how he really got started.

"Well, yeah. Actually, my partner won some lawsuit money, and I had money of my own, so we decided to put it together and open our own record company. At first it was rough, but now I have enough money to take care of myself, my home, and my parents."

At first I tried to hold back the tears as he spoke about his parents, knowing I couldn't do the same for my parents. But then my tears began to land all over his cashmere suit.

"What's wrong, baby?"

"Parents are a touchy subject."

"Why?"

"My parents are dead." A small cry escaped my lips.

"I'm sorry to hear that. I didn't mean to bring up something that could hurt you." He held me close in his arms.

"It's okay. It's just that it hasn't been brought up in a long time, so I kinda pushed it to the back of my mind, and now . . ."

"You wanna talk about it?" he asked, while using his fingers to wipe the tears from my face.

"Might as well to get it off my chest." I took a deep breath. "It was a winter night, and my father decided to work late because he had just come off a court case. My mother had a date with him that night, so instead of going home to change, we just rushed over to the base," I explained, hoping that a flicker of recognition would show in his dark brown eyes. Nothing.

"So your mother and father were both drug dealers?"

"Naw, my father was a warehouse distributor, but my mother was a parole officer."

"Wow," he said, searching my eyes. "Now *that's* a stretch."

"We got there, and he was upstairs counting money. A pregnant female asked my father to use the bathroom. Since she was pregnant, my father told her to wait. Then he put the money away."

While telling my story, Chin's normally slanted eyes began

to open wide to the point where they looked as if they were about to pop out.

"Are you OK, sweetie?" My soft voice penetrated the sounds of the water flowing under the balcony.

"Yeah." He gulped and took a deep breath.

"He took her to use the bathroom downstairs," I continued, never leaving Chin's face, "but before he could close the door, a couple of guys rushed in, shot him, then went upstairs and killed my mother, too. After they got what they wanted, they gave the pregnant girl a Columbian neck tie— slitting her throat, dissecting her ass, removing the baby, and stabbing the fetus a couple times. The girl died minutes after her baby."

"Damn shame," Chin said, loosening his tie a bit.

"I was hiding in the closet," I said, choosing my words carefully. Besides, the old lady who lived across the hall, you know, one of those peeping tom types, saw the whole situation, but she couldn't identify anyone because it was a little dark outside." Then I moved in for the kill. "I've given it some thought. Maybe I'll have the police reopen the case. I might have to go back and talk to the old woman. She did say that one had some sort of tattoo on his neck, sort of like—"

"Could you excuse me for a minute?" Chin whispered and jerked up from the lounge chair.

"Sure." Using my arm, I dried my tears. My performance was easy. But every bit of pain I felt about losing my parents came out as I spoke.

CHAPTER 57

CHIN

As BabyGirl looked at me through the glass door, I dialed Tony's number and waited with impatience as it rang four times.

"Hello," he answered, sounding out of breath.

"Tony, what up man?"

"Just here chilling, watching some NFL. How's the date going with your little mamacita?" he inquired, his voice irritatingly calm.

"Tony, that shit started off good, but it's getting ugly man, *real* ugly."

"What do you mean by ugly?"

"Remember that stunt I told you I pulled with my boys a few years back?"

"Yeah. If it weren't for that, you'd still be at nickel and dime bag level."

"Well, guess what?"

"I'm listening," he said, and somehow I could feel that I'd pulled his attention away from the NFL, and he didn't like it.

"The man and the woman that were killed were BabyGirl's parents."

"Get the fuck outta here!" Tony said, loud enough to bust my eardrum. Now I had his fucking attention! "Does she know you're responsible for her parents' murders?"

"PitBull was the trigger man, but how the hell am I supposed to tell her about that, after she soaked my cashmere suit with tears?"

"So what you gonna do?"

"I don't know. Just keep her distracted so she don't realize."

"Well, she don't know. And besides, the police didn't have a description to go by anyway."

"That's where you're wrong, Tony."

BabyGirl shifted in the lounge chair, but she didn't take her eyes off me.

"Some old lady across the hall managed to see someone with a tattoo on the neck."

Tony busted up laughing over the phone.

"What the fuck's so funny, nigga?"

"Chin, a million and one people have tattoos on their neck. So what are you worried about?"

"The old lady! If she sees it again she might remember. And we still have business in Harlem in that same building."

Suddenly Tony's voice became cold. "So what are you suggesting, Chin?"

"There's only one solution to the problem."

"Who, BabyGirl?"

"Naw, I'm staying with that," I said, turning my back to the balcony. "I say the old lady. She's definitely a threat right about now."

Tony sighed wearily. "Now you know I don't do women or children, and especially old ladies, unless they're holding a gun to me. Then, it's personal."

"You won't have to. But I'll need you riding shotgun."

"Chin, I think you're overreacting. The woman hasn't said anything all this time."

"And I'd like to keep it that way." I spoke in a dictating manner. "Until now, no one's asked the right questions. BabyGirl might change all that."

"A'ight, you know I have your back."

"Thanks, Tony."

"Who's a definite threat?" BabyGirl snuck up behind me placing her hands around my waist.

"Oh, um . . . we were talking about . . . Dragon's mother. She's a threat right now because she's scared her son's gonna end up being murdered like other rappers in the game."

"Well, all mothers worry. That's what they do. Shoot, I wish I had a mother to worry about me right now."

I grimaced, wishing at that exact moment I had never met the beautiful woman with the soft, sad, brown eyes.

CHAPTER 58

BABYGIRL

The full moon shone brightly on the still East River, giving the water a beautiful glow as I rested comfortably in Chin's embrace. I lifted my head and spoke.

"I am having a wonderful time."

"Are you?" he asked.

"Yes." I nodded

He kissed me on the forehead. "Sweetheart, are you okay?"

"Yeah." I smiled while burying my head in his chest.

"Ummm, you ready?"

"Yeah, I just wanna sleep right now."

"Do you want to go back to the hotel, or go straight home?"

"To the hotel, but only if you're going to stay there with me."

He glanced at his watch, grimaced, and then looked at me. He opened his mouth to speak when I cut him off. "Oh, how could I forget? You *live* with a woman."

Chin winced at my dry tone, but said, "I could stay until four, but I have to go home."

"That's cool. I'll leave when you leave, sweetie." I kissed him passionately on the lips.

"Damn, where did you come from, girl? I wish more females were as understanding as you."

Placing his hand in mine, I said, "Well, it comes with mastering the art of playing the game. With one roll of the dice, a female should know up front if she's wifey or not. Eventually, she'll either have his heart, or she won't."

"You think so, huh?" He palmed my ass, squeezing it gently with his massive hands.

"No sweetheart, I *know* so." I winked, and then smiled a sly smile as I saw the opportunity to drive another point home. "That way the game works in my favor. I can leave at anytime I choose."

As expected, Chin's expression turned dark. His grip tightened on my waist. "But what if I don't want to let you go?"

"If that's the case, you know exactly what you need to do."

The journey back to my house in the cab was filled with memories of my time with Chin. I cursed fate and blessed it all in the same breath. Under any other circumstances, I could have really fallen in love with him. And truthfully, I did have feelings for him. The only thing that kept me focused, was remembering what he did to my parents. Even though I overheard him say that PitBull pulled the trigger, Chin was still there. And if the situation was reversed, he would have killed my parents, too. Love couldn't factor into our relationship. I had a job to do.

I'd rather he didn't know where I lived, so I let him drop me off at another location. I slipped off to the side and called a cab once he drove off.

No one, except my father and Dragon, had ever treated me like Cinderella. As the cab passed Bronxdale Avenue, one thought stood out in my mind: *How am I going to kill him?* Sleeping with him would only make things harder.

Dear God, how did I get myself into this? But the better question was how would I pull my plan together without PitBull finding out? PitBull certainly had it coming.

"I know my father's money helped start Chin's business," I muttered to myself. "So it's only right that I take everything he has."

3:40 a.m.

"Where are you coming from this early in the morning?" Dimples inquired, stopping me dead in my tracks.

Shrugging, I tried to move past her. "I just had dinner with a friend."

"And might I inquire if this is the friend who's supposed to make you five hundred thousand dollars richer?"

My eyes popped wide open. "Excuse me?"

"BabyGirl, I've known you from day one. And I've never kept a secret from you. So why was it so hard for you to tell me about that deal?"

"You know, I'm going to hit you off with something, so don't worry about it," I assured her as I sat on the sofa to take off my shoes.

Dimples' hand snaked out and landed on her hips. "Hitting me off is no problem. I just don't understand why you didn't tell me in the beginning."

"Because I was trying to hide that shit from Sandy. And sometimes you let shit slip that should stay between us."

"When did I do that?"

"When haven't you done it? PitBull and Sandy know more about my business than they should. You side with him at times when you should have my back."

Dimples squinted her eyes as she raised her index finger to my face, making me wish I'd kept my thoughts to myself.

"Well, the bitch already knows and she's acting all jealous, so be careful."

I hugged her. I knew all was forgiven. "Thanks, girl."

"You're welcome." Suddenly, a plan formed in my mind. A test to see how loyal my girl Dimples really was, and to test PitBull's true intentions. Besides, I had a feeling that someone else was pulling the strings. PitBull couldn't possibly have the brains for this.

"Can I talk to you, Dimples?"

"What's wrong?"

"I'm falling for him," I whispered, but not too low.

"Him who?" Dimples screamed, though she tried to whisper. "The mark?"

"Shhhh, don't let Sandy hear."

The wind whipped around, suddenly bashing viciously against the window. Sandy's shadow had edged around the corner, listening.

"You're falling for him, BabyGirl? That wasn't the plan." Dimples joined me on the sofa.

"I know, but I can't fight it. I mean, I'm not there in full, but I am starting to feel a little sumthin sumthin."

"PitBull's gonna fuck you up if he finds out."

"I know, and I don't wanna fall too much for him, Dimples. He's got a woman."

"Fuck her. You need to worry about PitBull."

"How am I gonna get out, Dimples?"

"Let me ask you this, do you want to get out, meaning PitBull's assignment, or just away from this guy?"

"Both."

"Then I have bad news for you. You can't get out of this deal with PitBull. And since that can't happen, there's no way you can get away from the mark."

"Why?"

"PitBull hired you to do a job, and that job involves that stud. So put your feelings aside and handle the business first, and you'll get something out of it anyway."

"I'm in some shit stream, huh?"

"Yup," She sighed, getting up off the sofa. "And stop worrying about the other woman. You ain't fucking her. Just do what you have to do, but don't fall too deeply. Chances are he ain't gonna leave her, and you might get hurt."

"I know, Dimples."

"Remember, your job is to win his heart whether it's for PitBull or for yourself. If dude's hooking up with you, then there's trouble on the home front. You have to just prove why you're better than her. Listen to what he can't stand in her, and be whatever she's not." She winked at me.

"You're one crazy bitch." I laughed and shook my head.

"Yup," she flashed off.

"By the way, how's Marquis, your Mr. Range Rover?"

"He went to England for a month. He'll be back soon, and then we're gonna hook up on another date."

"A'ight." I fell back on the couch, propping my feet onto the armrest. "Looks like both of us are in for a rough ride."

"Yours will be rougher than mine."

Now that was something that wasn't news to me.

CHAPTER 59

CHIN

Chin's Office

Swiveling in my leather chair to face the security cameras— which I was not really paying attention to—my mind drew a blank.

"Still thinking about how you're going to deal with the situation?" Tony asked while pouring a glass of vodka.

"Yup!"

Tony took a long sip of the clear liquid. "Let me ask you this question, Chin."

I nodded, still keeping my eyes glued to the screen. The cameras had been secretly installed without anyone's knowledge. Not even Tracey knew they existed. I had one discreetly wired in every important area in the building, and Tony had come up clean.

"What are your feelings for this girl? And be honest."

"I don't know, Tony."

Tony's golden skin brightened as he smiloed, which was frightening because I didn't get to see that much. "Yes, you do. You're just trying to hide your feelings."

"Please, I told you already. No one pussy whips me."

"I think you need to rephrase that statement, because not only did the pussy whip you, but it's got you on lock."

"Whatever, man." I flashed him off, laughing.

"Seriously, Chin, is it that good?" he inquired, sitting back in the chair and staring at me.

"I'm gonna be honest with you, nigga, I haven't hit it, yet. I tasted it though."

"Wow." Tony laughed. "And she got your mentality fucked up like that already?"

"Nobody's got my mentality fucked up."

"Then how do you explain the fact that you were day-dreaming in today's meeting when we were going over Dragon's marketing plan? How do you explain that very little work's getting done around here, and we have a shipment coming in tomorrow? Did you remember that?"

"Oh shit!" I couldn't help rubbing my temples. A serious headache was throbbing its way through my brain. "I forgot about that."

"Once again, how do you feel about this girl?" Tony leaned back in the chair waiting for an answer. "I'm your dawg, so keep it thorough, man."

"Tony, she's different. I mean Porsha's wifey, but there's something about BabyGirl that excites me even more than Porsha. She's like my comfort zone. When I'm around her I feel stress-free—something I haven't felt in a while." Snatching the glass, I took a sip of the clear substance. "We had a good talk the other night, and that feisty personality of hers is sexy. I love it. I get the sense that she has a street edge, but underneath that street edge, she's vulnerable. And I have a feeling that with what happened with her parents, I've made her this way. She's special."

"Maybe it's her beauty, her personality, or the fact that you're feeling guilty that you killed her parents."

"Not even that Tony. I didn't kill them. PitBull did."

"That's technical bullshit, Chin, and you know it. You had

a part in the scheme and you'd spend just as much time in jail as the one who pulled the trigger."

The silence between us was thick.

"I kinda felt something for her on the dance floor *before* I knew who she was."

"Is it interfering with your relationship with Porsha?"

"Naw. How is it supposed to when Porsha don't know about her? She knows about Porsha, though."

A brief moment of silence fell upon the room, and an uneasy feeling began to come over me for the mere fact that my feelings were becoming stronger. "Damn, I wonder if Porsha noticed a change in me too?"

Tony shrugged. "All I'm saying is be careful, man. You can't lead on both females."

"Well, she knows I have a wifey."

"I agree with that, Chin, but think like a female. Do you think she really likes that shit, although she's pretending she's cool with it?"

"I don't know. She can't expect that I'm gonna leave Porsha for her, especially when I just met her."

"She's not asking you to do that, Chin. Right now it's a game."

Adjusting his shirt, he placed the glass on the table and leaned forward. "Let me break it down for you. Porsha is wifey so she has nothing to prove. Y'all live together. Now BabyGirl has all the proving to do. That's why she seems better than Porsha, and why she's gonna make you leave Porsha for her. Now all she has to do is get you right where she wants you, and boom, you'll be so fucking blind to it."

"It's never gonna happen, man. I'm not leaving Porsha."

"And nobody said you were," Tony said solemnly, "but remember this: sometimes it's best to stick with the one whose shoulder you have been crying on, but you have to be open minded, too. Look at the fact that there might be something *better* than Porsha. Treat both of them right, and don't disrespect one or try to play the other because toward the end, the one you might play could've been the one who was supposed to help you through life. And stop trying to fight your feelings. Ain't nothing wrong with loving two females. It's just that they both possess different qualities you are attracted to."

"That's deep, nigga. Good looking out."

"Somehow, I just wish I could fix my own problems at home."

"Don't sweat it, dawg. Everything will work out for the better."

"It better, because my bags are packed and ready to go."

"Thanks for the advice, cuz." I held out my hand for a pound.

"Anytime, son. I'm here for you." He sighed and nestled back in the chair. "Now that I just helped you, snap the fuck out of fantasy world and come back to reality. Tomorrow supplies are coming in, and the meeting spot is Hunt's Point."

"Yeah, I got that."

"Are the cameras in place?"

"They're gonna install them after everyone has gone home."

Tony propped his feet on my desk and said, "Sounds like a plan."

CHAPTER 60

BABYGIRL

White Plains, N.Y.

There was no way I could avoid sleeping with Dragon. I was too curious. My body became excited just thinking about him.

Guilt washed over me as I thought of Chin going down on me at the restaurant. Dragon was my main love, and I never wanted anyone to take my virginity except him. As I lay restless under the comforter, I picked up the phone to dial his number, but hung up. The wind whipped through the open window of my room, sounding like a wolf standing on top of a mountain howling. I dialed, and then hung up again.

C'mon, BabyGirl. The worst he could say is no. My inner thoughts pushed me on. I picked up the phone, dialed, and this time I let it keep ringing.

"Hello," he answered in a sleepy voice.

I listened instead of answering right away, knowing that someway, somehow the caller ID would give me away.

"Hello." He sounded a little more awake this time.

I could hear him fumbling in the background, as if he was struggling to turn on a light. It wasn't like I was scared of

Dragon. The attraction was there between us. But somehow I was scared of rejection—again. It hurt like hell when I first wanted to make love with him, and he didn't want me.

What if his love for me only extended to a love for a lil' sister? Had his feelings changed somehow?

"BabyGirl, I know you're on the line. Talk to me. Is something wrong?"

Tears welled up in my eyes as I blurted out, "I love you."

This time the pause came from his end of the line.

"I love you, too," he replied softly, but somehow his words didn't reassure me like they should have. "What's wrong?"

"There's nothing wrong. I've been in love with you for the longest, Dragon, and I'm tired of hiding it. I'm tired of waiting. You wanted me to be all up in Chin's grill, and I've done that. Now he'll expect more. And now I want more. I want to be yours. I want to make love, and I want to wake up to you in the morning."

Dragon cleared his throat. "You sure about that?"

"Yes, I am." Hopefully my sniffles didn't alert him to the fact that I was crying. "First it was my age, and then it was your time in jail, now it's something else. I'm tired. I want you. Chin is getting to me and I might do something stupid."

"I'll be there to get you in half an hour."

"Okay." A smile managed to come across my lips. "I'll meet you at the corner of Watson and Harrod Avenue. Pit-Bull's watching me too close these days."

"It'll be over soon."

"I'd like it to be over now. Let's just go somewhere and forget all this bullshit. I have a lot of money; enough money for us to start our own business or something."

"BabyGirl, would you be comfortable letting your parents' killers go free? You've wanted this for a long time. I've wanted to be a rapper for an even longer time."

He had a point. A damn good one.

"Yeah, okay. See you soon."

Somehow I'd have to slip by Sandy's room without waking her. And her old creaky floors could give away any criminal.

As I waited for Dragon, I wondered where my life was heading, and if it would be better anytime soon.

The pearly white Lexus jeep pulled around the corner and came to a halt in front of me. He got out of the car and opened my door, taking a quick glance at my long, knee length dress. Dressed in sweatpants, socks, slippers, and a white T-shirt, he looked so sexy. Little droplets of rain began to form on Dragon's car window, definitely proof that this summer was gonna be a wet one.

"You okay?" He used his right hand to rub along my legs.

As he sped along the Bronx River Parkway, the rain pelted the window at a faster rate. The road became slippery and dangerous. Sort of like my life. Jaheim's "Anything" flowed out of the speakers and soon became the only sound in the car. Dragon didn't say a word. Neither did I. Turning off at Exit 21, he stopped at a red light and glanced over at me. Our gazes locked and our lips followed. As he got deeper into the kiss, his tongue circled mine and I ran my hands along his six-pack. The blaring of a truck horn signaled that the light had changed from red to green and back to red again.

As we drove on Main Street in White Plains, New York, we made a right onto Mamaroneck Avenue. Five minutes later, he parked the jeep around the back in the parking lot, which was on Mitchell Place. We took the elevator up to the fourth floor. Fumbling to get the door open to 4G, he cursed a few times until he eventually got it. His home was very simple, yet elegant. The dark green leather sofa matched the green wall-to-wall carpet. Just like Chin's office. What was with men and the color green? A fifty-one inch plasma television stood in front of a bay window. His center and side tables were made of smoked tinted glass. Two statues of Dalmatian dogs stood watch at the entrance.

"You want something to drink?" he asked, hanging up the keys on the hook.

"Yeah, thanks. But no liquor. I want to keep a clear head. No soda either. I'll just take apple juice, please."

He gave my lips a brief peck.

I scanned the room and noticed that one of the pictures hanging on the wall was familiar. It was of my dad, Dragon, my mother, and me on a trip to Disney World.

"You still have this picture, Daquan?"

His head popped out of the kitchen. "What did you just call me?"

Whirling to face him, I said, "Daquan! Is there a problem?"

"Naw." He shrugged. "I just haven't heard anyone call me that in a long time."

I moved to another picture of little Dragon on a tricycle.

His footsteps crunched against the carpet as he came closer. "There was no more apple juice, so I gave—"

I untied my belt and let my dress fall to the floor.

He choked on his last word as he glanced over my curves. I stood in his living room in my bra and thong.

Taking slow steps over to him, I took the glasses out of his hand, resting them on the table.

My body ached from wanting him so bad. Using my tongue, I parted his lips as he held me around the waist and kissed me. He kissed along my neck and down to the center of my chest. He scooped me up in his arms and carried me into his bedroom. The Ingrid, a king size bed with elaborate Roman designs, would be the perfect place for me to lose my virginity. Leaning back on the soft comforter, his lips trailed across the tops of my breasts and down to my navel. Then he turned, allowing me to straddle his thighs.

As he kissed my stomach, he reached up, unhooked my bra, and looked me in the eyes once more. Biting my lips, I nodded. I didn't dare speak. My voice would have betrayed every emotion I felt. As he caressed my breasts, using his tongue to gently play with my hardened nipples, soft moans escaped my lips. Moistness formed below, creating a sticky wetness across my inner thighs. I ran my fingers through his neatly cut hair. My whole body trembled with anticipation.

As he kissed along my entire body, he slowly flipped me on my stomach, kissing my spine all the way to my butt cheeks, while using his massive hands to caress my breasts. Fluids pooled in the small nestle of curls at the base of my stomach, as though someone had poured a bucket of water on me. Case bellowing out "Touch Me, Tease Me" only added to the excitement.

Dragon turned me over, rested his head between my thighs, and kissed a line of fire to my pearl. Grabbing one of his pillows to brace myself, my body shivered from his wet lips and teasing tongue, which dipped into my center and back to my pearl. As I clenched the pillow tighter, he continued licking my insides and making me ready for him. Moans escaped from my lips rapidly, and I soon shouted to the world how much I loved him, how bad I wanted him, and how much I needed him. Just as I reached my peak, his dark brown eyes glanced up at me, and I grabbed onto his head, nearly slamming my pearl against his tongue.

"Baby . . ." I twitched my head from side to side. "BABY . . ." My screams became louder as my fist gently beat on his smooth back. Slowly coming up from between my thighs, he kissed me from the center, back up to my lips, and whispered in my ear, "You like it?"

"You can't tell?"

"We could stop right here, we don't have to . . ."

"There's no way you're pulling that bullshit! Make love to me."

Within seconds, his boxers hit the floor. My eyes popped open when I looked down. He looked down, also. A sly smile came across his lips as he positioned himself between my thighs. He kissed me deeply, trying to distract me from the pressure down below.

"Ahhhh. Baby, it hurts."

"You sure you want to?" he asked.

"Yes, I still want to."

Again he tried entering me as gently as possible. I grabbed onto him, closing my eyes and allowing him access into the deepest part of my body. The pain shot through me, but soon my body stretched to greet him, and I started to move to his rhythm. The pleasure was intense. He thrust in, then pulled out, and then thrust in once again. The wet sounds of our lovemaking drowned out the sounds of AZ Yet's "Last Night." My climax roared through my body like a lion cub calling for its mother.

After my body stopped trembling, Dragon lay still as he softly sang the song along with the group: "I kissed your lips, you felt my body slip into your soul. I heard you moan, I almost cried 'cause it was so beautiful."

We made love all night as the rain cried along with us. I woke up in his arms the next morning, kissed him on the lips, closed my eyes, and went back to sleep knowing that I had made the right choice. This was where I wanted to be and always would be. Chin be damned!

The Base—145th & St. Nick—Harlem

Heavy submachine guns were laid out on the table. Everyone had dressed in their disguises as Federal Agents or the ATF. PitBull recruited a lot of niggas for this assignment. I didn't know half the people around me. Where did PitBull get all of these people?

Dimples, Sandy, two other strange girls, and myself were the only females along with about seven men, including Shotta, Chico, and PitBull. Big, black vans were parked outside next to black jeeps with red flashing lights and sirens on top.

"Damn, motherfuckers plan their shit thorough," Sandy whispered in my ears.

"You're telling me." Making sure my bulletproof vest was fixed right, I scanned the area.

Dimples sat in the corner holding on to her Uzi and looking like someone who had just come out of intense military training. I walked over to the corner, gave her a hug, and wished her good luck.

"Okay, listen up," PitBull commanded. "The drop off point is a warehouse on Halleck Street in Hunt's Point. Once they open the back of those trucks, we jump out of the vehicles and tell them 'Freeze. FBI.' If they comply, we arrest each and every one of their asses, cuff them, take the supplies, and execute them one by one."

PitBull went on to explain the finer details of the plan for the fiftieth time, then he said, "Don't lose focus, because the minute you do, it could mean disaster for you or somebody on our team. Now, are there any questions before we leave? Because once we walk out that door, there's no turning back. And so we have to make sure you understand shit."

Dimples raised her hand. "I have a question. We won't be held responsible if we see a person on the other team shooting at somebody on our team, and we refuse to help that person because they're an enemy?" She inquired while glaring at Sandy, wishing she could shoot the bitch on the spot for all the grimy things she had done.

PitBull stormed over to Dimples and growled, "I don't care what problems you and that person have. At this point, there should be no doubt in your mind that, that person will have your back, even though y'all are not seeing eye-to-eye right now. Let me tell you this, we're a team, and a team fucking sticks together no matter what." He looked at Sandy and winked. She smiled.

"You damn right we're a team," Sandy mumbled under her breath.

Dimples grimaced as she looked at me. I shrugged. Now Dimples knew better than that. Why would she give up her game so easily? Stupid!

"Any more questions or does anyone have something else they need to get off their chest?" This time PitBull looked at me.

For a minute, I wanted to raise my hand and tell him I wanted out of the game, but I hesitated. I decided to tell him after tonight, when I could prove myself by how thorough I held shit down.

"Okay, since there are no more questions, let's grab our weapons and get the fuck out of here. We got ten minutes to complete this job, not a second more."

As we walked outside to get into the van, Dimples looked at me and spoke, "I can't wait for my date tomorrow with Marquis. I need a break from all these assignments."

"You're happy, right?"

"Yup. It's about time I got to him. Shit, we spoke on the phone a couple times, had one date, and now it's time for us to know each other." She nudged me in the side, smiling. "If you get my drift."

"I don't mean to cut you off, Dimples, but I wanted you be the first to know that after this robbery goes down, I want out."

"Word!"

"Yeah, I don't have plans to do this for much longer."

"Me neither. I just need one more robbery and I'm out," she responded, glancing over to PitBull and Sandy.

"Things are getting deeper each time. One more robbery could put me in a body bag."

"True that. But hey, we haven't been in a bag yet, so stop thinking like that," she whispered.

The van came to a complete stop at a red light as we turned off Bruckner Expressway.

"A'ight, listen up. Kill every mothafucka in sight. Don't hesitate." He glanced at us one by one. "And good luck." Pit-Bull faced the team as the red light turned green and we sped off to our destination.

CHAPTER 61

CHIN

Hunt's Point

Tony sat next to me as we watched the truck backing in. We were sitting in the car with two briefcases filled with cash.

"This is the big boy right here," Tony said, clapping his hands and laughing out loud.

"Word kid, we 'bout to have New York on lock after this. If we wanted to, we could open up two more bases, one in Brooklyn, and another in Lower Manhattan."

"Yeah, we could do that if we were expanding our territory," Tony agreed.

"Exactly. Then everyone would be buying from us."

"But we're moving on to bigger and better things, right?"

"Right."

The truck was finally in, and we waited for the shutters to slowly close before we got out of the car.

CHAPTER 62

BABYGIRL

Hunt's Point

Positioning ourselves around the warehouse, we leaned against the wall one by one waiting for PitBull's signal.

"Everyone in place?" His voice crackled in the headsets.

Everyone's right hand went up at the same time.

"Okay. Wait for my final signal, and then we move in."

While PitBull and Dimples held on to Uzis, two nine millimeters were behind my back, waiting for PitBull's index finger to point forward.

"Ready, move," he shouted.

Doors were kicked in. "Freeze! FBI," could be heard coming from the majority of our voices. "Drop your weapons and put your hands in the air," Sandy yelled.

Tension slipped into my body like a lion creeping up on its prey, and I knew without a shadow of a doubt that the situation was about to get ugly. None of the men sprinkled throughout the warehouse were willing to drop the weapons or the drugs. And our team wasn't willing to drop ours either. We couldn't turn back.

"This is the last time! Drop—" before Dimples could finish the sentence, shots were fired, and within seconds the warehouse looked like Macy's Fourth of July fireworks. I wasted no time firing my weapons, but froze when I saw Chin and his partner Tony coming from their hiding space and shooting at everything in sight. Knowing he was a part of this and seeing it in person were two different things.

"Dimples, I gotta get out of here," I said, backing out of view. "Chin's here and my cover's about to get blown."

"Oh, shit!"

While still firing, I looked around for a place to escape, but didn't see an exit. PitBull spotted me, he glared at me with a look that said, *Bitch, don't fuck this up. Keep shooting.* I ignored him. All he managed to do so far was take away some of Chin's supplies. He hadn't fully succeeded in taking down the empire. He still needed me, and the last thing I needed was for Chin to see me.

"Get behind me, BabyGirl. And find a way out of here," Dimples instructed me over her shoulder while firing to cover me.

Shots were still being exchanged, and so far three men on their side had died, and one was injured. I finally made it from the spot behind Dimples and opened the back door when something made me turn back.

"Look out!" I yelled to Dimples as she turned her back to look for cover.

By the time she heard my words, it was too late. Chin had managed to pump two shots into her body before the remainder of his crew escaped.

"No!" The distance to reach Dimples seemed to expand with every step. "We've gotta help her! Somebody call the fucking ambulance."

Nobody lifted a finger to help as they grabbed their bags and ran for the van.

"C'mon! Leave!" PitBull grabbed my shoulders.

I yanked away from him. "Fuck you! She needs help."

Giving me the look that said "you're making a serious mistake," he took one last look at us and fled the scene.

Searching frantically in my pocket for my cell, I finally realized it was still in the van. I searched Dimples' pocket, and sure enough her cell was there.

"911," the operator answered.

"Yes, I need an ambulance!"

"Where are you?"

I glanced around the place and came up blank. "I don't know. I'm at a warehouse in Hunt's Point somewhere"

"I need a street location, ma'am."

"I'm by a warehouse on Halleck Street in Bronx, N.Y., right across from the prison boat."

Whatever else the dispatcher said to me fell on deaf ears because Dimples' raspy voice pierced the air.

Lying helpless in my arms, she struggled to keep her eyes open long enough to say her next statement. "He didn't see you, right?"

"Don't worry about that, girl. I could care less if he saw me right now. I have to get you some help."

"BabyGirl," she said, then swallowed hard, "If you love Chin, then go after him. Don't worry about PitBull because tomorrow's not promised in this game. Take me as a perfect example."

"Don't say that. You gonna make it, girl. You have to. I can't see myself without you." I dragged her by the shoulders out the door as tears rolled down my face.

"Thank you for everything, BabyGirl, and remember play your cards right," were the last words she said before her eyes closed and her body went slack.

Pain tore through my heart. "No, you can't leave me," I whispered.

The ambulance was right out front, and paramedics rushed over.

"You gotta help her," I said walking side by side with them.

The dark-skinned paramedic leaned over, felt her pulse, and looked up at me. "She barely has a pulse."

"Get her help quick, so we don't lose her." I leaned over his shoulder looking on.

"Miss, we're doing the best we can, but—"

I backed away from the scene as fast as I could. Though I had wanted to ride to the hospital with them, police cars had pulled up and the place was now flooded with cops. There was no explanation I could give anyone, especially since I was still in an FBI uniform.

My heart hurt so badly. First my parents, now Dimples, and they both fell victims to the same man. Just at the point when we had decided to get out of the game, it looked like the game had decided other things for us.

CHAPTER 63

PITBULL

145th Street, Harlem NYC

The package I had been waiting for had arrived, and I couldn't wait to see what was inside it. Ripping open the brown envelope, I took the pictures out one by one and smiled.

I told her falling in love with Chin was like crossing me, and that's exactly what she did. So now she was going to pay the ultimate price.

"That's fucked up what she did," Chico, who was looking over my shoulders, said.

"Yup, and her ass ain't getting away with it," I responded.

"Can't, or else our other females are gonna think it okay to pull shit like that too."

"Exactly! She has to be the prime example. I made her, I built the bitch's career, and now she's gonna walk out on me because a nigga's laying gold in the street for her! Let's see if he'll lay out any more gold once he finds out about her," I said.

Shotta laughed hard. "More than likely, he'll put a silver bullet in her ass."

CHAPTER 64

BABYGIRL

Watson Avenue

Tonight I had to break the cycle. Being cooped up in the house for three whole weeks since Dimples had been in a coma wasn't doing me any good. I demanded that PitBull give me the money she would have made from the job, and I placed some of it in an account for her at the hospital, so they would keep her machines going. There was still some brain activity, so there was a chance that she would come back. I prayed for her every day.

Closing my left eye, I stroked the white eyeliner over my eyelids. I needed Chin to take my mind off things tonight. PitBull was angry with me, of course. He didn't want to fork over Dimples' share of the cash, and I refused to sleep with him for it. I told him, "If you don't give me the money, I'll walk out and you can deal with Chin the best way you can. Maybe Sandy will help out."

He forked over every single dime, scowling like a mad dog every dollar of the way. But at that point, I could have cared less. I didn't intend on losing anything else. I didn't get paid for that assignment because he said I fucked up by losing focus once I saw Chin. I didn't argue with him, because he was correct. The only thing that mattered was for him to fork over Dimples' cash. On top of that, after a huge argument, I told him I wouldn't take any more assignments.

I still lived in the house, though. Sandy and I didn't speak much, except to say hi and bye and relay messages. I knew she was still clocking me for PitBull, but I was looking for my own space, so that wouldn't be an issue anymore. My cell rang and it was Chin letting me know he was outside waiting. Grabbing the house keys off the table, I closed the door behind me and headed downstairs.

"What's up, baby?" He kissed me on the cheeks.

I gave him a fake smile. "Nothing."

"Yes. Something's wrong. I've known you long enough to know when something's wrong with you. You wanna talk about it?"

I leaned my head on his shoulder. "No, sweetie. I need you to take my mind off it."

"A'ight, I can do that. But where you wanna go? You wanna go eat, watch a movie, or what?"

"None of the above."

"So what you wanna do?"

"I wanna be alone with you."

"A private setting? You sure?"

"Yes, Chin. I need you to make love to me." He put the car in drive. "I need it more than ever. Then we need to talk. There's something I need to tell you and I don't think you'll like it very much. I've done some things—"

He stared at me a while before saying, "That's okay. We'll talk about it later."

Then he stepped on the gas and the Denali peeled off down the street.

CHAPTER 65

PORSHA

Staten Island

Unfortunately, after searching through Chin's files and other places in the apartment, I hadn't come up with anything tangible to use against him.

I still baited Chyna and Chin at every possible moment, just waiting for them to slip up. Chin had lied to me and there was no way I was walking away from the relationship without something to show for it. I deserved a piece of the record company and the restaurant since I had helped set up all the paperwork and had taken care of the legal end of things. But I had also put them on hold the moment I found out Chin's dick had been straying. Something as simple as a "name change" could hold up things for weeks.

Just at that point I remembered that Chin kept some of his things in his gun case. I turned toward the closet. The doorbell rang. I did a quick sweep of the place, making sure I had put everything back in its place.

After the second ring, I punched the intercom. "Who is it?"

"Chyna."

"This better be good, Chyna, for you to be strolling up here this late at night."

"It can't wait," she said.

"Drive in and come up to the door."

I opened the door just in time to see her walking toward me with a brown paper bag. She pulled out a video, telling me, "Look at it and let me know what you think."

"Aren't you gonna watch it with me?"

"Naw, I'm in a hurry. But tell me what you think tomorrow."

Hurrying back to the room, I quickly popped in the tape. First, Chyna appeared talking about how close our friendship had grown, and how much she considered me a real friend, and why she couldn't go on with this secret any longer. She blabbed on for a few more minutes, then uttered the words, "Chin and I used to be lovers."

Shocked by what Chyna said, I rewound the tape again and again. She went into details of how they met, what he used to do in the past, his friends' names, and how the day he took me to lunch and said that he was going in Chyna's office to talk business, it was business to make sure I never found out about their past.

When I played the tape one last time, I saw a longing stare on both Chin's and Chyna's faces, which was followed by them kissing. A tear began to fall down my face, and my insides started to burn with hatred and the need for revenge. I picked up the phone.

"Why?" I cried into the phone.

Chyna sighed softly. "I'm sorry, but I wanted you to know the truth,"

"No you didn't, you lying-ass bitch. You wanted to please yourself. All those times you would vent your frustration about him wasn't because you hated him, it was because you loved him and couldn't get him because I was standing in your way."

"Nothing like that, Porsha. I told you, I valued our friendship, and I just wanted you to know."

I hung up the phone, got dressed in some sweatpants, a white T-shirt, Nike sneakers, and a scarf. I went to Chin's sports closet and pulled out a baseball bat, then I went in another one of his closets and pulled out something more serious. The Jaguar was too stylish for what I had in mind, so I jumped in the Honda and tore out of the parking lot.

Rah Digga's "Party and Bullshit" thumped through the stereo. The only line from the song that I identified with was "I beat that bitch with a bat." I took a glance at the baseball bat lying in the passenger seat and smiled. Two people would feel my wrath tonight.

Pulling up to Chyna's new house she had recently bought in Scarsdale, N.Y., I peeked through the living room window and saw Chyna sipping a clear, bubbly liquid from a crystal goblet.

I thumped on her door with the tip of the baseball bat.

"Who is it?"

"Porsha," I said, speaking in a deceptively cheerful tone.

The door swung open. "You okay?"

My fist snaked out, slamming straight into Chyna's mouth.

"What the fuck!" Chyna staggered backward, holding onto her mouth.

"You ain't feel shit yet," I yelled, before using the bat to break everything within swinging distance.

"Get the fuck out before I call the police," Chyna screamed, cowering in the corner with the phone in her lap.

Pointing Chin's gun at the shaking woman, I said, "I dare you."

"A'ight, what do you want?" she asked, slamming the phone back down.

"Revenge, that's all, you trifling-ass home wrecker. With

women like you, people can't have a decent home. Instead, we gotta be watching our men twenty-four, seven."

Chyna stood, her laughing a sad, bitter sound. "So you think you're the only bitch your man is fucking?"

Now that brought me up short. Chin was fucking someone else? Then I would deal with that bitch, too. But first things first. I charged at Chyna, pushing her to the floor.

"Porsha, get off me," she yelled, using her hands to shield her face from the next blow. "You didn't watch the end of the tape, did you?"

"What the fuck you talking about?" I backed away, searching Chyna's eyes for some understanding.

"Your man's fucking a girl by the name of BabyGirl Smith," Chyna spat, rubbing the places where she was injured.

"You're lying 'cause you don't want me to bust your ass some more."

"Believe what you want, Porsha, but I have the number right here, and we are gonna call now to give you the real deal on your man and the bitch he's actually fucking."

CHAPTER 66

BABYGIRL

Mandarin Oriental Hotel-Manhattan

Chin went into the bathroom to take a shower, and I sat on the bed drying off when my cell rang. I didn't recognize the number, but I answered anyway. "Hello!"

"Bitch, why you fucking with my man?"

"Who the fuck are you? And who the fuck is your man because if you can't recite a name, then obviously he's not yours."

"Keep getting smart Miss BabyGirl and see if you don't get hurt for fucking with my fiancé."

"Again, who is your man? Do you want me to name some niggas and let you pick him out?"

"This is Porsha Hilton, bitch. And you're fucking my man, Chin."

"You're his fiancée? He didn't say anything about being engaged."

"I suggest you keep your hands off before it gets worse than it already is. You're a low class ho, and Chin will never settle for someone like you."

A long silence grew over the phone, and I smiled.

"Baby," I yelled to Chin as I strolled to the bathroom and

cracked the door open. "Tell me again, how was the pussy, Chin?"

"Damn good," he said laughing. "Perfect. With pussy like that, you make a nigga wanna wife you."

"So you're trying to say it's your pussy?"

Turning toward me, he stopped drying his hair. "Hell yeah, that's mine right there."

"So what about wifey at home?"

"Don't worry about her. As long as you and me are doing our thing, it's all good."

With that, I ran back over and sprawled across the bed.

"You heard that?" I asked into the phone. "I didn't go after him, Porsha Hilton, he came after me. Check yourself!" I laughed, waiting for her smart ass to say something. I was disappointed. "What happened? Wifey, you can't talk?"

She hung up without another word.

"What's so funny?" Chin came out drying his braids.

"Nothing." I kissed him on the lips. "Just something I was sharing with one of my girlfriends."

"What did you tell her about the dick?"

"How good it was." We both laughed.

CHAPTER 67

PORSHA

Bronx River Parkway NYC

Iwas completely crushed and at a loss for words as I ran from Chyna's house to my car. *How could he betray me like this after I had worked so hard to bring his empire from an illegitimate business to something legal? Is this the thanks I get after years worth of free services?* I was the dedicated fiancée, living up to the code of sticking by my man through thick and thin. Was I that much of a difficult person, that Chin couldn't approach me with the truth? What was this other girl offering him that I couldn't?

As tears streamed down my face, driving on the Bronx River Parkway became difficult. Confused as to what to do next, I stepped on the gas a little harder so I could escape this madness as quickly as possible. Two Hundred Thirty-Third Street was the next exit. My sister's house popped into my head. *Maybe I'll find peace of mind there tonight.* Stepping on the gas a little harder so I could reach my destination, I ignored the big red and white stop sign. I screamed when I realized there was no way to prevent the accident as an oncoming truck plunged right into my car and dragged me and the car to the other side of the street! I lay still, with blood gushing from my head and I silently prayed that medical attention would get to me soon.

CHAPTER 68

CHIN

Central Park West

A week straight I stayed in bed. I was not taking any phone calls. Porsha's near death experience had taken a toll on me. I was unable to do anything. BabyGirl had called me twice, and I didn't return any of her calls. BabyGirl hadn't tried again—and I doubted if she would. What hurt the most was the fact that I couldn't see Porsha because her family had requested that I not come to the hospital.

Thinking over things, I began to wonder what the purpose of my life was, and when anything would seem right. Here I was, all alone, thinking about myself playing with these females' feelings, and now one of them had almost died.

"I'm ready, man, I'm ready." I repeated while pouring the gin down my throat. "I can't go on like this. I need one chick in my life who I can ride with. All this running around ain't worth it.

After a few more minutes of deep thought, I picked up the phone and called Tracey.

"So tell everyone you'll be in on Monday?" Tracey asked.

"Naw, not everybody. Just the ones who are important.

Next weekend is the shooting of Dragon's first video, and I want to make sure I'm there."

"How are you holding up?"

"I'm still breathing, so I can't complain."

"We miss you, but we need you to regain your strength before you come back."

"I know. Thanks, Tracey. Tell Tony to holler when he gets in."

After hanging up with Tracey, the next phone call I made was to BabyGirl.

For a few minutes we caught up on things, like how she was doing, and how I was doing. Then I opened my heart. "I can't understand how the hell she found out about me and Chyna."

"She's a female, Chin. It doesn't take long for us to put two and two together and figure shit out."

"It's something else."

"I miss you," BabyGirl whispered.

"I miss you, too, sweetheart."

"You want me to come over and keep you company?"

I paused for a moment before saying yes. BabyGirl was just the distraction I needed.

CHAPTER 69

PITBULL

Albert Einstein Hospital, Bronx

Porsha's trip to the hospital couldn't have come at a better time. Chin would be off his game a little now that his woman was out of the picture. Chyna could make her move on Chin and I could still get what I wanted.

The next step would be to take BabyGirl totally out of the picture.

"I'm so sorry about your daughter, Mr. Hilton," I said to Porsha's dad as we sat in the hospital waiting room.

"Wait until I get my hands on him." Mr. Hilton clenched his fist while angry tears rolled down his face.

"Just let it go." I patted his back. "Trust me, he has to answer to God for this one."

"It ain't that easy when your child could be taken away from you over stupidity."

Porsha's mother came out of the bathroom. Her face looked a lot better than it did earlier, when the tears and makeup were mixing together.

"She had so much going for her," Porsha's mother said, "and she got caught up in that nasty boy's life and his world of drugs, crime, sex, and murder." She sobbed again.

Chyna hugged the brown-skinned, short-haired woman. "I know," she said. "I tried to warn her, but she never listened. You know Porsha can be stubborn when it comes to things."

"I wish she was like you, Chinetta," Mr. Hilton said while rubbing his wife's leg. "That's one thing I liked. You never mixed with those nasty thug niggers."

My gaze connected with Chyna's. *If he only knew*, I thought.

"To each their own, Mr. Hilton. To each their own," I said before patting him on the back, thanking God I had decided to come here wearing decent clothing. Maybe Pops would've remembered that I had been a thug, too.

CHAPTER 70

BABYGIRL

Central Park

Chin looked horrible. His hair wasn't braided and he wore some bleached-out sweatpants, a white tank, and some worn-out slippers. The smell of liquor drowned out his natural smell.

"Baby, you don't look so good," I told him while closing the door behind me. "Listen, why don't you go take a shower? Then I'll hook up your hair because I'm positive you don't want to go out of the house like this."

"I'm tired." He dropped right back onto the couch and poured himself another glass of gin.

"Oh no! Get your ass up and go take a shower," I said while taking the gin out of his hand. "You've had too much liquor in one week. Right now you need to stop and get yourself together."

Placing his towel on the hamper, I gauged the water so it was the right temperature, stripped him, and dragged his ass in the bathroom.

"Shower," I snapped, before closing the bathroom door.

I stood outside until I heard him splashing around.

The kitchen was a mess, so I took the garbage out, placed

the dishes in the dishwasher, and mopped the floor, hoping the disinfectant would take out some of the liquor smell. Pouring the rest of the gin down the drain, I prayed I could keep him sober for the rest of the night. When he finished putting on his pajama bottoms, I braided his hair with fresh Sprewell designs. He fell asleep just before I completed the last braid, so I fluffed his pillow, rolled down the blanket, helped him into bed, and covered him up.

The cool night breeze blowing from the open bedroom window brushed against my naked back as I lay cuddled in the bed with Chin. Earlier he went downstairs to spend a little time in his office. When he came back his mood was ice cold. Something else was bothering him and I could sense it.

"What's wrong?"

"Nothing, baby. Just make love to me," he whispered in my ear.

"Anything for you, sweetheart."

Slowly, I got up from beside him and climbed on top of him.

"I said, make love to me, not *fuck* me." He spoke in a demanding tone.

"Are you sure you're okay?"

Instead of replying, he caressed my breasts in a circular motion while using his thumbs to rub against the nipples.

"Make love to me," he demanded, while sitting upright so he could suck on my breasts.

I watched as he used his tongue to lick around my hard nipples, blowing cool air on them. As he proceeded to play with my breasts, I started to ride him. At first I started off slowly, but then he demanded me to ride him faster. It was so different from the first time we made love.

Immediately I erased all my questions of *why* from my mind, and brought myself back to the sex, which, for some reason, was not giving me the pleasure it should have.

"Baby, ride me faster." He began to yell while grabbing onto my hair and squeezing my breasts to the point where blood couldn't flow to them.

Leaning over, I whispered in his ear, "Baby, you're hurting me."

"I'm hurting you, huh?" His aggressive tone frightened me.

"Would you stop acting like that, Chin, and tell me what's wrong?"

For five minutes we looked at each other in complete silence.

"What the fuck is going on?" I asked. "Now I'm starting to worry."

His dark brown eyes narrowed to slits. "You should worry, because I'm about to blow your fucking brains out." He placed a nine millimeter against my forehead.

I laughed. "Nigga, you better stop playing and remove that shit from my head."

"Stop playing. Get the fuck up off of me before I blow your brains out."

The smile I had on my face earlier was now gone. A sliver of fear raced up my spine. I smelled bullshit. I smelled Pit-Bull.

"That's right, bitch, worry. Because I was wondering when the fuck you were gonna tell me that you were the one robbing my supplies," he shouted, hitting me with the end of the gun across my cheeks. "Not to mention the night when we were at the hotel you were on the phone with Porsha."

"What the fuck are you talking about?" I sobbed, as the biggest thing I feared began to unravel in front of my eyes.

"You don't know what the fuck I'm talking about, huh?" Still pointing the gun at me, he threw an envelope in my direction. "Well these pictures should freshen your memory. And let's just say a good friend of mine told me all about that phone call."

I didn't move.

"Open that shit," he shouted while kicking me in the side.

By now I was curled up in the corner, shivering and crying because this was a side of Chin I had never seen before.

"You won't open this shit?" He moved toward me. "Well, I'm gonna open it for you because one way or the other, you're gonna see for yourself, bitch."

Opening the envelope slowly, he spoke. Each angry word hurt worse than each kick he gave my ribs. "I was thinking before you came over about how my life's gonna change. I was ready to settle down with you, and eventually marry your little lying ass. Then I remembered that Tracey told me to open this envelope. It took me a minute, but I'm glad I got around to it."

He was pacing back and forth. Each time he would turn and point the gun at me, I would squirm. "At first I told her to put it to the side and I would look at it later, but she insisted that I take a look. I didn't then, but I did a little while ago. You know what was in the envelope?" He shouted while tears began to roll down his face.

"No, I don't have a clue," I responded, trying to sound stronger than I really felt.

"This, bitch!" He shoved pictures in my face showing me and the crew doing that last robbery.

"What do you have to say for yourself?" He asked, still holding the gun to my head.

I held back my tears. "I can explain. I tried to explain the last time we were together, but you cut me off and didn't want to talk, then—"

"Explain? You should've fucking explained from day one." He continued kicking me in the side.

"Get up, and get the fuck out," he growled.

"No! Not until your ass listens to me."

"You want me to listen to you, huh?"

"Yes, because there's more to the story than just—"

"So, you're trying to tell me you're not gonna get up?"

I didn't even have a chance to explain when the next thing I felt was a burning in my eyes. Chin had sprayed me with mace!

"Get up," he shouted, stomping on me, kicking me, and pulling my hair as he dragged me across the floor. My head felt as though it was on fire.

Struggling, I got up and stood at the top of the stairs, pleading with him to let me wash my eyes out and explain.

"Shut the fuck up!" He hit me with the gun in the face. "I would've given you every fucking thing. Your ass wouldn't have needed anything. You played your fucking games, betraying me, and then fucked up Porsha's mentality so you could get what you wanted." His foot came down on my side, and then swung again, this time sending me airborne. I landed at the bottom of the stairs. A solid crack from some breaking bone in my body assaulted my ears.

Blood poured from my mouth, my eyes were burning, and every joint in my body hurt like hell. As I lay curled up at the bottom of the steps unable to move, I heard his footsteps pass me. Hanging on to the staircase railing, I tried to get up to see if I could find my way to the door.

As if by some sort of fate, my mind flashed back to the damaging photos and something stuck out in my mind. Everyone's face was in those pictures except one. I knew instantly who had given Chin that envelope. I heard Chin's footsteps and turned to speak, but only managed the word, "PitBull" before something hit me across the head, knocking me back down on the ground as the world faded to black.

CHAPTER 71

CHIN

Central Park NYC

I continued to beat her across the head with the shovel as I watched her lifeless body lay at the bottom of the stairs.

"How could you do this to me?" I screamed. "I loved you." Anger was driving my every move as I continuing to beat, kick, and stomp her ass. The white carpet was filled with blood, leaking from her mouth like a burst pipe. Her body was bruised from head to toe. I was certain she was dead. I had only meant to hurt her, not kill her. If BabyGirl was dead, I couldn't let his ass live either. PitBull's bullshit had caused so much trouble.

In a way, it was my fault that she had come into this life. My fault. If her parents had lived, she would probably be in college right now instead of playing a game she should have never been in. Tears rolled from my face onto her naked body as I picked her up, cradling her body in my arms. I cried for Porsha. I cried for BabyGirl. And mostly, I cried for myself.

I picked up the phone and dialed.

"Tony," I whispered when he answered.

"What the fuck's wrong with you?" He asked, smacking noisily in my ear.

"I need you over here. I lost it man. I just lost it."

"Can you tell me what's wrong?"

"BabyGirl. She's dead." I hung up the phone before he could ask any other questions.

Grabbing the bottle of gin, I cursed loudly because it was empty and sat on the white leather sofa. When my brain started to calculate how much money I had lost, anger came back full force. But then again, I also wondered who else was behind the robberies. BabyGirl was smart, but she didn't do that shit by herself. PitBull could pull some shit together, but this was too organized to be him alone.

I didn't even realize when Tony came bursting through the door.

"What the fuck did you do to the girl?" Tony asked, pulling me away from her body.

Tony reached down, placing two fingers to her neck. "She ain't got long to live, man. Let's dump the body, or else your ass is going to jail for murder."

Slowly reality sank in. "I'll put some clothes on."

CHAPTER 72

PITBULL

145th Street, Harlem

"What are you so happy about, nigga?" Shotta asked upon entering the base.

"Celebrating. Yup, me and my boy Chico here are celebrating."

"Before y'all give me the rundown on what the fuck you celebrating, pass the smoke, so my ass can be high, enjoying whatever it is," Shotta said.

Chico took one more pull and passed it on to Shotta. He started laughing out loud.

"Is this boy a'ight, PitBull?" Shotta questioned.

"Hell yeah, we fine. What you need to worry about is if your girl BabyGirl is fine."

"Why she wouldn't be fine? The bitch turned her back on us after we built her career, bought her car, introduced her to the finer things in life. And all because Chin gave her even better things."

"Well, she won't be getting anymore finer things because homeboy is over there probably fucking her up right now. Knowing Chin, he won't hesitate to kill her over his money."

"Say word? What y'all did?"

"Simple, when she was robbing the supplies, I had a little camera taking pictures of them, you know just for *security* purposes," I said.

"Let me guess the rest. And since she betrayed you, you made sure those pictures got to Chin?" Shotta asked.

"Exactly!"

"That's what I'm talking about. We gotta show these bitches that this shit ain't no ordinary game. There are fucking consequences to face if they disobey the rules."

They all laughed as smoke filled the room.

"All I got to say, man, is for her sake, she better pray that she's dead," Chico added.

"Why is that?" Shotta asked.

"Because I ain't through with her ass yet," I warned. "This is a man's world *and* a bitch better recognize that *and* the fact that a male will always dominate the drug game."

"That's right. My man James Brown never said it better." Shotta laid back, smiled, and blew out the smoke.

"Actually, you're both wrong."

Looking to the entrance, a single female stood watching over our celebration. My anger had made me forget that she was there.

"Tell me, Chyna, what are the new plans and why did you want to take down Chin in the first place?" I asked her.

"Long story." She pushed my question away.

"Oh, believe me when I tell you we've got time. Especially since I'm trying to understand why you wanted to be with Chin instead of me. Especially when you were my girl before his."

"A'ight, I didn't like the way he treated you when you went upstate. And I definitely didn't like the way he treated me after you left. He did some serious wrong, PitBull. I just never told you about it. I'm taking everything back that he took from you, and I'm also making him pay for what he did to me."

Chico asked, "Damn, ma. You gets down dirty like that?"

"Trust me, I get down dirtier, especially if what I want is worth my interest."

Pulling on the blunt and exhaling, Shotta asked, "So don't you feel no remorse that you're responsible for his wifey being in the hospital?"

"Hell, no. She brought that shit on herself," Chyna said, sitting on the sofa next to the window. "I told you I achieve what I want by any means necessary."

"What about the empire, Chyna?" I asked before taking the blunt from Shotta and taking a single pull. "I thought we were gonna control that, you know like *partners*."

"Oh that! Well, I figure y'all got enough money to start your own empire."

"Shit don't work like that, ma. We kept our end of the bargain, so why can't you?"

"I did. I made sure y'all got paid," she snapped while putting her pocketbook over her shoulder.

"I thought we were partners. Spades." I got up off the chair and followed behind her. "You know, trying to outdo the other opponents."

Chyna made a quick turn and stared at me. "Yeah, but sometimes in Spades in order to win you can't play by the rules. You have to get a little dirty to win, even if you have to fuck up your partner's hand."

I shook my head slowly, eyeing Shotta and Chico. "I see."

"I want his companies. You're more familiar with the drug business," she said softly, holding onto the entrance door handle. "You understand how the game works."

"Yeah, but I hope you can understand this." With that, I aimed my gun toward the middle of her forehead. A look of shock took over Chyna's face as her impending death paralyzed her at the door. BOOM! The gun went off, leaving a hole in the middle of her forehead.

I looked at the body slumped in a heap at the door. "Sorry, baby girl. I have plans too—plans I most certainly can't have you ruin."

CHAPTER 73

CHIN

Soundview, Bronx: August

BabyGirl's nearly lifeless body lay in the back seat of the Denali. The clock on the dashboard read 3:37 a.m. as we exited off the FDR onto the Bruckner Expressway. At first we wanted to dump her body in the East River, but Soundview in the Bronx behind the projects would be a perfect spot, and Tony had to make a stop at the warehouse in Hunt's Point to survey the damage anyway.

We were now close to Rosedale Avenue, and somehow a guilt trip took over as I remembered that because of my actions, the sins of my past had come back to haunt the success of my future. *Fuck that!* I reasoned in my head, pushing my sadness away. From this point on, I'd make the right choices. Porsha would be my focus. It shouldn't be hard to pull our relationship back together. A little talk with her parents would put them in check.

Tony drove along the side of the curb where the brick buildings were.

"Pull over."

"Right here?" Tony asked coming to a complete stop.

"Yup, right here." Opening the back of the truck, I

scooped BabyGirl into my arms, then dropped her in the back of the projects right next to the dumpster. Scanning the area to make sure there were no eyewitnesses, I then took one last glance at the woman on the ground. My heart grew heavy, but I couldn't change the past. I wished, once again, that I would've listened when she said she wanted to talk—before I saw those damn pictures.

I jumped back into the truck and stared out at the dark night sky.

"Chin, you gonna be okay?"

"I'm tired of all this killing and shit. I'm tired of not knowing who to trust anymore."

"Man, don't pull this soft shit on me, we—"

"Yes, I know, we have to finish off the rest of these mothafuckas."

Tony hesitated at the wheel. "There's still time to save her."

Didn't I already know that? Didn't I know that leaving her here was signing her death warrant? Someone was bound to find her and they wouldn't help. They'd probably rape her and then finish the job.

"Just drive, Tony. Just drive."

CHAPTER 74

BABYGIRL

Albert Einstein Hospital

My surroundings were unfamiliar. A loud beeping noise pierced the air. Bright white lights assaulted my vision. It hurt just to open my eyes.

Moments later, I was able to keep them open. Damn! I was right back where I didn't want to be—in an uncomfortable bed, with tubes strapped to my body, wearing a night robe, and smelling the sterile smells that could only come from one place.

"I want out of here."

I repeated my request again, this time shaking the bed rail to make my point.

"Calm down," one of the three nurses said as two of them came running toward me.

"Get me the fuck out of here."

"I said, calm down," the taller nurse commanded.

"No! Get me the fuck out of here." I began to scream, and at that same moment I felt an eerie feeling in my body, as if I was about to throw up. "Fuck!" I couldn't understand what was happening to my body.

I looked at the nurses for some sort of explanation. They

looked at each other, coming to a silent understanding that the brunette would give me the news. "You're pregnant and—"

A pounding in my head blocked out everything else. Then the world faded to black.

CHAPTER 75

CHIN

Chin's Office

A month had passed since the incident, and I had no idea whether BabyGirl was alive or dead. All I knew was that one of the other girls in the photographs PitBull had given me showed some girl Tony remembered. He remembered a few details about Sandy because she tried to holler at him after the night I first laid eyes on BabyGirl. She even went as far as slipping her number in his pocket, which Tony remembered was still in his office. I thought Sandy might have the information I needed.

Tony slid the number across the desk. I dialed.

"Sandy."

"Who's this?"

"Chin. You remember me, right?"

"How could I forget a big spender like you? BabyGirl was practically in love."

I closed my eyes and blocked out the images of the beautiful girl who had captured my heart.

"Listen, Tony and I need for you to do us a favor, sweetie. You know that shit can't be discussed over the phone, but we thought we could drop by and speak to you about it. There could be a lot of money in it for you."

"What time do you wanna come?"

"Hmm."

Tony flipped both hands up, then flashed a single finger.

"Like around eleven tonight."

"A'ight, that's cool with me. It gives me enough time to prepare something for ya'll to eat," she said.

"Okay, so we'll see you later."

"Bye, Chin."

"Bye, Mrs. Moreno," I said, gassing her head, which earned me a little giggle on her end.

After I hung up the phone, I said, "Dumb-ass bitch."

Tony nodded.

"Is *she* in for a surprise," I said.

"You're good, Chin."

"Now the real key is to find out who's been behind this all along, because one by one I'm gonna knock down each player until I get to the final person. I'm saving the best card for last."

CHAPTER 76

BABYGIRL

Albert Einstein Hospital

My body felt drained, and I was still a little drowsy from earlier. Situated in the room were a nurse, a doctor, and an Ob-Gyn. A monitor displayed a gray and white image, and someone rubbed something on my stomach.

"What are you doing?" I asked.

"Checking your baby's heartbeat."

"Baby's heartbeat?" I shouted while trying to sit up in bed. "What baby?"

The Ob-Gyn eased me back down. "You're two months pregnant."

"Two months pregnant by who?"

"Miss, I'm sorry I wouldn't be able to tell you that because we have no idea who you are, much less who got you pregnant."

"What is your name, sweetheart?" The nurse asked while taking my blood pressure.

"I don't know," I replied.

The doctor sighed wearily. "Oh boy, we have a long way to go."

Not even a second after the doctor said those words, a tall, slender African-American woman neatly dressed in business attire walked in. Those little indentations in her cheeks reminded me of my friend, Dimples. She wore glasses, had brown eyes, dimples on both sides of her cheeks, and long hair extending to her shoulders.

"Good evening," the woman said before extending her hand to shake mine.

"Good evening to you, too."

"My name is Dr. Whitfield and I'm a psychologist."

"Hi Dr. Whitfield," I replied, wondering for a moment if I was crazy.

"What's your name?"

"I don't know my name, and I don't know how I got pregnant so stop asking me these questions," I lied smoothly as pain shot through my ribs. Every second, details of my life came back, including the last encounter with Chin.

Dr. Whitfield's eyes landed on the other women. "Could everyone please leave the room so I can have a talk with this nice young lady?" She asked.

Without hesitation, the doctors and nurses grabbed their belongings and trailed out the door.

"Now, since you don't know your name, would you like us to make one up together?" She asked, sitting on my hospital bed. She rubbed the tops of my hands.

"I guess so. I don't have any other choice."

"What would you like to call yourself?

"I don't know."

"Well, do you have a favorite person, actor, singer, comedian, or someone you would like to name yourself after?"

"Sanaa Lathan."

"You like Sanaa, huh? What is it about her that you like?"

"Practically in every movie, she's determined to go after what she wants."

"Okay, so I guess we're going to call you Sanaa. Is that okay with you?"

"I would rather be called Mystery." I looked up at her. That beautiful smile reminded me of my mother, but I could barely smile back because my jaws were hurting like hell.

"First, I want to say that I'm glad you came out of the coma." She opened her briefcase. "Although you have a lot of rehabilitation ahead, I'm glad that the baby is doing okay. They are still, however, trying to determine if the baby might suffer any trauma due to the beating you received and the injuries you sustained."

"What coma? How long was I out? What injuries?"

"Well, I don't want to push too much, but I can fill you in on a few details, and later on through our sessions, I'll fill you in some more. You were in a coma for a month. Actually, someone found you on the street corner near someplace called Soundview Projects." She glanced over her glasses at her notes.

"How long will all of this take?" I asked. "Rehab, I mean."

"I don't know. It all depends on you, but the more determined you are, the faster the process goes."

"Okay, well believe it when I say I have all intentions of remembering."

"That's good." She grinned. "Listen, we can't rush this process because . . ."

I didn't even give her a chance to finish when I cut her off.

"Dr. Whitfield, I'm determined to remember," I said, knowing damn well that I remembered everything. I just needed time in the hospital to plot against Chin. The hospital couldn't call anyone if I didn't remember anyone. And they couldn't release me unless someone was responsible for me. At least I hoped it worked that way.

She sighed loudly and said, "Okay." Then she stood, pulling her stuff together.

"Thank you, doctor."

"You're welcome. Intense sessions. Just remember that."

The door closed behind her. *Intense my ass.* The first thing I needed to do was get shit straight, then get the hell out of there and deal with the mothafuckas who put me there.

CHAPTER 77

CHIN

Chin's Office

Evening was winding down. In another hour, we would travel to Sandy's. As I sat behind my desk, I counted out one hundred thousand dollars, knowing that since there were no more of my bases that could be hit, Sandy's source had dried up. She would spill her guts for far less. After handing her this cash, she would start speaking to a point where she wouldn't shut up.

My thoughts were interrupted by a knock on the door.

"Who is it?"

"Dragon."

"Gimme a sec. Let me clear up some things."

Scooping the money into an envelope, I made sure the briefcase was shut tight, then shoved it into the safe.

"Come on in," I said.

Dragon walked in, a smile plastered on his face. "The single is tearing up the airwaves," he said, before giving me a pound.

"I know, nigga. We should go celebrate your success tomorrow night."

"Tomorrow night? I got the drink and the weed right

here," he said, pulling out a bottle of Cristal and three ounces of good yard weed.

"That's what I'm talking 'bout—puff, puff, pass."

I stood and rubbed my hands together. At the mini bar, I grabbed two wine glasses.

Tony and Tracey were at the office, and it would be unfair if we kept this celebration to ourselves. I picked up the phone and dialed Tracey's extension.

"Tracey, order some Chinese, and then come join us. Make sure Tony knows what's up."

CHAPTER 78

BABYGIRL

Albert Einstein Hospital

A nurse trying to check my temperature woke me up. "What time is it?"

"It's 1:45 a.m.," she replied while quickly eyeing the chart and filling in the information.

"Is Dr. Whitfield coming in today?" I asked.

"Darling, I have no idea," she stated as she looked at me over her glasses. "You would have to ask your doctor that."

"Well, is the doctor here?"

"She's at the desk. Could you give me a minute? Let me finish with the other patient, and I'll call her for you."

As she pulled the blood pressure monitor across the room, I lay back on my pillow, turned on the television, and began to drift. What the hell had I done to him to deserve such harsh treatment? How could I have had feelings for him? At this point, it didn't even matter. The plan that formed in my mind was downright evil.

CHAPTER 79

CHIN

Chin's Office

Celebrating Dragon's new single made us lose track of time until two in the morning.

"Nigga, how the hell we gonna go over to Sandy's tonight?" Tony whispered. "It's two o'clock."

"Simple. Call and tell the bitch we're on our way. She won't trip. There's money involved."

Tony, Tracey, and Dragon all left the office, so I walked back over to the closet and pulled out the briefcase.

Tracey walked back in the office seconds later. "Ah, I left this paper here."

"You left this paper, huh?" I watched her closely as she bent over and picked up something off the floor. The girl wasn't wearing any panties.

I knew from day one, Tracey had wanted me, but since I was caught up with Porsha, then BabyGirl, I didn't give her the time of the day.

"What's the rush, ma?" I held onto her hands and she didn't pull away.

"Since it was so late, I thought you were in a hurry to get home."

"Me? I'm in no hurry." I used my index finger to trace along the center of her breasts, causing her to tremble. Her shirt was open to the point that all I had to do was lean in and wrap my lips around her nipple.

"What are you doing?" she asked in between giggles. She inched closer.

Smiling, trying to cover the fact that I was high as hell, I whispered, "Please, you know you like it."

"Says who?"

"Says me. Because if you didn't, you would've stopped me a long time ago." Pulling her to the place between my legs, I lifted her short skirt and cupped her soft ass in my hands.

Tony burst through the door and froze. "You ready, man?"

Tracey didn't flinch.

"Give me a few minutes, man."

"A'ight man." Tony grinned as he closed the door behind him.

"So, what's it gonna be, baby? Because we ain't got all night here."

"I don't want you thinking I'm a ho," she whispered.

"A ho? Now where the hell did that come from? Girl, I don't hire hos, much less fuck 'em," I assured her, while sliding my hand under her skirt.

"You sure?" she asked, letting out a small moan.

"You want me to stop?"

"Do you *want* to stop?" she challenged, her dark brown eyes intense.

"Only if you want me to." Pulling her dress up, I slipped a finger into her pussy. "Ouch, you wet, ma."

"Umm-hmm," she groaned, lifting her head to the ceiling.

Unzipping my pants, my dick jumped out into my waiting hand. I put on a condom, centered my dick at the tip of her pussy, looked down into her eyes, and rammed my dick into her, balls deep.

Her scream tore through the air.

Watson Avenue

The angry expression on Sandy's face indicated that not only did we wake her up, but she was also furious at us for not being on time.

"Get your late asses inside," she said, yanking open the door.

Walking toward the living room, I could tell that Tony would soon have a hard-on. The red, sheer lingerie exposed her ass, tiny breasts, and shaved pussy. Her nipples hardened the moment we walked in. I licked my lips once, grabbed my dick, and followed her to the living room.

"You better hit that," I mumbled to Tony, "or I will."

"Hell yeah, nigga," he whispered back. "I'd never let an opportunity like that pass me by. Plus, we need to soften her ass up."

Sitting on the black leather sofa in the living room, I switched on her big screen television and flipped through the channels. The furniture and ornaments in the house let me know that not only was this bitch fucking big time ballers, but they were letting off big time dough.

"What can I do for you?" she asked, bending over to pick something up from the floor.

Tony walked up behind her, squeezing her ass. "You can let me hit that."

"Nigga, please, get the fuck off me."

"Be easy, ma. Just let me slide up in that for a quick minute." He placed one of his hands around her waist and slid a finger inside her pussy.

A big smile came across her face as Tony began to move his fingers back and forth along her clit.

"Girl, you better let the nigga hit that. I bet your ass wouldn't regret it."

"Shut up, Chin!"

"A'ight, I'm gonna shut up, so my nigga Tony can fuck you up." I laughed, and they began to laugh, too.

Tony eyed me, grinning. He pulled a rubber from his jacket pocket and said, "Give us a few, Chin."

Sandy excused herself while pulling Tony toward the bedroom.

"Go ahead. Do y'all thing. I'll be right here making myself at home."

Settling into the sofa, I propped my foot on the table and went to sleep.

An hour later Tony strolled in the living room, buckling up his belt.

"How was it, man?" I asked.

"The coochie felt kinda loose." He fixed his shirt over his pants. "She's fucked plenty this week, but shorty did her thing in the bed and gave good head. I give her mad props for that."

"So where is she now?"

"In the bathroom. She'll be out in a minute."

"Still wanna go through with the plan?"

"No doubt, kid. A nigga gotta do what a nigga got to do. Can't let pussy knock you outta your plan, know what I mean?"

"Don't remind me."

"Just checking to make sure the kid is down."

Sandy came strolling into the living room looking all tired and acting weird.

"Girl, you look like you been through hell and came back."

"Fuck you, Chin. What the hell you want from me?" she snapped.

Now why was she mad at me?

Picking up the briefcase sitting beside me on the floor, I opened it, exposing the Benjamins stocked inside. Her eyes nearly popped out her skull, and her mouth opened wide.

"What have I done to deserve such good treatment, gentlemen?" she inquired.

"A nigga can't hook up a sista?" I asked, as she still stared at the money.

"Yeah, but he ain't hooking her up like this without wantin' something. And when I say something," her eyes glazed at the money, "I mean something real big."

I shrugged, leaning back in the chair and watching her intently. "Well, since you put it like that, let me break it down."

She plopped down on the sofa across from Tony.

"You know that our supplies have been robbed, right?"

"Yeah," she said cautiously, eyeing Tony, then me. "So what's this got to do with me?"

"It has *everything* to do with you, Sandy, because you and I both know that even if you didn't have anything to do with it, you *know* something about it." We pulled her strings.

"Well, that's where you're wrong. I don't know nothing about no robberies."

"Oh yeah, then how come I only mentioned that we'd been robbed and you said *robberies*, like it was more than one? And that's not what PitBull told us."

"PitBull?" She jerked off the sofa. "What the fuck did Pit-Bull tell you?"

"Well, PitBull gave us pictures showing you, along with some other chick and BabyGirl robbing one of my places."

"And you believe that?" She laughed while counting the money, but her jaw twitched just a bit and she didn't look us in the eye. A sure sign of a liar if I ever saw one.

"And I meant robbery." She *still* hadn't lifted her head.

"So tell us your side," Tony said, pulling out the .45 from his waist. "Maybe PitBull's lying, and if he is, we'll deal with it accordingly."

She looked up at Tony and smiled nervously.

"What's the gun for?" she inquired.

"Hmmm," he said, shrugging. "Just for security purposes."

"Security purposes?"

"Yeah, warehouse security," Tony replied. "We can't get to the bottom of it, so if someone doesn't start talking, we're going to start killing from A to Z 'til someone does."

"Well I—I—I don't know much—much—much," she stammered. Her hands lifted away from the cash. "But I know a few things."

"Well, start talking." I went over to hold her hands while Tony still held onto the gun with a sour expression on his face.

"First of all, we have been robbing supplies. I ain't gon' front on that. But we didn't know *whose* supplies we were robbing. PitBull always arranged everything."

"And . . ." I said. She fell silent and didn't say another word.

"Is that all you know?" Tony broke the long silence, his voice hard and angry.

Sandy's legs began to shake and her hands trembled though she tried to hide it. I could feel the vibrations of her fear run from her hands and into my body.

"All I know is that PitBull wanted BabyGirl to seduce you and find out as much as she could about your empire. At first she was up for the plan, and then she told Dimples that she loved you and couldn't hurt you—"

Suddenly, I winced. Although I didn't mean to show that Sandy's words had affected me, they had. BabyGirl had loved me? She wasn't frontin' on that shit? My heart felt like a vice grip had closed around it. The girl had loved me as much as I had loved her. And I killed her before giving her a chance to explain. Damn! Life was so fucked up.

"Chin, listen up," Tony said, noticing that I had zoned out for a minute.

Sandy's flat voice continued the tale. "So she stopped reporting information to PitBull, and that's all I know. And that bitch deserves everything she gets."

Suddenly, I slammed Sandy's frail body against the wall. "She didn't deserve a damn thing. If she hadn't been sold out by PitBull, she'd still be alive. So watch your mouth, bitch."

Tony pulled me away from the trembling woman. I felt a sudden rush of anger at all that I'd lost recently—both Porsha and BabyGirl—all over some bullshit.

"Call PitBull," I growled at Sandy.

"For?" she asked.

"He needs to be dealt with for lying to me."

"And then we'll be cool, and you'll let me go?"

"Yup!"

Tony and I listened as Sandy used her charm to bring Pit-Bull to the house.

"He'll be here in two hours."

"We'll wait. All we have is time."

CHAPTER 80

BABYGIRL

Albert Einstein Hospital

I was finally being released from the hospital. Dr. Whitfield had come to visit me a couple times, but I declined her services. I didn't need therapy because I remembered everything perfectly. Accomplishing my mission would be all the therapy I needed. My stomach had a little pooch, and every chance I got I rubbed it just to confirm the impossible. Me? A mother? Hell no! What would I do with a little brat? Was the baby Chin's or Dragon's? It had to be Dragon's. I didn't use a condom with him.

One of the nurses walked in. "Ready to go home?"

"You better believe it." I looked up while tying my shoelaces.

"Well, you'll be out of here in no time, as soon as Dr. Gail comes in to check you out."

My roommate was also awake, eating breakfast.

"Good luck," she said, slowly spooning the food into her small mouth.

"You too."

For the first time, we exchanged words. She had spent

most of her time crying since they brought her in. A gunshot wound made her paralyzed from the waist down.

I didn't know much about her, but for some reason we kinda connected. She had a street edge that even her pretty face and delicate features couldn't hide.

As my life played out in my mind, I suddenly remembered the exact words Murdera spoke that day on that fateful trip to Philadelphia: *A majority of the people who enter this game don't know the rules. They know that flashy cars, flashy clothes, and money are a part of the game, not realizing that the game's about the survival of the fittest. One has to follow the rules in order to survive. This game consists of winners and losers. The side you're on doesn't depend on you, but on how well you play the game.*

Looking back, I realized how much I'd been through, and the risks I had taken to move to each level of the game. I stole, took lives, and watched my best friend nearly die while protecting me. Closing my eyes for a brief moment, I decided to have a talk with God. I told Him, "If you let me get through this and I can take care of each one of my enemies, I promise I'll go legit. No more dangerous activities. Amen."

At this point, I couldn't say I survived the game, because there was a lot more for me to accomplish. But I could say that I was one of the fittest, because I'd made it this far. Whether I was a winner or loser wouldn't be determined until I completed my final mission.

"Ready for your checkup?" Dr. Gail asked.

"Ready and waiting."

Dr. Gail rolled up my sleeve and took my blood pressure. She then placed a thermometer in my mouth to check my temperature.

"Everything seems okay," she said. "I just need for you to sign these release forms and you will be out of here in no time. Natasha Crawford is waiting for you downstairs."

"Who?"

Dr. Gail stopped writing on my prescription and looked at

me. "A young woman with brown, curly hair and really deep dimples."

"Oh, sorry about that. I forgot Dimples' real name."

As I was pushed down the corridor, a familiar name was tagged on the nurse's station's board. *Porsha Hilton Room 735.* Porsha Hilton? Chin's wifey!

I turned to the nurse who was wheeling me to the elevator. "Hey, I need to make a quick stop. I'll let you know when I'm ready to leave."

Opening the door to Room 735, my eyes connected with the dark-skinned woman who wore the same gown I had just taken off. It barely covered her ass too.

I didn't know what to say, so I decided to let everything flow.

"Porsha, I'm BabyGirl and I'm sorry. I know you are probably wondering how I know you, but your name was on the room door."

Instead of an answer, she simply turned her head the other way to face the window.

"Porsha, you have to listen to me." I rolled my way to the other side of the bed so I could get her attention.

"Listen to you," she said in a tone of disgust.

"We can't let Chin get away with hurting you, with hurting us."

"He has already gotten away with everything. While I was in here, my partners found out about my dealings with him, and now I'm out of a job. By the looks of things, I can tell he sent you in here, too."

"Exactly. That's why we have to get back at him. Not only did he play you, but he used you to get what he wanted. Then on top of it, he insulted you by dating me. He had no intentions of staying with you after the paperwork was done."

"How do you know that?" She struggled to sit up in the bed.

"You can wait things out and clean up the mess, or you can

grow some balls and get revenge." She stared openly at me as I continued, "So are you gonna punk out or be a woman and help me teach that mothafucka a lesson?"

Anger toward Chin now replaced the disgust she had for me earlier. I had finally struck a nerve.

"Take me with you. If you have a plan, I want to be a part of it. Then I'll tell you my own plans." She slipped out of the bed and pushed her feet into her bedroom slippers.

Minutes later, Porsha was ready for war.

As she pushed me toward the door, we stumbled into a plump nurse who tried to stop Porsha from leaving.

"Bitch, if you don't get the fuck out of the way," Porsha said, "you will be laying up in here instead of working in here."

Without another word, the nurse backed up, her dark skin flushing red with anger as Porsha wheeled me down the hall and through the double doors.

CHAPTER 81

CHIN

Watson Avenue

"You sure he's coming?" I asked Sandy.

"Yeah, I said he'll be here in two hours," she repeated.

"So, is that all you know, Sandy?"

She looked at the gun Tony held and said, "I know there's a female behind everything."

"A female!" Tony shouted along with me.

Sandy grinned. "Yup, a female masterminded this."

"Who?" Tony asked as he moved closer toward her with the gun.

"I don't know because PitBull never went into details, but I heard a couple of times he talked about the female frontin' the cash to get the equipment for the robberies."

"You lying to us?"

Looking up at the concrete ceiling and letting out a big sigh, she replied, "Why in the fucking world would I lie to you, Chin, especially when you frontin' me this much cash? I would even spill the bitch name if I had it, but unfortunately I don't. Now leave me alone and let me count my money."

I changed the topic, asking, "So since you're so disgusted

by BabyGirl's actions, what do you think we should do with
. . . you?

She froze. "Nothing, I've already told you that I didn't
know it was you who PitBull had set up," she said nervously,
and began pushing herself up on Tony.

"And we appreciate the information," Tony said, spreading her legs apart and dipping two fingers inside of her. I
watched as he moved his fingers in and out of her, and my
dick began to get hard.

"Now, I want you to be a nice girl," Tony said huskily, "and
do Daddy a favor."

"What's that?"

"You see that guy over there," he said, while pointing
across the living room at me. Her eyes followed the direction
of his fingers. "I want you to go over there, and give him
some head."

"Naw, I can't do that. That's your friend."

"Oh yes, you *will* do it for Daddy," Tony demanded while
pressing the gun to her ribs. "It's only fair. The man lost a lot
by your hands, and you can't pay him the money back. So go
hook a nigga up with some good head, and we'll call it a
night."

"A'ight," she flashed Tony off, put the money back in the
briefcase, and walked over to me.

He didn't have to tell her twice. By the time she stood in
front of me, my dick was out of my pants, stiff as hell, and
ready for her mouth to take it in.

Pushing my legs apart, she got down on her knees and
wrapped her moist mouth around my hard dick.

I looked over to Tony and grinned. "Man, this is the second time in four hours. This must be my lucky night."

Shorty was doing such a good job that I busted off in minutes. I held her head in place, forcing her to swallow every
drop. She glared at me, but didn't say a word as that shit trav-

eled down her throat and spilled out of the sides of her mouth. She almost choked.

"A'ight," she snapped, dark brown eyes flashing with anger. "Y'all got the information you wanted. I called Pit-Bull, fucked you, sucked his dick, so what else y'all want?" she inquired, trying to clean her mouth with her shirt.

Tony leaned over, placed the gun at her temple, and said, "Your soul."

Sandy didn't get a chance to reply. The blue flash of light from the gun sparked, and then dimmed, along with her sad little life. Marrow splattered across the wall, and blood drained from her head, pouring out onto the carpet like a river running downstream.

"Well, our job is done," Tony said, brushing off his shirt. He tucked the .45 into his waistband, scooped up the brief-case with the money intact, and followed me out the door. We would pull the car down the street, take in a bite to eat, and await our next victim.

Dinner at the restaurant down the block from Sandy's was good. Tony and I sat there for an hour barely saying a word. I think Tony knew exactly what was going on in my head—BabyGirl.

"What if—?"

"There's nothing you can do about it, Chin. Let it go. She's dead. Yeah, you made a mistake, but you didn't know the whole story. That's not your fault."

As we sat parked in the shadows, a few houses down from Sandy's behind a black Ford Expedition, Shotta pulled up in front of her house. PitBull and Chico got out of the car first, with PitBull scanning the area quickly before reaching the door.

"You take Shotta and I'll go after Chico and PitBull," Tony said, crouching down in the seat to strap on an extra gun.

"Why do you get to kill PitBull? I wanted—"

"Because this is way too personal for you. And more time is going to be spent arguing—how could you do this, and yeah I got you now mothafucka. Instead of one, two, three, shooting and that's it."

Damn, the man had a point. There was a whole lot I had to say to PitBull. None of it mattered now.

Tony opened the door and followed closely behind his victims while I turned off the engine to the Denali. I reached Shotta just as he pulled the driver's seat into a reclining position.

"Whaddup kid? What you doing over here?" Shotta asked, blowing smoke out of his mouth.

"Sandy was having a little celebration so she invited us," I replied.

"Word?"

"You're not going in?"

"Yeah, I'll follow you."

"Hold up. Open the back of the truck, so I can get in and count out the money I have in this briefcase."

Freeing up the lock, he opened the door. I sat in the back pretending as if I was counting money while he blabbed away about how business was looking at the base. I kept him distracted by pretending to agree with a few of his statements. Then, as he glanced at the mirror, I saw my opportunity. Slowly I pulled the knife out of my pocket, grabbed him by the neck, and slit his throat. Blood spattered all over the jeep's windows. I picked up the pace, running to the house to see if Tony needed help. I nearly knocked him over as he ran out of the house and simply said, "Let's go."

"You killed them?"

"Chico took one in the head. If PitBull's heart is where it's supposed to be, it's not working anymore. But just to be sure I put one, up close, in his head."

"If business is done, why are we running?" I questioned.

"Because PitBull confessed before I shot him. There's someone else running the show. And I certainly don't want to be here if Chyna shows up with the other workers. We're not fully prepared to deal with them. Their weapons outnumber ours."

Freezing at the door of my truck, I said. "Get the fuck out! *Chyna* is behind this?"

"C'mon, nigga. We can discuss that in the car later." Tony motioned for me to get in.

"Chyna!"

"Chin, if you don't get moving, I'll put a bullet in you my damn self."

After scrambling into the passenger seat without another moment's hesitation, I said, "I dare you to try and shoot my ass."

Tony grinned. "I don't see you still standing outside either."

Tha Hustle Records

A month later and things were still going well with Dragon on the label. Tracey and the other employees had left for the evening. I had asked Dragon to come on down to work on this track I wanted him to lay later, with some new girl named Temptation we had just signed to the label. Dragon was still having his dinner, so I sat on the sofa watching while Tony set up everything in the studio.

"Time to bust some sweat, Dragon," Tony said as he clapped his hand on my shoulders and looked at the talented young man seated in the chair.

"Word." Dragon nodded while he pulled on the blunt that he had in his hand. He was high, and ready to take on anything. "A'ight kid. Let's go."

As Tony adjusted the buttons on the panel board, he shouted to Dragon.

"Give us another hit, boy!"

"You know that's all I drop," he said in a cocky manner.

"Hey, team," Tony said. "All those drinks from our pre-celebration last night just kicked in. Gimme a few. I gotta go to the men's room."

"A'ight, the kid will still be here."

CHAPTER 82

BABYGIRL

Tha Hustle Records NYC

My prey made his way down the hall. *This was going to be easier than I had thought.* I had just finished explaining the strategy for taking him down, and the victim walked right into my trap. With one hand, I urged Porsha to go on while I wheeled myself back to hide in the shadows.

She stepped out into the lobby.

"Porsha," Tony said in a startled voice as he stared her up and down.

"Tony. What's up?"

He held out his hands for a hug. "Glad you okay, ma."

Porsha swallowed hard before hugging the big man back.

"Chin's in the studio, so go holler at the kid. I'll catch you in a few."

Porsha pointed the .45 with the silencer to his chest. "You ain't going nowhere, Tony."

"That's right nigga," Dimples agreed.

"What's this all about?" Tony jerked his head to look at her, his hands held high in surrender.

"It's called winners take all, and losers get nothing," she

said as I popped my head from around the corner and joined in.

"We don't have no beef, Porsha," Tony said, while raising both his hands, "so what's the deal?"

"You're right we don't have any beef, but you and a friend of mine have beef."

"What friend?"

"BabyGirl!"

"You mean to tell me all this time y'all were partners?" Tony asked with his mouth wide open.

"Yup," I lied smoothly.

"Wait—"

The gun fired. Tony jerked once and fell to the floor as the shot tore through his muscular frame.

"Hello," I said as I rolled into Chin's office.

The coffee Chin held in his suddenly trembling hands spilled onto his white Fendi shirt.

"Surprised?"

Chin threw a quick glance in Porsha's direction as Dimples placed her weapon on her lap, waiting for anyone to make a wrong move. Chin let his hands fall to the side of the chair.

"Well, well, if it ain't the resurrection of the dead, right?" I pulled my nine at him. "How are you, baby?" I asked, pulling on every ounce of strength I had to stand and walk away from my wheelchair to face him.

"What do you want?"

I shrugged, placing my rear end on the studio controls. "Nothing. I just wanna talk."

"You're crazy, you know that?"

"Be careful. You weren't saying that when you were fucking me," I said, smacking his head with the butt of the gun. "Let me tell you a little story—"

"Please spare me the drama and get to the point, Baby-

Girl," he snapped. And he had the nerve to use a sarcastic tone.

"Boy, you must really want to die fast."

"Is that any way to talk to the lady?" Porsha dipped in, keeping the gun pointed on Chin.

"You ruined my life, Chin." I spoke.

"I don't know what you're talking about."

"Well for one thing, I'm pregnant."

"So what, are you looking for child support?" he snapped, glaring at me, but taking a quick look at my pooch. I did hear Porsha's sharp intake of breath, and I knew when everything was said and done, I'd have some explaining to do.

"Don't fuck with me, Chin." Leaning forward, almost at a kissing distance, I said, "My hormones ain't right, and I'll shoot your ass just on g.p."

Finally, the moment that I had prayed for had come, but suddenly my heart felt empty. This whole game had left a hole deep in my soul and I didn't know what it would take to fill me up again.

"A few years back you and PitBull walked into my father's place, robbed him, and after killing him you killed my mother. You took everything away from me. She didn't have anything to do with the game, but you killed her anyway. You're probably wondering how I knew you had some connection. The tattoo on your neck was a dead giveaway. I vowed that I would get back at both killers. I was the one who called the police and sent PitBull to prison, and you'd better believe that I dished out a lot of money to find out about you and how your whole organization was set up."

"You had to have help, you weren't smart enough to play the game that way," he said.

"Oh, I thought you would have figured that out by now, seeing that you played the game so well, and I learned from the best."

"Sorry to disappoint you," he informed me. "But it feels like you're the one playing games."

"What a shame." I walked over to his bar and poured three glasses of Hennessy. "Spades, baby. It was just like spades. You see, it was just like a tournament. All I had to do was get in the game and prove myself. Once I did that, I watched everyone until I ultimately challenged the top player for his empire."

"PitBull and Chyna were partners, you and Tony were partners, Sandy and PitBull were partners," I continued as I took a sip of my drink. "And I had to play my hand by myself. I never had a partner, until recently. Now I have partners—both women—and fortunately they can think on their feet, which is more than I can say for your stupid ass. While you were sitting there thinking you had the upper hand, you did all my dirty work, eliminated the other players, and now it's down to you and me. The King of Spades and the Queen of Hearts."

"Yeah, I killed your father, and so fucking what? I was starving. Your father was flossing, so I took what he had to get what I needed. That's how the game is played," Chin spat.

The door to his office opened slowly. It was Dragon walking in to ask Chin a question. He was in total shock to see that three females had Chin under their control. He just stood there quietly.

I held my gun to Chin's head and pretended as though I was about to pull the trigger, then I pulled the gun away.

"I can't kill you. That's too easy. So I'm going to play this out a little bit. I've waited too long for it to end this quickly. I want you to suffer just like I did."

"C'mon, speed this up," Dimples said in an agitated tone. "People could come in. We don't want to kill anyone else."

"No! Don't rush me. I deserve this." I shot her a *don't fuck with me or I'll kill you, too* glare. She shut up real quick.

At that moment Tracey walked in, interrupting our little meeting. Her dress was unzipped, exposing her naked body. "What the fuck is going on, Tony is—"

"My, my, my, look what the cat dragged in." I shook my head.

Her eyes widened to the size of saucers, and then she tried to run her ass out of the studio. "Looks like someone was expecting a little nookie."

"Sit your ass down," Porsha commanded.

Tracey slumped down to the floor.

"You, oh yes, I have something planned for you." I pointed the gun at Tracey.

"Just let her go. She ain't got shit to do with this," Chin said.

"Trust me, her mean ass has a lot to do with this. Not only did she work for you, but she was the one who told you about my father's place, hoping you would only kill my mother, so she could have my father all to herself. She's just as responsible for his murder as you are."

"What happened to the sweet BabyGirl that would spread her legs for me anytime I wanted?" Chin asked as an evil grin spread over his lips.

"She was just a pretender."

"Pretending my ass. Sandy said that you told your girl you were in love with me. So what's that all about?"

"Don't add insult to injury," Dragon dipped in.

"Sandy lied." I turned to Dragon, who stood staring at me. "Dragon, if you want to keep your record contract and your life, deal with Tracey. I continued playing it off in front of everyone. No one can leave here without some ounce of guilt on their hands. Porsha already took out Tony. Her job's done. Since she was looking for dick, give her what she wants."

Dragon glared at me. "Think about that shit. I can't believe you're asking me to sleep with this bitch."

"Think of it as a job. Your performance is required."

When he continued to hesitate, I said, "If it's a matter of loyalty, give it to her up the ass."

At that, Dragon flipped Tracey over and whipped out a condom from his back pocket.

I laughed. "So much for just loving me, huh?"

Dragon flipped me the finger. He bent Tracey over the desk and spread her cheeks. Dimples ran over and covered the woman's mouth with a single hand, but kept the gun on Chin.

Dragon rammed his dick in. Her scream was muffled by Dimples' hand.

Tears sprang from Porsha's eyes as she shifted uncomfortably.

"Anytime you want to leave, go right ahead. But remember that this bitch fucked your man, too. And she's known you a lot longer than me."

Porsha's shoulders stiffened. Her tears dried up as she watched every thrust of Dragon's hips.

Blood flowed down the woman's thighs, landing on the carpet. He continued to fuck her until he reached an orgasm. Tracey's limp body lay on the desk. He took her head in his hands. A solid crack tore through the air as he ended her life.

"Dimples, put a shot in her ass just to be sure."

Dragon turned to me, out of breath. "After all this time, you don't trust me?"

"Trust has nothing to do with it. When you worked for my father, he always trusted you because you were the only runner to never come up short. And I even remembered when you helped me into the ambulance that day after Chin shot my parents. Then you took care of me the best you could. But I had to fend for myself when you went away. But right now that's beside the point. This is the new me. Love me or leave me."

I looked at Dimples, Porsha, and Dragon. "I don't want nobody snitching to the police. So everyone in this room who walks out alive can't say they're innocent. The only reason Porsha didn't shoot you on sight is that she now holds your contract as the new owner of Tha Hustle Records. If you have a problem with that, she can kill you later. It'll probably sell more records—at least it worked for Biggie and Tupac."

Dimples chuckled. "Damn, BabyGirl, you're cold as hell."

Dragon shook his head. "You weren't supposed to be like this."

"I wasn't given a fucking choice."

Dragon then helped me put duct tape around Chin's wrists. I looked up at Porsha who shrugged and said, "It's up to you." I unzipped his zipper and took his dick out.

He glanced down at my stomach since my blouse didn't quite cover the distance to my waist.

"That ain't mine," he said. "You probably done fucked the whole damn town and you're trying to pin that shit on me."

Porsha laughed, causing all heads to turn in her direction. "Sounds like the same shit you said to Chyna before she had that abortion."

Chin looked into the cold glint of Porsha's eyes. She wouldn't lift a finger to help him, but I also noticed she didn't lift a finger to hurt him, either. I didn't quite understand what that meant.

I reached out for his dick, put it in my mouth, and sucked and played with it to the point where he froze, unable to move. As his erection struggled to aim for the ceiling, I took the knife off the table and leaned over him.

"You should've believed in me." I sliced upward and soon placed the little bleeding member next to him on the floor.

After the initial shock, Chin shouted.

"Ahhhhhhhhhhhh! You crazy *bitch*. Get the fuck away from me!" He struggled to stop the flow of blood from his dick. "You better pray my ass don't get fucking loose. I'm gonna kill you."

I laughed—hard. I couldn't help myself. "Kill me? Didn't you try that already?"

"This time, you won't be so lucky," he spat at me.

"Mothafucka, I've walked through the valley of the shadows of death, so I'm ready for anything."

Chin surged forward, nearly taking the chair with him.

Dragon pressed the gun to the back of Chin's head. "Take another step and you'll be dead. Damn girl, you're cold. Cutting the nigga's dick off! What you trying to be, the black Lorena Bobbitt or something?" Dragon asked, while holding a solid hand over his Polo jeans as though protecting his own dick.

"Naw, that's what happens when you fail at your assignment, and give an opponent a chance to come back," Dimples said while giving Chin a cold stare.

I placed Chin's hand on the desk and stabbed him with the knife straight through the top of his hand, cutting off one of his fingers.

"Let this be a lesson to teach you not to steal from people." I warned everyone before poking out Chin's right eye. Porsha winced, but she stayed silent as I finished and Chin's screams pierced the air.

Chin yelled out, "How could you do this?" He gasped and nearly passed out from the pain. "You deserved that ass whipping. You betrayed me."

"And you killed my parents, so now we're even."

With that, the gun went off, and my last enemy could no longer take a breath.

"Good for you, you fucking bastard." Dimples rolled her eyes at Chin's lifeless body.

Porsha, on the other hand, had a puzzled look on her face as she watched Chin. I made a mental note to keep an eye on her later.

"That's what you get for fucking up people's lives." Dimples walked over and kicked Chin.

"Girl, you had all of that in you?" Dragon asked, wrapping his arms around me like he once did so many years ago. I held onto him, letting the anger seep from my body as he kissed my temple and held me close. Something about his embrace and kiss seemed a little odd. I made a mental note of that.

"Believe me, everyone has it in them if they're pushed to the limit. This was for my father and mother. He took away their lives and didn't give it a second thought. I took his life and had plenty of time to think about it first."

"True, well time for a nigga to get paid and be out of here," Dragon said before pulling open the studio door.

The sun had dipped behind the clouds to allow darkness to take over. I took one last look around Tha Hustle Records and shook my head in disgust at the fact that one man had so much ambition, but had ruined so many lives.

Nothing brought a smile to my face more than to see the man who killed my parents die under worse conditions than even my father could dream up. But that part of my life would be over. Looking back at it, I realized my father was guilty, too, because he knew the consequences of the game. He should have never brought my mother and me to a place where he conducted business.

I turned to Dimples and Porsha.

"New beginnings from here on out," I said. "I want no part of my old lifestyle. So from this point on, everything's legit since we have no enemies to speak of." I glanced at Porsha to see if she had recovered. "I don't have any more enemies, right?"

"It's all water under the bridge," Porsha replied.

With that, I put on my Prada shades and waited out front as Dragon pulled his SUV around.

We then dropped three packages off in the East River.

EPILOGUE

East River NYC

Cars raced past on the FDR as she pulled under the bridge. The cell phone sat defiantly on top of her red duffle bag. The radio had been turned off. The only sound echoing was her heart slamming against her chest. A sickening moisture pooled in the palm of her trembling hands. She reached out her fingers and slowly pressed the buttons on the keypad one by one.

Gently lifting the phone to her ear, she listened for several rings, hoping someone would pick up before she changed her mind.

"19th Precinct, Officer Gomez speaking." The woman's deep voice sounded unnaturally warm.

"Can you transfer me to D. T. Garfin, please?"

"What's this about ma'am?"

"I'd like to tell it to him . . ."

The line buzzed three times before Garfin's husky voice bellowed, "Garfin. How may I help you?"

The woman sighed wearily, then rushed ahead. "I'm calling to tell you that there are three bodies in the East River, near the Water Club. There's a possibility that one of 'em might still be alive."

"How do you know that? What's your name, Miss?"

"I suggest you quit with the questions and get on it." Her voice wavered. She cursed herself for not being stronger.

"Who is this?" he demanded, making her a little angry, but no less willing to finish the business.

She answered his question with a simple, "Someone who knows more than she should. I'll be in touch."

Detective Garfin stared into space with the phone still in his hand. He gazed at the map of New York City on his front wall. The East River was known for tossing up bodies from its deep waters. But what the woman said had struck a nerve.

Suddenly, he sprang into action, yanking his coat from the wooden chair. He dialed a number and said, "I need two cars at the Water Club."

Five minutes later, as the silhouette of the woman stood off near the Water Club, she flicked the last of her cigarette into the river. She waited for five minutes. Then she heard exactly what she had hoped for, sirens blaring a short distance away and growing closer with each passing second.

Sotto Cinque Restaurant, Manhattan

The crispy November wind brushed against BabyGirl's face as she stood next to the limo ready to join Porsha, Dragon, and Dimples.

"Ahhh . . ." she inhaled the fresh air and wrapped her jacket even tighter around her shoulders.

"C'mon, girl, we're gonna be late. Sotto only holds reservations for fifteen minutes," Porsha said, pulling on her jacket.

BabyGirl managed to settle down next to Dragon and enjoy the ride into the city.

When they arrived, the table was ready. As they requested, a bucket filled with ice and Cristal awaited them.

"Let's make a toast." Porsha held up her goblet. "For a successful future and my departure from the legal field."

"Amen to that," Dimples joined in. "And don't forget the new owner of Tha Hustle Records. Please, girl, change that name."

"I will, and I am owner as long as Tony and Chin are still rolling in their graves." Porsha laughed a sad, hollow sound.

"Let's make a toast to the man above for taking us safely out of the illegal business," BabyGirl added, lifting a glass of sparkling apple juice. "To Dimples, my new partner and co-owner of the Exquisite Restaurant and to Big Tymers nightclub, which we also plan on buying out."

"To the new CEO, a damn record contract, a hot single, and hopefully a platinum album," Dragon said.

As they touched their glasses together, BabyGirl stopped everyone, adding one last comment. "Listen up," she tapped her glass with a fork. A brief silence fell at the table as she had everyone's attention.

"Chin, Tony, and PitBull may have been the Kings of Spades, but from here on out we are the Queens of Hearts and the King of Diamonds, right baby?" She laced her fingers with Dragon's as she placed a kiss on his lips.

"Right," he responded with a wary glance at BabyGirl's belly. He knew there was a possibility that it could be Chin's child growing inside of her. And also, with a custody battle on the horizon for BabyGirl's little sister, Tracey's little girl, things would be rough. Much to Dragon's dismay, BabyGirl was about to become a mother to not one, but two unwanted brats, if Porsha won her case.

Dragon wasn't so sure he wanted to raise the children left behind by two scheming and dangerous people. No matter how much BabyGirl swore that the baby wasn't Chin's, he didn't believe her. She refused to get an abortion. He also wasn't so sure he wanted to be an underling in an empire run by women. Things would definitely have to change. He wanted to share in the wealth, too. And he knew voicing his opinion might create problems.

Regardless of BabyGirl's title for him, he knew that the women would kill to keep what they had fought so hard to win. Dragon wasn't a stranger to killing to get what he wanted. Maybe he should remind them of that fact.

BabyGirl was now a tiger in bed, but her ruthlessness surpassed even her father. That alone made Dragon worry. She frightened him. With so much power in her hands, she would be hard to control. He'd left an innocent girl when he went to prison. Now, somehow, he had a monster on his hands.

"Queens of Hearts," BabyGirl said as she watched Dragon closely and the other girls tapped their glasses to hers, glancing in his direction.

"Queens of Hearts," he said cautiously, taking a slow slip of Cristal as a plan formed in his mind.

FOOD FOR THOUGHT

"The game of life is like the game of boomerang. Our thoughts, deeds, and words return to us sooner or later with astounding accuracy." Florence Scovel-Shinn

About the Author

Kiniesha Gayle is originally from Kingston, Jamaica. She is a graduate of John Jay College of Criminal Justice where she holds a B.A. in Forensic Psychology. Her passion for the written word began with writing poetry at age nine and was further encouraged by Prof. Conrad Wynter just before completing her college studies.

After completing the first manuscript in 2002, she sent it out to several publishing houses and received a few rejections. The rejections only strengthened her desire to become successful. After experiencing a number of wrong turns and a few con artists, she was finally introduced to Lissa Woodson, a developmental editor who not only edited her first novel, but also restored her faith in becoming a published author. Later, she received a book deal from Mark Anthony, an author and publisher of Q-Boro Books.

Kiniesha Gayle currently lives in Bronx, New York with her son and is working on her second novel, *Queen of Hearts* - the sequel to *King of Spades* .

Visit Kiniesha's website at www.KinieshaGayle.com.

ALSO AVAILABLE FROM
Q-BORO
BOOKS

DOUBLE BOOK!
DOUBLE BOOK!

DOUBLE BOOK!
DOUBLE BOOK!

LOOK FOR MORE HOT TITLES FROM

Q-BORO
B O O K S

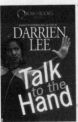

TALK TO THE HAND - OCTOBER 2006
$14.95
ISBN 0977624765

Nedra Harris, a twenty-three year old business executive, has experienced her share of heartache in her quest to find a soul mate. Just when she's about to give up on love, she runs into Simeon Mathews, a gentleman she met in college years earlier. She remembers his warm smile and charming nature, but soon finds out that Simeon possesses a dark side that will eventually make her life a living hell.

SOMEONE ELSE'S PUDDIN' - DECEMBER 2006
$14.95
ISBN 0977624706

While hairstylist Melody Pullman has no problem keeping clients in her chair, she can't keep her bills paid once her crack-addicted husband Big Steve steps through a revolving door leading in and out of prison. She soon finds what seems to be a sexual and financial solution when she becomes involved with her long-time client's husband, Larry.

THE AFTERMATH
$14.95
ISBN 0977624749

If you thought having a threesome could wreak havoc on a relationship, Monica from My Woman His Wife is back to show you why even the mere thought of a ménage a trios with your spouse and an outsider should never enter your imagination.

THE LAST TEMPTATION - APRIL 2007
$6.99
ISBN 0977733599

The Last Temptation is a multi-layered joy ride through explorations of relationships with Traci Johnson leading the way. She has found the new man of her dreams, the handsome and charming Jordan Styles, and they are anxious to move their relationship to the next level. But unbeknownst to Jordan, someone else is planning Traci's next move: her irresistibl ex-boyfriend, Solomon Jackson, who thugged his way back into her hear

LOOK FOR MORE HOT TITLES FROM

LOOK FOR MORE HOT TITLES FROM

Q-BORO
B O O K S

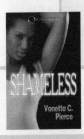

Attention Writers:

Writers looking to get their books published can view our submission guidelines by visiting our website at:
www.QBOROBOOKS.com

What we're looking for: Contemporary fiction in the tradition of Darrien Lee, Carl Weber, Anna J., Zane, Mary B. Morrison, Noire, Lolita Files, etc; groundbreaking mainstream contemporary fiction.

We prefer email submissions to: candace@qborobooks.com in MS Word, PDF, or rtf format only. However, if you wish to send the submission via snail mail, you can send it to:

Q-BORO BOOKS Acquisitions Department
165-41A Baisley Blvd., Suite 4. Mall #1
Jamaica, New York 11434

*** By submitting your work to Q-Boro Books, you agree to hold Q-Boro books harmless and not liable for publishing similar works as yours that we may already be considering or may consider in the future. ***

1. Submissions will not be returned.
2. **Do not contact us for status updates.** If we are interested in receiving your full manuscript, we will contact you via email or telephone.
3. Do not submit if the entire manuscript is not complete.

Due to the heavy volume of submissions, if these requirements are not followed, we will not be able to process your submission.